Praise for Lisa Ball...

'Se... Sp... d, sus...
Lee C...

'[A moving, insightful debut . . .
To Sleep, I'll e...
Guar...

'A gripping and emotionally charged story. Just brilliant'
Clare Mackintosh

'An absorbing psychological debut'
Company

'Grips like a vice'
Daily Mail

'One of the most readable, emotionally intense
novels of the year'
Richard Madeley, Richard and Judy's Book Club

'A cracker of a story . . . a page-turner with real emotional depth'
Daily Express

'Thought provoking, brave and challenging, this book is an
unsettling and compulsive read'
Rosamund Lupton

'Lisa Ballantyne has written a first novel that is both
moving and suspenseful; richly detailed, yet with the
eerie simplicity of a parable'
Joyce Carol Oates

'Subtle, suspenseful and sophisticated'
Sunday Express

'Gripping stuff'

DORSET COUNTY LIBRARY

400 267 190 T

Dorset Libraries Withdrawn Stock

'This is ... ding work of fiction, and the real
crime would have been if the talent of Lisa Ballantyne had
never been discovered'
Daily Record

'Will touch your heart, even as it leaves you unsettled'
Hallie Ephron

'It's a work of genuine substance about real human beings
with real human flaws, in which nothing can be tied up neatly
because life doesn't work like that. *The Guilty One* puts her
firmly on the list of writers to watch'
Irish Independent

'An emotionally compelling tale of old sins and lingering ghosts'
Chris Brookmyre

'Fast-paced and emotionally charged, we were tearing through
it well into the night. Keep a tissue handy – you'll be a wreck by
the end'
Emerald Street

'I couldn't get this book out of my head. It kept me up all night
and guessing the whole way through, I loved it'
Jenny Colgan

'A page-turner'
Cosmopolitan

'Lisa Ballantyne has conjured a world that is both utterly
believable, and horrifying ... a story that will keep you turning
the pages late into the night'
Joyce Maynard

'Gets better as you read it ... a novel that grips ... engrossing
the reader who will want to find out what happens'
Dulwich Book Reviews

Lisa Ballantyne is the author of the Edgar Award-nominated and Richard and Judy-bestselling *The Guilty One*, which was translated into nearly thirty languages. Her second novel, *Redemption Road*, was a *USA Today* bestseller.

Originally from Armadale in Scotland, she now lives in Glasgow.

Little Liar

LISA BALLANTYNE

piatkus

PIATKUS

First published in Great Britain in 2018 by Piatkus
This paperback edition published in 2019 by Piatkus

1 3 5 7 9 10 8 6 4 2

Copyright © 2018 by Lisa Ballantyne

The moral right of the author has been asserted.

*All characters and events in this publication, other than those
clearly in the public domain, are fictitious and any resemblance
to real persons, living or dead, is purely coincidental.*

All rights reserved.
No part of this publication may be reproduced, stored in a
retrieval system, or transmitted in any form or by any means, without
the prior permission in writing of the publisher, nor be otherwise circulated
in any form of binding or cover other than that in which it is published
and without a similar condition including this condition
being imposed on the subsequent purchaser.

A CIP catalogue record for this book
is available from the British Library.

ISBN 978-0-349-41992-3

Typeset in Goudy by M Rules
Printed and bound in Great Britain by
Clays Ltd, Elcograf S.p.A.

Papers used by Piatkus are from well-managed forests
and other responsible sources.

Piatkus
An imprint of
Little, Brown Book Group
Carmelite House
50 Victoria Embankment
London EC4Y 0DZ

An Hachette UK Company
www.hachette.co.uk

www.littlebrown.co.uk

Grateful thanks for the project funding
awarded to me by Creative Scotland, without
which the writing of this novel would
not have been possible.

Dorest County Library	
400 267 190 T	
Askews & Holts	05-Jun-2019
	£8.99

Part One

'Light, which is positive, holds dominion
over darkness, which is negative.'

Joseph Mallord William Turner

1

Angela

Fight, fight, fight.

Angela looked down at her knuckles and saw they were red. It wasn't her blood. The crowd had formed so fast, pupils from her year – twelve- and thirteen-year-olds – being elbowed out of the way by lads of fifteen. The ring of people around her pulsated as one. The eye of the fight, where she stood, was only three or four feet wide. Kids pressed as close as they could to get a look, climbing on shoulders and pulling on school bags, but they also stayed back, gave room for the violence, so the circle where Angela stood contracted and dilated like an iris. She didn't know how many people surrounded her. Everyone wanted to watch a fight and a girl fight was even better, so long as it was a real one.

This was a real one. She hadn't started it, but she was going to finish it. She was going to teach Jasmine a lesson.

Blood was running from Jasmine's nostrils and her eyes were streaming, although it didn't look as if she was actually crying. Angela would sort that out. She took her by the hair and forced her down onto the ground. Jasmine's hair was easy to get a hold of because it was so big and bushy. As soon as she was on the ground Angela began to kick her. Jasmine rolled up into a ball and covered her face with her elbows and hands and so Angela kicked her hard on her thighs. She kicked her so hard it jarred her hip, but it wasn't enough. She wanted to really show her.

Angela heard deep male voices and knew the teachers had arrived to break up the fight. She didn't have much time. She grabbed another fistful of Jasmine's hair and at the same time put one foot on the girl's waist, pinning her body to the ground. Angela gritted her teeth and pulled as hard as she could, just as the eye of the crowd ruptured and separated.

She was pulled away by one teacher, while another knelt to tend to Jasmine, who was now screaming and writhing on the ground. Angela felt dizzy, happy, high. She didn't recognise the teacher that was marching her by the elbow to the main building. All her limbs felt heavy and she allowed herself to be led, a smile of achievement on her lips.

'Sit down,' the teacher ordered, when they reached the corridor where the head's office was. It was only her second year of high school, but Angela knew this corridor well.

She did as she was told and sat down. It didn't matter. She shrugged to show that she didn't care. In her fist, she held a large clump of Jasmine's light brown frizzy hair. Angela hunched over to inspect it and saw that there was blood on the ends of it. She'd ripped it right out.

If only her dad had come to get her, but of course it was her mum.

An hour later, she and her mother were sat side by side at the head teacher's desk. The head was called Mr Pickering and Angela noticed that he had a food stain on his pale blue shirt. Angela had been at Croydon Academy for just over a year and this was the second time she had been in Mr Pickering's office. She slumped in her seat as she half-listened to them going on and on.

'Angela is a bully,' said Mr Pickering, his thin lips pressed together, 'and we do not tolerate bullying at Croydon Academy. This is the third incident of unacceptable bullying behaviour towards other pupils and the level of violence today was really quite shocking. The pupil that Angela attacked needed medical attention and would be within her rights to press criminal charges. It could have been much *more* serious if staff hadn't intervened when they did.'

Angela's mum smelled of cigarettes. She would have had one on the way here, walking from the bus stop to the school. She always stank more when she'd had a fag outside.

'What do you have to say, Angela?' her mum asked, turning to her. Her voice was always different when she talked in front of the teachers, as if she was putting on a big act.

Angela shrugged and turned away. She heard her mother sigh lightly.

There was the sound of Mr Pickering shuffling papers on his desk. 'I note Angela's behaviour and academic performance in primary were almost exemplary.'

'Yeah, she was top of her class. I suppose the work's easier at primary . . .'

That was typical for Donna. If Angela did well it was because the work was too easy; if she did poorly it was Angela's fault.

'It still doesn't explain this extreme change in performance and behaviour.'

They were talking about her as if she wasn't there.

'Do you have an explanation for this, Angela?' Mr Pickering raised his eyebrows as he waited for an answer. His hair was grey but his eyebrows were still black, so they looked fake, stuck-on.

Angela glanced at her chipped nail polish. With her thumbnail, she tried to scrape a little more off. Her hands were still dirty from the fight.

'It's just teenagers, isn't it?' her mother offered in the silence.

'But you're not thirteen yet, are you Angela?' said Mr Pickering, raising his voice a little, as if she had hearing problems.

Why did he keep saying her name all the time? *Angela, Angela, Angela*, as if she didn't know who she was?

'She's thirteen soon enough, but it all starts earlier now, doesn't it?' her mother answered for her.

'And there are no problems at home?' Mr Pickering looked over his glasses at them both. Angela wasn't sure who he was talking to this time so kept her mouth shut, glancing at her mother.

'The normal ups and downs, y'know. I separated from her father recently, but it's been fairly amicable.'

She still had that stupid voice on but it was getting even more high-pitched. Her mother liked to pretend everything was fine, even though it had been a year since her dad had left home.

They started talking about her again and Angela looked down at her feet. *A safe environment for pupils and staff. Zero tolerance. Penalties. Blah, fucking blah.*

She wanted to die. She just wanted to die.

'So,' Mr Pickering said with such finality Angela looked up at him. 'I have spoken to my senior colleagues and the decision is that we are suspending Angela for two days. The reasons for exclusion are abusive and bullying behaviour, and violence towards another pupil.'

Blah, blah, blah.

On the bus home, her mother was more upset about having to leave work early than about the violence and the suspension. It was raining outside and the bus smelled of damp clothes.

'I just get a promotion and then you start acting up. This is the third time in almost as many months I've had to leave work and go to the school.'

She made out that she was some kind of high-flyer instead of a college finance officer. Her mother's job sounded stupid and boring.

7

Angela rooted in her school bag and found a half-eaten packet of Haribo. She hunched down in her seat and began to chew. The intense sweetness and the rubbery texture soothed her.

'Where did you get those?'

'Bought them, *Donna.*'

'I told you before, don't call me that. With what?'

'Dad gave me money on Saturday.'

Her mother exhaled down her nose. Angela smiled and put another two sweets into her mouth at once.

'Well you shouldn't be buying sweets, that's for sure. You have to be careful, young lady. You're getting heavy. It's not very attractive.'

Angela put three sweets in her mouth, and faced her mother for a few seconds as she chewed with her mouth open, but her mood had darkened and she no longer felt the same comfort from the sugar rush. As if *Donna* was the hottest chick in town, with her fat thighs and her charity-shop clothes and her home-dyed hair. No wonder her father left. *You don't make an effort,* she'd heard him say to her mother once, when Angela had been listening from upstairs.

She looked out of the bus window at shops passing on the Portland Road: The Star Café Sandwich Bar, Diva Cuts, Morley's Chicken Burgers and Ribs, Portland Wines. The bus moved slowly around the green curve of Ashburton Park.

'Well, you're grounded anyway,' her mother continued. 'No tablet, no phone and no sweets till the end of the week.'

Who gives?

They got off the bus and tramped in the rain to the house. Angela hated home since her father had gone. It felt empty. It smelled different.

She let her school bag fall to the floor and brought her hands up to her face. They smelled of blood and Haribo, salt and sweet.

She wanted to die. She just wanted to die.

'Why are you standing there like that? Hang your coat up, put your stuff away. What's wrong with you?'

'*You're* what's wrong with me,' Angela screamed suddenly, so loud that it seemed to come from her belly. The scream scratched her throat and brought tears to her eyes as it left her.

She felt as if she had a monster inside her. She felt like two parts, the inside and an outer shell. The shell was thinner than an eggshell; it offered little protection. Every so often the inside reached out, and people saw who she was for real, and everyone hated her just as much as she hated herself.

Her mother, who had been too tired for anger until now, was shocked at first, but then her face set itself for combat – low brows and white pinched lips. Angela stood waiting, needing something from Donna and hoping that it would be strong, that it could match the rage that was welling up inside her.

Rage – that was it – *that's* what was possessing her; *that* was why she had beaten skinny, stupid Jasmine, made her bleed, ripped out her hair. *The rage* – that was why she refused to get A grades any longer. It wasn't that high school was too hard or her hormones were surging, it was because she was *seething*.

As they faced off, whatever anger Donna had mustered began to evaporate and her eyes shone with tears. 'Why are you like this? Why do you have to be like this? I'm left to do everything and I don't get any thanks. You love your dad but what do I get?'

'*He* loves *me*,' Angela screamed again, the scratchy, scaly, clawed fist of her voice punching into the hallway.

Real tears now. Donna was crying real tears. Angela hated when her mother cried – the awful shape of her mouth, as if it had been torn.

'Yes, you love him. With him you're all sweetness and shite, but what do I get? Just the shite.'

'I hate you,' Angela cried. The rage was in her fingertips now, tingle and itch, and she wanted to fight again, wanted to rip out hair and bloody lips and noses, wanted to kick and punch and scream.

'I hate you, too. You're a freaking monster. Go to your room and stay there.'

It was enough.

It was the strength that Angela had needed, but not what she had wanted. She had wanted something physical, a shake or a slap. She had wanted toughness, grounding physicality. But what she had been given was enough. Donna hated her. She had never actually heard that before, although she had suspected it. It was calming. It set her mind.

She wanted to die.

She. Just. Wanted. To. Die.

*

10

She went upstairs and slammed her bedroom door, then went to the far corner of the room and sat down, hugging her knees. She pushed her kneecaps right into the sockets of her eyes. She liked the bright lights that came and the pain in the middle of her head. After a few moments she had to uncurl herself and take a breath. She had done this since she was little, but now her belly was so fat it cut off her breathing. She had put on a lot of weight recently. It was true, but she didn't care. She wanted to be massive. She wanted people to turn away when they saw her. She wanted everyone to see the monster that she was on the inside.

She looked up at her bedroom walls, decorated with her drawings and paintings. She had won a national prize when she was in primary for her drawing of a flamingo. The certificate was framed on her wall, alongside a huge poster-sized painting of Katy Perry's face that Angela had done in art class on her first week at Croydon Academy. It wasn't perfect, the teacher had said, but all the other kids in her class had crowded round her when it was finished and said it was amazing. Whenever Angela looked at the painting she remembered that feeling, of having created something to be admired. It had felt like love – or how she had expected love to feel.

On all fours, she crawled to the bed and pulled out her old music box that she had hidden underneath. The music box no longer made a sound, but it still had the tiny ballerina on a spring – although she, too, no longer danced. Inside the box was a diamond ring on a chain.

As she had done many times before, Angela slid the ring onto her finger and admired it, tilting her fingers up at the end as she flashed the ring from side to side. Even though her fingers had got fatter, the ring was still too big for her. She unhooked the chain and fastened it around her neck, closing her fist over the diamond and holding it against her heart. Diamond was the most expensive jewel. The ring meant that she was beloved. She had wanted to be loved more than anything, but it didn't feel as she had expected. Love was such a shock. It felt like being held under water.

Also inside the music box was a packet of thirty aspirin tablets that she had taken from the kitchen earlier in the week. She had been keeping them for a moment just like this. She popped the tablets out of the packet onto the bedspread. When all of the tablets had been punched out, Angela scooped them up into her fist. She glanced up at her drawings on the wall, wondering if she could really do it, but then remembered that her mother hated her.

With the same absent compulsion that she had eaten the jelly sweets on the bus, Angela put one tablet after another into her mouth and washed them down with flat Coke that had been sitting opened on her dresser since the day before. She didn't have enough Coke for the last few pills and two got stuck in her throat, so she had to rush to the bathroom and drink straight out of the tap to wash them down.

She went back to her room, put the light out and curled up in bed, her clothes still on, pressing the diamond ring against her chest.

She had left no note.

That was all right.

You are born and then, you die.

2

Nick

It was a Friday like any other. Marina was washing fresh shrimp while Nick was upstairs bathing the children. A Rioja was breathing and the kitchen filled with the smell of garlic as Marina's famous paella cooked on the stove, the rice fattening with the juices of tomato and onion. Fridays Marina got home from work about six, and they liked to stay in, get the kids to bed so that they could relax and talk. Friday nights they could focus on each other. It was their favourite time of the week.

Nick had fed the kids just before Marina got home: fish fingers and baked beans at five. Now the children were in the bath together – Ava, four, was making cakes with the soapsuds, which Nick had to pretend to eat.

'Es delicioso,' Ava said, grinning with her tiny shoulders raised to her ears in joy. Both the children were bilingual.

13

They weren't too strict about it, but Marina tried to speak only Spanish to them and Nick stuck to English. Ava still sometimes mixed it up.

Six-year-old Luca was making a Mohican with his wet hair.

'Dad?' Luca said, face suddenly serious, studying his hand, his hair still on end, 'what makes the tops of your fingers go all wrinkly?'

'Just 'cause the water makes them soft,' Nick replied, not looking at his son but massaging shampoo into Ava's hair. It was another question of Luca's that he was not sure how to answer. If he answered too fully, then Luca would ask another, even more difficult question. Nick lathered up Ava's dark curly hair.

'That hurts,' she cried out, tears sudden but brief. 'Hurting me.'

'Sorry.'

Marina was naturally gentle. She said Nick didn't realise his own strength.

'I hate you,' said Ava, sullen but no longer crying.

'You've not to say *hate*,' Luca corrected, by rote.

'Well, I love you,' said Nick, reflexively, using one of Ava's Tupperwares that she used as pretend cake tins to rinse her hair.

'Dad?' said Luca, frowning earnestly.

'Uh huh.'

'You know how all of us in our family have got brown eyes . . .'

14

'Yup.'

'But you've got blond hair and me, mum and Ava have got dark brown ...'

'Yeah?' Nick raised his eyebrows as he waited for the question. Luca still had his Mohican. The solemnity of his face beneath the ridiculous hairstyle made Nick smile.

'Well, why didn't one of us get your blond hair, like I have your big toes?'

'Um ... I dunno. I think the gene for dark hair is stronger, so it cancels mine out.'

'The gene?'

Nick panicked, knowing he'd got himself into trouble. It would go on for weeks, if not months, and would culminate in hours on the internet learning the facts so that he could break it down for his son. 'I'll look into it and explain tomorrow.' He was sure that other fathers got away with that as an answer, but his son *always* remembered. Luca never, ever forgot when an explanation was owed to him.

He lifted Luca out and towelled him dry, leaving Ava in the bath as the water drained. She liked to lie down and feel the pull of the water sucking her to the bath, or else she would kneel and watch the whirlpool up close.

Dry, Luca left the bathroom and streaked down the hall and then back. 'Look at me. I'm running about naked,' he giggled, wiggling his bottom and making a funny face.

On his knees, Nick couldn't help laughing at him. 'Go get your pyjamas on.' He looked down and saw that his T-shirt was soaked through. 'C'mon, missy.' Nicholas lifted Ava out of the bath and wrapped a towel around her, swaddling her like a baby. 'Have you forgiven me?'

She nodded abstractly. Lashes wet over huge brown eyes.

'Do I get a kiss, then?'

She tilted her head coyly, then lunged forward and kissed him on the lips. He sat back on his heels, stunned.

'That's my girl.'

He scooped her up. Luca was at the top of the stairs, battling his pyjama top – head in an armhole. Rusty, their ten-year-old Border terrier, lay with nose on paws watching them, only his eyebrows moving.

Marina and Nick had got Rusty when they lived in the flat in Balham, and the dog had become used to life with them before the children, when he had been the centre of attention. He was silently disapproving but stoic – allowing ears and tail to be gently pulled and fur to be stroked against the grain. The dog always seemed grateful for the children's bedtime. Now Rusty watched as Nick passed with Ava in his arms.

In the bedroom, Nicholas unwrapped Ava from her towel and bunched up her pyjama top so that she could put her head through. She ran away from him, climbing on the bed and jumping up and down. He caught her and tickled her, blowing a raspberry on her round belly, and then held her between his thighs as he put the top over her head and tugged her arms through. He bent to kiss her hot cheek as he pulled on her bottoms.

Then it was story time on the big beanbag in Luca's room. Marina was reading them Aesop's Fables in Spanish – the

Hare and the Tortoise – but when it was Nick's turn the children always tortured him by asking not for a story but a performance.

Nick's hungry caterpillar slurped and lurched, antennae tweaking underarms and ears. His witches cackled camply and screeched. His giants made the floor shake, *fee fi fo fum*, causing Ava and Luca to squeal with laughter.

Sometimes he would try to read something quietly and normally, but they would always plead for the characters and the voices, promising not to get too excited and to go straight to sleep. Tonight, he tried to be a timid Rumpelstiltskin, but Luca was unimpressed.

'Dad, read it properly.'

'I am.'

'Do the funny voice and the jumping up and down.' Luca stamped his foot in imitation.

'Tomorrow.'

When Nick finally made it downstairs, barefoot, jeans still damp but wearing a fresh T-shirt, Marina had lit candles and poured him a glass of wine. He picked up a prone, juice-stained bunny on the stairs and fired it into a toy box in the corner of the room as he let out a long sigh.

The kitchen windows were steamed up, and the smell made his stomach rumble. He was hungry. He had spent most of the day at a school in Croydon, his fourth week delivering a series of drama workshops to the lower school, and he hadn't eaten properly since breakfast. A Snickers and a flat white in the car before he picked up Ava and Luca from the childminder.

He sighed as he looked at the long, bare wood table, daring to relax for the first time that day. He rubbed his eyes with the heels of his hands. Two plates were on the table with cutlery set on top. Crusty bread had been torn open.

'Tired?' Marina was standing by the stove, her dark hair swept up into a messy bun. She was wearing her favourite navy tracksuit bottoms tucked into his old fleece-lined hiking socks. A bright blue sweatshirt, off the shoulder and cut off so that her brown stomach showed when she stretched to turn off the extractor fan. The bone of her wrist was exquisite as she reached out for her wineglass.

Nick circled his arms around her before she caught the glass. He put his two hands over the gentle swell of her stomach and then ran them under the easy give of her waistband to cup her bare behind in both hands. She leaned her head back towards him and rested it on his shoulder. He kissed her neck and she turned, draping her hands over his shoulders. She backed against the counter and he leaned into her, pelvis to pelvis.

'They asleep?' she looked up into his eyes.

He loved her face. Oval, olive skin, eyes like their daughter's – fathomless chocolate brown. The careful arch of her brow and the cut of her cheekbone, almost jarring with her eyes, making her seem sculpted, detached, intellectual. Full lips and a space between her front teeth. Crinkles at the corners of her eyes and a mole just below her left lower lid, like a black tear.

'Of course they're asleep. I'm the master.'

'You refused to do the voices, so they fell asleep out of boredom?'

'No, I gave one of my best performances, actually. Put a lot into it.'

'You're a little liar.'

They rocked back and forth for a moment, breathing each other in. They didn't always make it, but Fridays, when they were good, were just like this – remembering that they were lovers and two distinct people. Often the week would rush past in a flurry of work and parenting and friends and family commitments, so that they felt they were only really together in the early hours of the morning, entangled in each other's warm smell. And sometimes not even then, if there were nightmares or monsters, little ones creeping the hall in fear. Luca would lift the covers and slip in beside Marina, but Ava always went to Nick, curled in a ball in the crook of his arm.

'Let's eat.'

The prawns were curled pink on top of the scarlet rice. Nick sank into a wooden chair and ran his fingers through his hair as Marina spooned portions onto plates.

'Could eat a horse,' he said, tucking in right away, biting into a succulent piece of rabbit.

They would each talk about their days, but Marina liked to go first. He was prepared to listen.

'So, you remember that DfID bid I was working on?' Marina peeled a prawn and licked her fingers, olive oil making her lips glisten.

Nick nodded. He had taken too big a mouthful and the rice was hot. He took little sips of air to cool it down as she continued.

'You won't believe it. Theresa found out about it and now she's trying to mastermind everything.' She opened her eyes wide then dunked her bread in oil and washed it down with wine. 'She is so patronising, so micromanaging it makes me insane. "This is a wonderful piece of work," she tells me with that stupid smile she has, "it has to go to the board."'

'That's bad, right? The bid going to the board, I mean.' Nick raised an eyebrow.

'Yes, of course; the board will hack around with it and it will become nothing like I wrote, but that isn't the worst thing. She wants me to increase the bid by fifty grand. Fifty fucking grand.'

Even swearwords were elegant on her lips, defused by her lilting, anglicised Spanish accent. Marina was director of Child International's London office, the breadwinner of the family, making more than twice what Nick brought in with his company, ACTUp, which he'd set up when Marina was pregnant with Ava. By then his own acting career had diminished into merely audition attendance. His company delivered acting workshops for kids and media training for adults. It wasn't what he had planned to do but he mostly enjoyed it.

'She drives me crazy.' A viscous tear of olive oil rolled from the corner of Marina's mouth to her chin and she caught it with the heel of her hand. 'She is a terrible woman . . . ' She shook her head and sighed, picking up her fork.

Her accent showed most on her 'r's. The terrible woman was Theresa Long, Chair of the Board of Trustees at Child International. Nick already felt as if he knew her intimately.

'Why is increasing the bid so bad?' he said, scraping his plate with his fork as he walked to the pot for more. 'Surely the more money the better – if you're lucky in getting it anyway?'

'If we increase it, it will cross the funding threshold and I will need to incorporate formal accounting, but it is not just that – the funders will expect more and I do not have the staff.'

She kept talking, one leg tucked under her, pausing every mouthful or so to gesticulate with her fork, her forehead wrinkling as she recalled the day's exasperation. Her work was stressful – more so than his.

When Luca was a toddler, Nick had been cast as a regular on the BBC drama *Scuttlers* about a street gang in the 1890s and had thought, *This is it*. He had paid a fortune for a voice coach, to get his Manchester accent just right. They had bought the house on Firgrove Hill and the following year took the whole family – Nick and Marina's parents, Nick's siblings and their children, on holiday to a villa in Portugal. When the show came out, someone had recognised Nick in Sainsbury's and asked for his autograph.

His character had finally been tortured and murdered. The series had then been decommissioned and other roles hadn't come his way.

Those that can't do, teach, his father had said woundingly when Nick started ACTUp to compensate for the lack of roles. Teaching was still performing, he had learned, and he liked working with the kids. He was good at it; and he was a husband and a father now. He had to support his family. His last real acting job had been reading Dante's *Inferno* on Radio Four – over a year ago.

'And *then* you know what she said to me?' Marina shook her head in frustration, teasing her prawn skins from the rice, then sitting up, posturing, imitating her boss, whom Nick had never met but could now visualise. 'She says, "You don't know how difficult my job is, Marina – I've got to persuade the rest of the board. It's much harder than managing the day-to-day operations."'

She turned her mouth to one side and waved her fork in a gesture of defiance that reminded him of the Marina he had met for the first time in the Marlborough Arms off Hampstead Road. He had been an out-of-work actor while she was doing a masters in Economics at UCL. They had tended bar together, working for five pounds an hour, and flirting heavily: flicking bar towels across the backs of each other's legs, brushing up against each other when a keg needed changing. Nick had waited until the last minute to make his move, when she was set to return to Spain. He had been ready to forget everything, teach English in Spain if he had to, but then she got a fund-raising job in London.

That was Marina. She seemed so relaxed, warm and unpresumptuous, but she aced everything she touched.

'I mean,' Marina continued, 'she tries to make out that I am just some office manager, when really she wants to do my job for me.'

The anger pinked her cheeks and he wanted to kiss her again, but knew he would be rebuffed as she was on a roll. 'She's awful,' he said, agreeing instead, raising both eyebrows and pushing his plate away. 'Is that final, though – will you have to increase the bid and send it to the board?'

Rusty had moved nearer the table since Nick got second helpings. Now he stood to the side, averting his eyes yet watching Nick wipe his plate with bread. Normal dogs begged shamelessly, while Rusty thought he had mastered seeming disinterest. No Olivier Award for him. Nick broke eye contact with Marina to give him the crust.

'Yes, and it will be a nightmare. The funders will expect me to change the world, and how can I do that with so few staff? They just expect miracles.' The tendons along her neck were tensing. 'I'm sorry,' she said, 'I thought I was going to explode.' She dipped her pinkie in the olive oil and licked it. 'I had to get it out of me.'

'I love you,' he whispered, head dipping.

She smiled, her eyes opening to him. They had been married for seven years, parents for six. Marina reached out and cupped his cheek. He turned to kiss the palm of her hand.

He poured them both another glass of wine. Marina was rubbing the back of her neck and he stood up and took over, kneading the brown skin. He noticed that she had a knot above her right shoulder. She moaned lightly, in pain or relief, and then looked up at him.

'So how was your workshop?'

'It was all right, I suppose.' He kept kneading her shoulders and she let her head drop. 'More of the same – driving me nuts. Cannot wait for it to finish.'

'You only have one more week?'

'Well, week and a half – they do their performances week after next.' He sighed loudly, sat down and drank another sip of wine.

'It's a rough school.' She raised an eyebrow at him as she dabbed crumbs from her plate with her forefinger.

'It's not a bad school – good arts programme – but I dunno, it's just that group.'

'The loud girl giving you trouble again?'

'Loud girl?'

'The fat one.'

'Angela. God help me. She wasn't there today. I dunno, I worry about her, but I have to admit that it was easier without her there.'

'Why don't you just send her out?'

'I could, but that's not the point, is it? It's about inclusion and building confidence. I think I just need to get better at controlling her behaviour. She's really quick though, y'know. One of those kids who has an answer for everything.'

'But you said she is aggressive?'

'Aggressive to the other kids, not to me.'

'Just be strict with her.'

'The other kids don't like it when you get serious. Drama's supposed to be fun. It kind of kills the mood. Let's change the subject.' He held up his arms as if surrendering.

'What about talking to the head teacher about her?'

'Nah, it's fine. I've made a special effort with her recently. I've tried to focus just on her when I can ... I think that's all she needs.'

There was a thump from upstairs and Rusty, who had become more anxious since the children arrived, jumped suddenly to his feet and watched the door. It was only a few seconds before the cries started.

Nick exhaled audibly.

'I'll go,' said Marina, pressing her palms on the table to raise herself to her feet.

'We should just get that bunk bed back,' Nick said. The noise was likely Luca, who kept falling out of bed since they had moved him from his high bunk into a normal bed. His old bed had had a barrier and he was used to rolling against it.

'Either that or put bars on this one,' Marina laughed as she slowly made her way to the stairs, 'like a hospital bed.'

Luca was calling 'Dad!' Because Nick was at home more, both children instinctively called to him when there was a problem. There was no worry that he would wake Ava, who slept like a stone, and Marina did not rush as she climbed the stairs.

Nick drank his wine, looking out of the window at the sun setting on the full-grown paper bark maple in the garden. The night was still and he could just make out clouds clustered like a fist on the horizon. He picked up his phone and flicked through his emails. There were a couple of messages from his accountant, signatures needed on company reports that showed his income had shrunk since last year.

An email from his agent, Harriet, mentioned an audition. Nick reached for his laptop at the far end of the table. He had to close down World of Zoo which Luca had been playing earlier, then opened Harriet's email. A young male actor was being sought for a TV advert for cold and flu medication. Nick grimaced. This was what it had come to – auditioning for adverts – yet there would be a lot of competition and he never seemed to be first choice. 'Your face is too pretty,' Harriet had once told him, sucking on her cigarette. 'You're not getting the parts because you look as if butter wouldn't melt.' He replied, asking if she thought he had a chance this time.

He closed the computer and opened a text message from his brother Mark, who was on holiday in Thailand with his long-term girlfriend, Juliette. There was a picture attached of their two pairs of sandy feet photographed before a blue sea and sky.

Hope you're not working too hard. Sod coming home tomorrow X

Nick smiled to himself as he noticed that Mark and his girlfriend had matching bunions.

He held his phone at arm's length and flicked through photos of the kids he'd been working with earlier. He had taken some group shots and then one or two of the pupils had Googled him and asked for selfies, even though they hadn't even seen *Scuttlers*. It was enough for them that Nick had a Wikipedia profile.

Nick took another sip of wine, smiling wryly as he remembered being at drama school and thinking he was going to be famous one day. He shook his head and tossed his phone onto the table, and then began to stack the dishwasher with their dirty plates. He heard Marina's feet on the stairs and turned, closing the dishwasher behind him.

She launched herself at him from the bottom of the stairs, a skip and a jump like a gymnast and Nick caught her and turned her around, shifting the weight of her and setting her on the counter. He pulled on the neck of her sweater and kissed her bare shoulder as Rusty began barking gruffly. He didn't like it when they hugged and tried to get in between, snaking in and out of their ankles.

Marina snapped her fingers at him. 'Quiet. You'll wake them.'

Rusty barked once more, as if insisting on the final say.

'Do you want to be bad with me?' said Marina, head to one side.

Nick bit his lip. 'Luca back to sleep?'

'Yup and I've built the bed up with pillows. Come on, it's been a week from hell.'

Marina opened the kitchen window wide as Nick stood on tiptoe and reached up to find their contraband hidden behind a large tin of pineapple slices: an old Ray-Ban sunglasses case which contained a few sprigs of budding marijuana, a thinned packet of Golden Virginia tobacco and some rolling papers.

They hung out of the window together, sharing a thin joint. Late autumn and the evening was cool. Nick inhaled, watching goose bumps rise on Marina's brown forearm. She took the joint from him and he reached up inside her top, unhooked her bra and slid a hand around her ribcage to cup her breast. 'Want to go to bed early?' Dope made him horny.

She looked over her shoulder at him, brow arching, and he leaned in to kiss her cheekbone. Each of them was seeking oblivion, the dispatching of the day into pleasure. Now he wanted her, needed the assurance of her, after his day of un-realised ideas, broken communication and searching teenage questions. Her smell – the soap of the morning lost to sweat and stress and smog – and now the garlic on her fingers, the grass and a musky hollow of perfume behind her collarbone.

As he ran his thumb up her neck and tucked a strand of loose hair behind her ear, the doorbell rang.

'Who the hell is that?'

Nick glanced at the clock. It was just after nine. He was hard and he tugged at his jeans as he peered through the small kitchen window that looked out onto the doorstep. Strangers – a man and a woman were standing there. The woman reached up and the doorbell sounded again.

'I think it's just Jehovah's Witnesses. I'll get rid of them.'

Marina covered her mouth to stifle her laughter as she stubbed out the joint on the stone windowsill. Nick went to the door, kicking a rainbow-coloured My Little Pony out of the way so that he could open it. He ran a hand through his hair and smiled, *thanks but no thanks* on his lips. Rusty stood at his side, tail wagging uncertainly at the people on the doorstep.

Before he was able to speak, the woman – sandy-haired, a

tired face without make-up – held up an identification badge that Nick didn't even look at.

'I'm Detective Sergeant Brookes from the police.' She glanced at the man beside her, who was strapping, taller than Nick with a deadened expression. 'And this is Detective Constable Weston.'

They weren't in uniform. Nick frowned, not understanding, then a prickle of panic about the weed.

'How can I help you?'

'Are you Nicholas Dean?'

'Yeah . . . ' Nick's heart began to thump in his chest and he hooked a thumb into his back pocket.

'Detective Weston and I work in child protection services. Do you know why we are here?'

'No.' His heart pounding and a rushing sound in his ears.

'What's going on?' Marina's voice.

His mind blank with shock, Nick opened the door and the two plain-clothes officers walked into the house. In the kitchen, Nick stood with his hands on his hips.

'Mrs Dean?' said Detective Brookes, forehead wrinkling.

Marina had her arms folded over her chest. 'We are married but I keep my own name, Alvarez,' she said, her face dark with suspicion. 'What is this about?'

Nick motioned towards the kitchen, pulling out a chair for Marina only to discover she was not behind him, but at the edge of the utility room, quickly fastening her bra. They had been smoking out of the window, but he wondered if the smell was on their clothes or had drifted into the room.

Detective Brookes straightened and said, 'Mr Dean, an allegation has been made against you.'

'What kind of allegation?' Heat at the nape of his neck.

'A child at Croydon Academy has alleged that you committed a sexual offence against her.'

Both officers' faces were impassive. Nick's mouth suddenly felt dry. Tongue furred: red wine and tobacco and fresh fear. 'What? I've been working at that school but ...' his eyes wide, looking from one police officer to the other, the mere accusation causing a reflex of guilt to curdle in his gut. The rice from earlier heavy inside him. 'I haven't ... done anything wrong.'

'What sexual allegation? Who said this?' said Marina, her voice indignant, two thin lines of anger between her brows.

Nick reached out and put a hand on Marina's arm.

Brookes looked from Marina to Nick. 'Mr Dean, we are arresting you and taking you down to the station to be interviewed. You do not have to say anything. But, it may harm your defence if you do not mention when questioned something which you later rely on in court. Anything you do say may be given in evidence.'

Nick swallowed. *Court? A defence?*

'Are you serious?' Nick pressed his fingernails into the palm of his hand.

The male officer, Weston, spoke for the first time. 'As part of our ongoing inquiry, we would like to take a detailed look at your electronic equipment – phones, computers – for evidence.' His eyes focussed on the laptop on the table. 'We ask that you let us take these now. If you don't consent we will get a warrant to take them at a later stage.'

Marina was flustered. She stood up, eyes shining and cheeks flushing. 'We work. We both work. You can't just take our computers.'

Nick felt a cold wave of fear wash over him. He watched Marina gesticulate, hands to her hair in anger and disbelief. 'This is a mistake. This is all a mistake. You can't just come in here and take our computers and tell us this . . . these lies.'

'We understand this is upsetting to hear,' said Weston to Marina, his face doughy, eyes cold and lifeless as a fish in the market.

Nick put a hand on Marina's shoulder. 'It's all right.' He handed over his mobile phone and the laptop from the table. 'Can you get your laptop? We'll get it back, I'm sure.'

Marina went into the other room and returned with her laptop zipped inside a grey padded carrier and the iPad that they shared. The children would miss that most. Her face was drawn, suddenly drained of all its luminosity – like the day they had briefly lost Luca in Tesco in Aldershot. She handed the laptop to Weston, who put it on top of Nick's and tucked them under his arm.

'When will you return them?' Marina said, frowning.

'It will be a minimum of four to six weeks . . .'

'Four to six weeks! Why on earth do you need them for so long? We are working people. We do work from home.' Marina had raised her voice and Nick put a hand on her waist but she twisted away from him. 'What are you looking for?'

'As I was saying,' continued Weston, slowly blinking his fish eyes, 'it will be four to six weeks ... assuming that there is no evidence of child pornography. If anything of that nature is discovered, the computers will have to be taken into evidence.'

'This is crazy,' Marina's 'r's ripped through the room. 'Of course there is no pornography.'

Weston nodded gravely, his voice measured and flat, devoid of all emotion: 'Paedophiles tend to search for on-screen images before progressing to assault, so the computers are important to assess Mr Dean's guilt ... or innocence.'

The air seemed to compress as before an explosion.

Paedophile.

3

Angela

At seven o'clock the alarm sounded and Angela opened her eyes. It was a few seconds before she remembered she was supposed to be dead.

She lay on her back, blinking at the ceiling, listening to the sounds of the morning: the steamy hush of the shower and her mum singing a song from the radio out of tune. She could smell coffee. Tears rolled from her eyes and pooled in her ears.

There was nothing else for it, so she got up. Carefully, she unhooked the catch on her necklace and tucked the diamond ring back in its box and slid it under her bed.

She hated herself. She couldn't do anything right. She didn't feel well, a strange fullness pressing upwards from her stomach, but she didn't feel like she was going to die, either. Maybe it was because she was so fat. Maybe she should have taken more pills. Maybe it was because she had eaten all those sweets. Maybe you needed an empty stomach so the pills could work.

She took off yesterday's clothes then spent about five minutes sitting on the bed buttoning her school shirt before she remembered that she was suspended and didn't have to go to school. She wanted to scream but couldn't. She just sat there in her half-buttoned school shirt looking at the floor.

She had imagined being found dead in her bed, and her mother crying, calling her father and telling him. Even though the chance was now lost, Angela still watched them in her mind, hearing the news and hugging each other like they used to when she was small. The grief for her might bring them together again.

Angela sighed, looking down at her bare feet. Even her feet were chubby. She watched the small round toes bunching up on the carpet. This little piggy went to market. This little piggy stayed at home. This little piggy cried all the way home.

She was *that* little pig, the crying one. She felt as if she were screaming inside her head all the time. She was just trapped inside, screaming and crying on the inside and no one could see.

She felt sick and wanted her mum to stay home and look after her, but there was little chance of that. She couldn't even say she was sick because she had brought it all on herself. She couldn't admit what she had done. Angela stood in front of the mirror and watched her pale, expressionless face.

4

Donna

Her daughter never got out of bed in the morning without coercion, so Donna was surprised that Angela was already up and staring at herself in the mirror.

Donna wasn't sure if she was getting dressed or undressing from the night before. They had not spoken since the screaming fight in the hall after school. Last night Donna had drunk a bottle of white wine to calm herself down and now felt the metallic shiver of it on her skin, but it was Friday and she would get through. She felt better now she had had a shower.

'I called your dad and he can come and take you to his at three. There's some stuff in the fridge for lunch. Make yourself useful and tidy the place up a bit. Do the vacuuming. I'll call you when I'm on my break.'

Angela said nothing, still turned towards the mirror. With her bare legs and her stomach sticking out, her daughter seemed like a miniature sumo wrestler. Donna watched the face in the mirror. Angela still looked babyish, the fat happy baby she had once been, although there was no happiness in her any longer. Donna was still not sure where it had gone, but she was sure it had to be all her and Stephen's fault.

Donna suspected that the root of her daughter's anger was her father being asked to leave. Donna hadn't done it lightly. Stephen was, if nothing else, a good father, but it had been a torturous marriage. Torture was not an exaggeration – there had been no violence, but Stephen's indifference to her had been crushing and absolute. Separation had been a relief, but it seemed Angela would never forgive her.

'Did you hear what I said?' Donna folded her arms.

Angela half-turned and then parted her knees and retched. To Donna's horror a gush of white foam rushed from Angela's mouth onto the carpet. It was like something out of a horror film.

'What on earth?'

Angela took deep breaths, hands on her knees, and then retched again. This time it was a thin white stream, almost like milk, turning green at the end.

'What's the matter with you?'

Angela put the back of her hand over her mouth. Tears were coursing down her cheeks.

'I was supposed to be dead.'

'What are you talking about?'

Donna put a hand on Angela's back and felt the after-shudder of her stomach and ribs.

'I took thirty pills, but it wasn't enough.'

'What?' A fist of fear in Donna's chest as she tried to process what her daughter had said.

Angela said nothing, wiping her face and looking down at the foam on the carpet.

'What do you mean? What did you take?' said Donna, spinning Angela round by the shoulders. Her daughter's eyes drifted to an empty blister packet on the floor.

'Dear sweet God.' Donna picked up the packet. It was aspirin, only aspirin. 'You took all of these?'

Angela nodded once. 'I wanted to die.'

Donna didn't know what an aspirin overdose meant. 'I need to get you to the doctor. Put your clothes on. Hurry up. When did you take the pills?'

'Last night.'

'Last night, dear sweet Jesus. You'll be the death of me, you will.'

Donna called a taxi. There was nothing else for it, as Stephen had taken the car. While they were waiting for it to pull up outside, Donna texted her colleague.

Taking Angela to A&E. Be in late.

The morning was damp and cold. They watched lashes of scarlet light easing above the roofs of the red-brick terraced houses. Angela was dressed in jogging bottoms and trainers, her white school shirt and a hoodie. She hunched as they waited, hands in her pockets.

'Why would you do something like that? Why would you want to hurt yourself?' Donna was aware that she sounded harsh, but that was how love was dished out in her family. She felt alone and frightened, overburdened and abandoned again. Other people didn't have to put up with this. Other mothers didn't have their twelve-year-olds trying to commit suicide by taking all the aspirin in the cabinet.

Angela shrugged. Her face was pale, a round, unforgiving moon.

'You really wanted to kill yourself?'

Angela nodded once. The skin under her eyes was shaded blue. She seemed different, changed, as if all the anger in her had been vomited out onto the bedroom floor.

'It's always got to be about you, doesn't it? You've got to be centre of attention no matter what.' Again, Donna winced at her own harshness. She wanted to be kinder but didn't know how. She had been brought up the hard way, when there had been no time for self-pity.

'No.'

Tears again. Donna stiffened. She realised that it had been some time since she had seen her daughter crying tears that were not born of rage. She was reminded of baby Angela again, the little girl that liked dandelion clocks and lie-down cuddles. She had been such a sweet child not so long ago.

'You get in trouble and so you do this to yourself just to try and get some sympathy.'

More tears. Angela wiped her chin with the sleeves of her sweater.

'Well why, then? Why did you do it?' She spoke more gently this time. It was hard to distance herself from her daughter. Sometimes Donna felt as if they were one person. She didn't like to admit it, but Donna could see herself in Angela even when she was being hateful. It was hard to see her daughter for what she was: a separate entity, a twelve-year-old girl.

Another shrug. Donna wanted to shake her. She looked out of the window but the taxi was not yet there.

'Why did you have to make Dad leave?'

'So surprise, surprise, this is my fault, is it?' Donna pressed her lips together and looked up the road in the direction the taxi would come from. She glanced at her watch. It was two minutes later than the last time she had checked. 'I didn't make him leave. I just told him what was what and he left of his own accord.' Donna swallowed hard. Her own pain and anger was swirling inside her. Her head hurt and her mouth was dry and she didn't need this today. 'Why don't you blame him for anything? Why can't something be his fault for a change?'

A strange look came over Angela and Donna wondered if she was going to be sick again, or pass out. She gripped her daughter's wrist.

'I just wanted it to stop. I don't want it again.'

'Don't want what again?'

Angela's bruised blue eyes looked away from her. Donna felt the tension between her brows and tried to stop frowning. She consciously tried to suppress her anger so that Angela would talk to her, but it had been a long time since they had really talked. Everything had changed between them in the last year or two. She had been a little girl that loved her mum and now she was nearly a teenager, and a bully. Hands in fists of anxiety at her side, Donna tried to listen, waited for an answer.

Angela began to cry again, big, fat, heavy tears that magnified the pores of her skin.

'I ... didn't want ... him to ...' gulping, eyes blurred, 'touch me ... again.'

Palpitating, words born and dying on her lips, Donna lowered herself to face Angela.

'Touched you? Who touched you? What do you mean?'

Real fear now pierced the skin of Donna's hung-over panic. Still she resisted the understanding that was already easing into her mind. She waited again for an answer, this time heart pounding.

'I'd had enough.' Angela fisted tears from her eyes and sniffed, looked up at the ceiling. 'I didn't want it anymore ... I didn't like it.'

'Darling,' said Donna, taking Angela by the shoulders, 'who touched you? And what do you mean ... touched?'

She was crying so hard that the sleeves of her sweatshirt were wet with her tears. 'Touched me down there, but I don't like it.'

Donna squeezed her daughter's shoulders. 'Who did this? Is it a boy at school?'

Angela shook her head, choking.

'Is it someone your age or someone older?'

'Older.'

'I'll skin him alive and kill him with my bare hands. Tell me now.'

'I . . . can't,' Angela was almost hyperventilating.

Donna stood up and folded her arms. 'You have to tell me right now, young lady. If someone's hurt you, we need to call the police. Can you imagine what your father'll have to say about this? He'll have him strung up.'

Angela crossed her arms over her body, protective.

'Tell me who it was. Angela, please sweetheart, I have to have a name.'

Angela wiped her face with both hands and looked at her mother. Donna saw the red face as at once defiant and vulnerable. Angela gasped little convulsive sips of air, trying to control her breathing.

'Who?' Donna prompted again, the pain in her temples now so dark and incisive that it felt as if there were a knife in her skull. 'If someone has touched you, we need to tell the police. Your dad'll make sure the right thing's done.'

The taxi horn suddenly, jovial, intrusive.

Donna pressed Angela into her. She was shaking, trying to say something into her shoulder and so Donna pushed her away, smoothed the hair off her wet face.

'Who touched you? Tell me, darling, tell me now.'

'It was . . . Mr Dean.'

'Who the hell is Mr Dean?'

5

Nick

'I'll be back as soon as I can,' Nick whispered, kissing Marina's hair. 'We'll sort this out. Don't worry.' He didn't believe his own words, but consoling her helped calm him.

'Don't worry?' she repeated. 'How can I not?' Tugging gently on his T-shirt.

Nick sat and put on his shoes, looking around the kitchen at the glasses still stained with red wine, the kitchen redolent of garlic and onion, twisted napkins spotted with tomato, breadcrumbs on the table. The spoils of their happiness. A dark thought shifted over him, that everything was about to change.

The unmarked police car in the drive was a black BMW. Nick sat in the back seat, hands between his knees, his mind a turning kaleidoscope of concern slicing into fear.

42

He wondered who had accused him, and of what exactly? A sex offence – what was that? Assault – rape? A thousand inter- actions flipped through his mind, clumsy stills of encouraging hands on young shoulders, casual touches that had been part of drama scenes or not part of scenes. Off-the-cuff remarks. Conversations that could have been misconstrued: jokes about rap lyrics, trying to be cool.

The police officers were silent. Brookes drove and Weston sat in the back seat with Nick. The hulk of the man was silently domineering. The dashboard of the car had a radio and some kind of computer system that was flashing. Nick let his head rest on the back of the seat behind him, wondering if he smelled of alcohol or the joint. It was Friday night, for Christ's sake.

The laptop computers were in the boot of the car. Nick's stomach lurched again as he looked out of the window at the suburban darkness, punctuated briefly by lit windows and LED lights on well-kept lawns. What would they find on his com- puter? When was the last time he had cleared his history? Did it matter if the history was cleared or was it all still embedded in the hard drive? He closed his eyes, trying not to remember late-night searches.

The lights of Farnham town centre came into view and then passed. Darkness again as they drove alongside Hankley Common, its green at night a stretch of nothingness blacker than the sky. They were in the car for no more than twenty minutes, but it felt like an hour as they drove to Guildford and Surrey Police Headquarters. Nick was suddenly very thirsty, his head throbbing.

Brookes parked, and they asked him to get out. Nick followed them round the back of the police station, a tired, three-storey 1960s block.

'Wait here and the duty sergeant will book you in,' said Detective Sergeant Brookes.

Nick waited at a reception desk. The duty sergeant, an older woman with a heavy, resigned expression was speaking loudly and repetitively to a young woman altered by drink or drugs.

A middle-aged man with a florid complexion and small eyes was sitting on a plastic chair in handcuffs. He watched as Nick clicked his knuckles and looked around for water.

The young woman was led away and then the sergeant turned her attention to Nick. Up close the duty sergeant smelled of the same perfume Nick's mother wore. He couldn't remember what it was called.

Detective Constable Weston came out of a door behind reception and stood as Sergeant Warner laboriously typed Nick's details into an on-screen form. *Name. Address. Date of birth.*

'Twelfth of August 1981,' Nick answered, clearing his throat, wanting to ask for water but deciding to wait.

The badge on the sergeant's white shirt said that her name was Pamela Warner. Nick was standing only a foot from her, yet she was still speaking as loudly as she had been when talking to the drunk woman, asking if he had been advised of his rights and if he had any physical or mental health conditions, any specific dietary or religious requirements.

Nick tried to keep his voice even and his breathing in

check as he answered, although it felt as if his whole body was trembling.

Suddenly, Sergeant Warner narrowed her eyes and regarded him.

'You look familiar.'

Nick swallowed.

'Have you been on TV?'

Nick felt his shoulders sag. 'Yes, I'm an actor.'

Sergeant Warner's face suddenly broke into a smile. She had big white teeth and the sight of them changed her face entirely, brightening it, if only for a moment.

'Hang on, were you in that murder mystery series, *Shetland*?'

'No, that was Douglas Henshall. I get it a lot.'

'I didn't think that series was very realistic,' said Sergeant Warner, raising her eyebrows as her lips turned down.

Nick shrugged, unsure what to say, trying hard not to scream at her as the young woman had earlier.

'And the reason for arrest . . . ?' Warner said loudly.

Weston straightened, and spoke to Sergeant Warner's computer screen. 'Allegation of sexual assault of an under-thirteen . . . '

'Sexual assault,' Warner repeated as she typed.

Nick pressed his teeth together, not daring to look over his shoulder at the others in the waiting room and the staff in the office. He could feel the man with the small eyes watching him.

'Sexual assault of an under-thirteen,' Warner said again.

Nick wiped some beads of perspiration from his hairline. It

was like a farce, only so serious it was terrifying. He looked over his shoulder. The man with the small eyes could be a murderer and yet Nick felt his accusation. The eyes of everyone in the room regarded him: the man who was sexually attracted to *under thirteens*.

'A solicitor called Mr Faldane just called to say your wife has asked him to represent you. Can you indicate if you accept this solicitor? You are entitled to another of your choosing, or a duty solicitor can be allocated to your case.'

Faldane. The name was familiar.

'The one that my wife has arranged is fine,' Nick almost whispered.

Sergeant Warner asked Nick to empty his pockets. He only had his house keys and some money on him and Sergeant Warner put these in a bag before taking him to the cells. She unlocked a door which revealed a small, bare room with a thin, blue plastic mattress on a concrete bench.

'Take off your shoes and leave them here.'

'My shoes?' said Nick, at first misunderstanding, then realising that his shoelaces could be considered dangerous. He hoped he wouldn't be in the cell long enough to think about harming himself.

When the door closed, Nick pressed the heels of his palms into his eyes and stayed like that for a few moments – darkness and bright lights, and a pain deep in his head. He let his hands fall to his sides and sat.

Faldane – Nick remembered the name – a friend of his brother Mike's. Nick hoped that Marina hadn't called Mike in

Thailand to ask for the contact details. If so, his parents would now be aware of the situation. He pitched forward, head in his hands. *Mum and Dad.* He felt sick, deep in his gut.

Without his watch he couldn't tell, but after what felt like an hour, Nick was taken to an area where he could meet the lawyer, and gratefully accepted a plastic cup of water that he downed and crushed as soon as the door was closed. He sat there alone for a few moments. The room was bare, wooden table and chairs. There was nothing to look at, no window or poster. He clasped his hands on the table and felt the nerves rippling through his body. He was still thirsty. He told himself to calm down. Thank God for Marina. She was always one step ahead of him. He needed a solicitor now, he realised, not because he was guilty but because he felt guilty. He didn't know what to do, or say.

No smoke without fire.

Mud sticks.

He took a deep breath in, from his abdomen, and out again, as he had been trained to do before going on stage. It didn't help and so he tried to focus and repeat. Just then, his lawyer entered and closed the door behind him. He was about five foot eight, in a suit that was just too small for him, a double chin when he smiled and a briefcase so full it didn't quite close.

'Hi, are you Nicholas?'

Nick nodded imperceptibly, getting to his feet.

'I'm your solicitor, Bob Faldane. Your wife called me.'

They shook hands.

47

'You got here quickly.'

'I live not far from here. You're Mark's little brother?' said Bob with an expansive grin, as if they were meeting at a wedding.

Nick nodded. 'Yeah, I've heard your name mentioned. How do you know Mark?'

'Met him in the union bar in Freshers' week at Leeds.' Bob's face lit up with nostalgia. 'I love him. Don't see him enough.'

Nick nodded, hands on his hips, trying to smile.

'The arresting officers are going to interview you shortly and take your statement. Is there anything you need to tell me before they begin?'

Nick looked the man in the eye. His eyes were grey and looked tired, full up with stories.

'I didn't do it,' Nick said plainly. 'I don't even understand what I'm being accused of ... '

'All right. Well, let's get started and then we'll know what we're up against.'

In the interview room, Brookes sat opposite Nick, while Weston turned on a recording machine in the corner. Nick noticed there was a camera fixed to the ceiling. Weston dragged his chair out noisily and sat down.

Nick felt his armpits dampen with sweat. It was now after ten at night and he felt underdressed in his T-shirt. Brookes had a closed brown file before her. It was too bright in the room and Nick felt exposed.

Two hours ago he had been eating dinner and thinking about making love to his wife; now here he was.

Brookes clasped her hands, mirroring Nick's posture.

'This morning we received a complaint that you had sexually assaulted a child under the age of thirteen,' she began.

'Who said that?' Nick's heart pounded. 'Which child made the allegation?'

Faldane raised a hand that Nick understood to mean he should calm down. 'You are currently working as a drama teacher at Croydon Academy?'

'No, I'm a private contractor, giving a series of drama workshops. I don't work at the school.'

'You are currently teaching drama to children in the lower school at Croydon Academy?'

'Yes,' said Nick, so weary that the skin on his face felt heavy.

'One of the children, Angela Furness, has alleged that you sexually assaulted her during drama class.'

Angela. Not Angela?

Nick's mind turned and jammed, like slides stuck in a projector. He saw her face – the mean little mouth and sneer. He didn't understand. They had barely been alone.

'Angela ... nothing happened – nothing happened at all. She's just a difficult girl in the group.'

Brookes glanced at her notes briefly and then met Nick's eye. She had a blue biro in her hand and she repeatedly pressed on the lid with her thumb as if she were a nurse dispensing drugs.

'Difficult how?'

'She's disruptive, that's all. Combative. Likes attention.'

'Likes your attention?'

'Yes ... but not what you're suggesting. She's just an out-spoken, attention-seeking child, that's all.'

'Angela has alleged that you asked her to go behind the stage to help you retrieve a gym mattress, and that when you were then alone together you pressed her against the wall and covered her mouth with one hand while you put your hand under her skirt and underwear and fondled her private parts.'

Detective Brookes' face as she delivered this information was devoid of any emotion. She did not even blink.

Nick opened his mouth in shock. He was trembling. It occurred to him that this was the one time in his life when he *needed to act*, needed to appear other than he was, but he couldn't.

Angela's face was stuck in his mind, a single still. A white moon of a face and her uncombed dark hair framing it. School uniform too tight. She looked younger than twelve. She still had that careless disregard for her physical appearance. Hair needing to be brushed, scuffed shoes, tummy pushing at the buttons of her shirt.

'Perhaps you could tell us in your own words what *did* happen,' said Brookes, her face expressionless, her blue eyes cold and reflective.

Nick looked at his lawyer, Faldane, who nodded in response.

He unclasped his hands and put them face-up on the table. 'What can I say, except that nothing happened? What she said is not true. The last part, anyway. I've no idea why she would say such a thing. I've been teaching this group for the past couple of weeks and I'm still getting to know them. I know Angela ... but I can't think why she would say that about me, as none of it is true. I did ask her to help me get the gym mattress from behind the stage.' Nicholas was warming to his story and the narrative in itself gave him more confidence, direction. 'We used it for trust falls and I used Angela as an example, so she was the first to fall. I joined her classmates in catching her and I touched her in that way. I caught her just as the other children did. I might have helped to right her and put a hand on her shoulder to check she was all right, but apart from that I never laid a finger on her.'

Nick looked down at his hands and realised that his fists were clenched.

'Trust fall?' said Weston, his expression blank.

'It's a common thing in drama and self-esteem workshops. It's often used as a warmer, to build trust and empathy in the group ... ' Nick began, feeling the breath uneven in his throat and aware of his still-trembling fingers. He wasn't sure if he had enough breath in him to explain. 'A person falls backwards without trying to stop themselves and the group catches them. It helps people feel supported – physically and mentally.'

'So if the group catches the person falling, why did you need a gym mattress?'

'I ... I shouldn't have needed it,' Nick stammered, 'it was just in case. Extra safety measure. They were a quiet group, a difficult bunch. They didn't seem to gel somehow. I used the trust game specifically to try and pull them together more as a group – to open them up. I set it up so the kids fell from the stage, which is a foot or so high. It is a fair distance – not the same as falling backwards from standing. I wanted a safety net.'

Safety net. The syllables and vowels of those words reverberated in the room.

For a moment, Nick felt as if he was falling backwards, gravity sucking him down to the earth.

'So you did ask Angela to meet you behind the stage to help you get the mattress?'

'Yes, well, no . . . we went together, but then we picked up the mattress and that was it. We threw it down off the stage and that was it.'

'So you admit being alone with her?'

'I was alone with her for the shortest of moments.' Nick put a hand through his hair, trying to laugh but only managing a strangled sigh.

'Why did you ask *Angela* to help you get the mattress?' Weston asked, his fish eyes fixed on Nick. 'Why her?'

'She was disrupting the group. She had been . . . challenging from the very first day,' Nick said, trying to smile again. 'I think I asked her because I thought if I involved her more she might behave better. She seemed to like attention. A lot of her behaviour was negative but attention-seeking. I think I thought it would be better to use her desire to be centre stage. That was the most I thought about it.'

'And you have disclosure for this post at the school, I see. No previous convictions.'

'Enhanced disclosure. Absolutely no convictions. Even my driving licence is clean.'

There was a pause. *Squeaky clean.* Was it too much?

Brookes leaned forward on the table and smiled. 'So ... you're married with children.'

'Yes.'

'Tell me about Marina.'

Nick held his breath. The question was innocent but invasive. 'She's my wife,' he said, castigating himself the minute he said it. It sounded stupid, superfluous. 'She's wonderful. Smart. Funny.' Words that he did not voice sounded in his head. *Beloved. Protector.*

'And you've been married for how many years?'

'Seven.'

Seven-year itch.

'And you're happily married?'

'Very.'

'And you have two young children?'

Nick cleared his throat. 'Yeah, Luca's six and Ava's four.'

The conversation's turn to family chat unnerved him further. His palms were suddenly slick with sweat.

'Young kids. It can be hard on a marriage. Do you find your sex life has changed?'

Nick sat back in his seat. 'I think that's my business.'

'Would you consider yourself as a man of average or greater than average sexual habits?'

'Average.' Nick glanced at Faldane, who was frowning, two fingers raised off the table, as if he was about to call a halt to proceedings.

'Do you have any sexual interests that you think some people would find unusual?'

'No.' Heart thumping against his ribcage.

Faldane punched the top of his pen. 'Is that everything then? Can we call this a night?'

Nick's statement was read back to him by Weston and Nick signed it.

Brookes stood up. 'Sure – let's get you bailed.'

'Bail? What does that mean?' Nick began.

'We're releasing you on police bail,' said Brookes. 'We need time to investigate as there is not enough evidence to charge you. As part of your bail conditions you can still live at home ... that's not always the case in these situations.'

Nick frowned. He and Faldane followed Brookes down a corridor where a young police officer processed the bail.

'The conditions of your bail are that you are to have no unsupervised contact with any under eighteens,' Brookes continued. 'Any breach of bail conditions and we will have to take you into custody.'

Nick looked up, hands on his hips and an incredulous smile on his lips. 'What does that mean? I have two children. You just said there wasn't enough evidence to charge me.'

'You must have no unsupervised contact with *any* under eighteens; that includes minors you may encounter through work as well as family members.'

'Are you saying I can't be alone with my own kids? Is that what you're really saying?' Anger consumed him for the first time.

Brookes' face hardened.

'This is fucking unfair.' Nick felt Faldane's hand on his arm, tempering him.

He and Faldane stepped out into the cool, still evening. Nick put two hands to his head as if surrendering and took a breath. He felt emptied out. Faldane lit a cigarette.

'Do you need a ride?'

'I guess so.'

Faldane's car was an Audi convertible, somehow incongruous with its owner. There was a child's booster seat in the back and when Nick got into the front he sat on a stuffed monkey.

'Sorry, that's my daughter's,' Faldane laughed, cigarette between his teeth while he buckled his seatbelt. 'I'll not tell her you sat on him.'

Faldane started the car and Nick's face fell into his hands. The lights of the police station faded as they headed down the dark road alongside Hankley Common. The radio was playing faintly.

'What happens next?' said Nick, turning to look at Bob, who was steering with one hand, his stomach pressing against the bottom of the wheel. He hoped his voice sounded calm, normal, instead of strung with the anxiety he felt in the pit of him.

'Well, nothing very fast. These things usually take a while. I know it's hard but you have to be patient.' The window was

open halfway and Bob blew smoke towards it, but the movement of the car meant it blew back in.

'How long?'

'At least until the bail date, perhaps longer. The best thing
you can do is try to put it out of your mind and let the process
do its work.'

Nick opened the window and looked out at the darkness,
feeling the breeze lift the hair from his forehead. 'Just like that,
eh?' he said quietly, into the wind. 'Just put it out of my mind.'

It was midnight when he got home. He stood outside the front
door for a moment, wondering what to say. He covered his
face with the crook of his arm. He wanted to cry, or punch
someone, break something, scream at the top of his voice. The
front door opened and Marina was there, her face pinched
with worry. He walked into her arms and held her close.

6

Donna

Her most horrible imaginings had not included her daughter being molested, but Donna had learned early in life to expect the worst. Expectation was preparation.

Waiting for Angela's father to arrive, Donna moved quickly around the house, tidying magazines, and dusting the surfaces. She did it because she was nervous about his arrival, unsure what she was going to say, rather than concerned that he would criticise the cleanliness of the home he had left behind, although Stephen had always liked things neat. He would take his time on chores, undertaking tasks that Donna never even considered – such as vacuuming the stairs and wiping down skirting boards.

Cleaning helped to calm her, taking her mind away from what had happened to Angela and how her father would react to the news. Sweat broke at her hairline as she polished the table in the lounge with big, muscular strokes. Angela's confession, the hospital and then the police: Donna had taken each blow like a seasoned boxer. She had been so little when she learned the reflexes that now formed the basis of her nervous system. She reached up and swiped her duster at a cobweb, tendrils of memory turning in her mind.

Donna was four years old and in her grandparents' house. She was pinching the skin on the back of her grandmother's hands – amazed that it stayed pinched and did not snap back onto her hand like her own skin. Her grandmother smiled at her with kind eyes as she held out her thin arm coursed with the deep worms of her veins. The coal fire was spitting and over the sound of the fire her grandfather coughed, hacking and wet, then lit another cigarette. The room and the furniture seemed huge, the ceiling high above her head and a single light bulb in the centre, competing with the light of the fire. Donna's head reached just over the arm of her grandmother's chair. The arms were covered in white lace that was ragged on the edges and yellow in the middle from elbows.

Donna was hungry and so her grandmother made her a slice of bread with butter and jam. She ate it in the dark kitchen as her grandmother leaned down to watch. Gran's eyes sparkled when she was happy.

There was a big clock on the mantel that ticked loudly, and soon Donna realised that it was nearly six. She couldn't tell the time properly, but she knew all the numbers and she knew half past, although she mixed up quarter to and quarter past. Six o'clock meant her mummy and daddy were coming to collect her. They had been at work and now it was time to go home.

Just as the old clock began to chime, there was a knock and the back door opened. 'Hello?'

It was her parents.

'Quick,' her grandmother said, eyes sparkling, 'it's them. Hide.'

It was the game.

Every week it was the same. Donna would hide behind her grandfather's big high-backed chair and pretend she wasn't there. Her father and mother would walk into the room and then Donna would bounce out, making a noise like a tiger. Her father would put a hand to his chest in shock, and then pick her up and spin her around the room, so that she could almost touch the light in the middle of the ceiling.

Donna crouched behind her grandmother's chair. She could see nothing but the slow hungry licks of the fire, the tiled fireplace and the tools at the fireside for shovelling the coal and brushing out the grate. She put her arms around her knees to make herself as small as possible. She heard the living room door creak open and her father's feet enter the room.

'Raaaaaaaaa ...' Donna pounced out from behind the chair.

Her father was covered in blood. He looked down at her with pinched, invisible eyes, then picked her up and put her on his knee. She was crying and choking and he kept saying that her mother would be fine, although Donna didn't care about her mother then, she cared about him, didn't want his face to be bleeding.

She hugged him and the blood of her mother and father smeared on her face and neck and arms.

Donna stopped cleaning and looked at the clock. It was just before six. She went into the kitchen to wait and soon saw his car pull up in front of the house.

Stephen was off duty, but anyone could tell he was police. He still wore the uniform trousers – black with a hard crease. His haircut stood to attention, as if shaped by the absent police cap, limbs stiff and impatient.

Donna watched him step out of the car and tweak his slacks into alignment, then smooth the right side of his hair. He was driven to authority, never happier than when he was in charge. The will to power. She supposed it gave him a sense of importance, even after everything that had happened.

He wouldn't talk about it, but even Stephen had fallen from grace.

Not long after they were married, it had happened. Stephen had been part of the riot squad detached to Upton Park after clashes between West Ham and Chelsea supporters. A sixteen-year-old boy, called Terrence Noaks, had stood watching as a West Ham supporter smashed up a car outside The Boleyn Arms. Stephen had pounced on Noaks, assuming that he too was a rioter and participant, fractured the boy's skull in two places and broke his nose. The boy survived but remained permanently disfigured and suffered from epileptic fits and seizures.

There had been threats of a court case and an inquiry but the boy had not been able to find a suitable lawyer to take on the Metropolitan Police. Instead, there had been an Independent Police Complaints Commission hearing. The attack had been described by the Metropolitan Police's lawyer as an *accidental collision*. Stephen had been legally exonerated but demoted to a basic beat constable with no chance of further promotion or transfer.

There was a small mirror on the kitchen wall and Donna glanced at herself and smoothed her hair before she opened the door.

She had never been sure if her marriage had fallen apart because of her, or because of that hearing. Stephen lived for his job. He was a police officer before he was a man.

Things were amicable between her and Stephen now, but she was anxious about telling him the news about Angela. She rubbed her hands together as if to gather energy before she opened the door, a wide smile on her lips.

'Hello, thanks for coming early,' she said, dipping her head in welcome and pulling her cardigan across her body. She was wearing thick socks in place of slippers and she looked down at them as she stepped back to allow him to enter.

Once inside, he smoothed a hand through his metallic-coloured hair that behaved like steel wool. Stephen sat down in the living room.

'Cup of tea?'

'Sure. Is she here?'

'Yeah. She's in her room, but I wanted to have a quick word with you first.'

She warmed her hands with the cup as she sat opposite him and muted the television.

'Is it strong enough?'

'It's great, thanks,' he said, leaning forward to take a sip.

The nights of screaming arguments were behind them. It was Donna who had done the screaming; Stephen's voice always lowered in anger and so their rows had been underscored by his hissed condescension. Hurtful words had always been whispered. Now they were polite. It broke Donna's heart, but she couldn't let him see that. Stephen's life, like his well-groomed body, was about order. Donna and her mess had never been right for Stephen's world, and yet he loved their fat, wild, violent daughter.

'You said you wanted to talk about Angel?'

He *still* called her that. It had always annoyed her.

'I hope you don't blame me for keeping this from you, but I really didn't want to tell you over the phone, and to be perfectly honest I was trying to get my head around it myself . . . I still am. It wouldn't have helped us for you to be there last night and so I made a decision to handle it myself . . . tell you face to face.'

'Handle what?'

Donna could still read his body – the stiffness in his arms and spine and a tension in his legs as if he might spring up from the couch at any moment. The flicker of nerves anticipating his reaction made her forget the words she had prepared. She always seemed to speak out of turn and managed to rile him before he even knew why he should be angry.

'Last night we were at the hospital and the police were involved.'

'What do you mean?'

The frown she was so used to confronting cut into Stephen's brow.

'Angela tried to commit suicide.' Donna waited just a second before she continued, just long enough for Stephen's lips to part under the weight of his jaw. 'She took aspirin, and I know now that was a fantastic choice. If she'd taken paracetamol, we'd've lost her for sure. She vomited in the morning and that's what alerted me. It all happened so fast. She was put on a drip right away, and then they gave her a drug called sodium . . . sodium bicarbonate which helped her to pee the aspirin out of her system.'

She spoke quickly, almost without breathing, and now took a sharp intake of air.

His hold on his tea slackened as her words reached him, so that the mug tilted, but not enough for the brown liquid to spill.

'Kill herself? Jesus Christ. She's only twelve . . .'

Donna swallowed as Stephen put his cup down hard on the lamp table. 'We were lucky, apparently. Almost *any* other drug and we would've lost her.'

'But why? Was it school?'

'I thought it was because of school. She'd been suspended for fighting again. I thought she was just acting out, being attention-seeking, but then she told me . . .'

Stephen met her eyes.

'She said a teacher at school, her drama teacher, sexually assaulted her.' Tears suddenly clouded Donna's eyes. 'I wish she'd just told me . . . ' She put a hand over her mouth, but then pinched her nose to halt her tears. She remembered Angela's bare legs opening to allow the white foam of her vomit to fall between her feet.

'Oh no,' Stephen whispered, wiping a hand over his mouth.

There was a germinating silence. He covered his eyes with his right hand, elbow on his knee supporting his head. After another painful minute, he spoke.

'So, let me get this right . . . she's sexually assaulted at school and comes home and takes all these pills. How did she get the pills? Why did you not notice?'

Not for the first time, Donna felt as if she were being interrogated.

'She got suspended from school and we had an argument. She just went to bed and I didn't know till the next morning.'

Colour flushed his face suddenly. 'You leave her all alone dealing with that, and what were you doing? Sitting down here guzzling the wine, I expect. Meanwhile she's upstairs thinking about this pervert who's attacked her and trying to kill herself.'

Tears fell and Donna brushed them away. She needed to defend herself against blame but she had never once won an argument with him.

'She's become very difficult. You don't see it like I do. They

64

wanted to expel her from school. She's a bully, they said. You should hear the things she says to me, the things she does to other girls ...'

He was shaking his head as if he wasn't even hearing her. 'So you call me and I'll deal with it. You don't know how to talk to her. You're her mother and she needs your support, but all you do is lose your patience with her. Last time she was with me, she told me she didn't think you even *liked* her.'

Donna looked away. She recalled telling Angela that she hated her.

'The minute this happened, you should've called me. I can't believe you would keep this from me.'

'I wanted to call you but the hospital was very intense,' she said, doing what politicians did on the news – deflecting, choosing to answer one thing instead of another. 'There were social workers and then police, and they all wanted to interview her, examine her ... but Angela was having none of it and you know her, once she's made her mind up.'

'I should have been there,' he said loudly, but seeming desperate.

'It just wouldn't have helped. Believe me it wouldn't.' Donna reached out to him, fingers turned upwards. 'It took me and the social worker a good few hours to persuade her to allow an examination.'

'And what did they find? I mean, was she ... raped?'

Donna blinked twice. 'They said there was no sign of penetration and she didn't have any STIs. They didn't get any biological evidence – hairs or skin cells or whatever else they hope to find ... I don't know,' Donna shivered, although the heating was on full. She pulled her cardigan around her again. 'The doctor did say that she was red, and a bit sore, but that could have been because of the assault or because of a normal rash or what have you.'

'So what did she say ... he did to her, then?'

'Covered her mouth, pushed her up against the wall and grabbed her down there, inside her underwear.'

Stephen was silent, his arms heavy on his knees, but Donna could sense the hurt and anger emanating from him. She couldn't stand it any longer. She got up and opened the patio door and then lit a cigarette, inhaling with relief and desperation. She was trembling so hard she could feel it all the way up her back into her shoulders. It was hard for her to be in the same room as him. It wasn't just this awful news and waiting for him to react, but it reminded her of how she had felt for years in his presence – stupid, irrelevant, unattractive. She had never been good enough, for him or his family. The first time Donna had met Stephen's mother, the old woman had turned up her nose. *Nice girls don't have tattoos*, she had said to Stephen after Donna had left. She knew that, because Stephen had told her.

Donna sucked at the cigarette and watched him.

He was staring into the distance, eyes reddened, a flush in his cheeks as if he were about to blow. Donna cleared her throat, preparing to say something pacifying, anything at all, but he spoke first.

'I can't believe this has happened,' he said, whispering at the worn carpet, 'But more than that, I . . . can't believe that you kept this from me. I should have known, right away.'

'It happened *yesterday*. I didn't keep it from you. *Yesterday morning* I woke up to this,' Donna shouted.

She turned towards the garden to smoke in the hope that it would help her keep her temper. This was what she had expected. Blame. 'I'm telling you now, aren't I?' she whispered. Smoke stung her right eye and she smudged a tear away with her thumb.

'Either she lives with me or I need to know everything that's going on. All the time.' He was speaking in that strange officious voice he had, that she knew he used at work. His police-officer voice, authoritative, hierarchical. It would be the voice he used handing out speeding tickets or asking people to step outside the car to be breathalysed.

'What do you think this is?' Donna screamed, feeling strain at her temples. She remembered Angela was upstairs in her bedroom and lowered her voice. 'Yesterday morning I learned that our daughter had been . . . ' she pressed her lips together, 'and tried to kill herself. I spent all day at the hospital dealing with it, and today I'm telling you—'

'Why didn't you call me last night?'

'Because she'd had enough. Because I wanted to tell you face to face. We'd both been through the wringer. I told you already. Don't you understand? They had a specially trained police officer talk to her, and she was examined at a specialist sexual assault unit. It wasn't the time and Angela was embarrassed. She didn't want me to tell you. In the taxi on the way to the hospital, before I even knew the half of it, she kept saying ... ' Donna inhaled hard, 'please don't tell Dad.' *Dad* brought the smoke from her lips in a cloud.

Stephen caught a tear on his cheek with the heel of his hand. Donna stubbed out her cigarette on the roughcast wall of the house and put the butt in a little plant pot that she used as an outdoor ashtray.

He took a deep breath and sat back on the couch, both hands on his head in a strange gesture of surrender. Donna slid the door closed.

'I'm just saying I need to know. I'm her father.'

'So what are you going to do?' she asked, folding her arms. He met her eye.

'They let him out, you know. They arrested him, took him to the police station, interviewed him and then they just let him out. The police say it will take weeks – months maybe – to be patient until they've completed the investigation. He could do it to someone else.'

Donna inhaled slowly, watching the thoughts turn in her husband's mind. 'He goes round schools teaching drama. And he's got two kids of his own.'

'How do you know? Did the police tell you?'

'They didn't have to tell me. I looked him up. He's an actor. He's on bloody Wikipedia.'

Stephen pitched forward, hung his head in his hands. When he finally looked up, they met each other's eyes. It had been months, perhaps years, since they had looked at each other with such unguarded honesty.

'You know I can't get involved. I can look into who's dealing with the case, but there is absolutely no way they will let me get involved in the investigation. It'll be CID. It'll be plain-clothes. And it's my own daughter – I can have no influence.'

Donna sat back in her chair. 'And you wonder why I didn't call you . . . ' She twitched her lips in a downwards smile.

The colour came to his face again. 'You're unbelievable. You really are.' He stood up. 'I'll go up and talk to her.'

As she heard his feet on the stairs, Donna slid another cigarette out of the pack. She opened the patio door and lit up, leaning her head against the stone of their house.

She inhaled deeply, remembering that night when she was a child, the blood of her parents on her face and arms. She had *only* been worried about her father.

'Daddy,' she whispered, breathing smoke into the yard.

It had been a head-on collision with a lorry. Her mother had died two days later.

Donna breathed smoke down her nose as she heard the floorboards shifting above and Angela laughing as her father entered her room.

7

Nick

'Why would the girl say such a thing? I mean *why* would she say it?' said Betty Dean, her voice low so as not to be heard by the children in the other room.

'I don't know, Mum,' said Nick, nudging his plate away.

He watched his mother, the kindness driven deep into her face. He had let Marina tell his parents – allowed her to choose the words. She had done well – handled it with her usual professional consideration: *allegation, teenager, touched*. She had managed not to say *sexual, twelve-year-old girl* or *assault*.

There was strain behind his eyes and so Nick pressed his thumb and forefinger against his eyebrows. He wanted to pour another glass of wine, but everyone was watching him. Since he had left the police station on Friday night he had just wanted to shut it all out, make it go away. Now he felt suspended between his desire to escape and the expectation of his family's gaze. The whole family was here, at his parents' house on Church Lane, not far from Nick and Marina's home. His father had been mostly silent, sitting far back in his chair with his arms folded. Nick found it hard to look at him.

It had been Marina's idea to tell the family – the main reason being that they would need help with childcare as a result of the bail conditions. Nick had argued at first. *How am I supposed to tell them this?* Marina had been insistent: *You're innocent and we need their support.* Besides, his brother Mark knew and would have at least told his sister Melissa, and if she knew there was a chance his parents would soon know anyway.

It wasn't so unusual for Marina, Nick and the children to be at Nick's parents' for Sunday lunch but when the whole Dean clan was present as they were now, it was usually a cause for celebration – Christmas or a special birthday. Mark and Juliette were just back from Thailand, and even his sister Melissa was there with her brood. She was a keen runner and often had races on a Sunday but had made it here.

There was no celebration today, but Betty had still made a feast. The main course had been roast lamb with three different types of potatoes (boiled, mashed and roast), baby corn and green beans. She had made a green salad with artichokes and for dessert there was homemade rhubarb pie, as well as ice-cream and fruit salad. Betty believed that most things could be made better by a square meal and a good night's sleep. Nick wondered if he was now testing that assumption.

The children had eaten in the living room and were now upstairs.

Melissa's kids were older: Rebecca was in secondary school, Jack was not far behind her and Jennifer was just eight. The older kids helped to look after Ava and Luca and so they had not been disturbed, although the sounds of their voices were audible downstairs.

Everyone else was talking about Nick as if he wasn't even there – making proclamations to the table. Under the table, Nick held Marina's hand.

'Bob Faldane's a good guy,' said Mark, his face and neck obscenely tanned from his holiday. His arms were pale brown, more normal, but his face looked like it had been slapped several times. His teeth and eyes shone white. 'He's always been a really bright guy,' he said, addressing their father, who raised an eyebrow.

Thomas Dean was still powerful even in his late seventies, broad shoulders and long back, thicker around the waist but still trim. His hair was greying at the sides but was still remarkably dark. He had brown eyes and a face that had reddened with age, hinting at his fondness for whisky and the quickness of his temper.

Tom nodded slowly. 'You need someone good,' he said, glancing at Nick.

Nick assented. He felt embarrassed, a child again, caught out, needing direction.

'It was just a precaution, to get the lawyer,' said Marina to Betty, who was nervously smoothing and folding her napkin.

'It's good to have someone there from the start, guiding us through it.'

Tom frowned deeply. 'But you *know* this girl ... the one that's made this accusation?' Again, he didn't meet Nick's eye, but glanced in his direction, touching a teaspoon and turning it in his fingers.

Nick let go of Marina's hand. 'Well, I worked with her class for a couple of weeks. I know her that much, but no ... of course I don't *know* her. She was just another kid in the group.'

'And do you think ... ' Tom cleared his throat and turned to Nick for the first time, pointing the spoon at him, 'you touched her some way that she could have misinterpreted?'

Touched.

The word settled on the table, gentle but alien, like dandelion spores blown inside.

'No, of course not.' Nick felt heat rising to his face and fought to control it. Here he was, thirty-five years old, a husband and father and yet still that child of his parents, facing inquisition, feeling shamed.

'You know what girls are like at that age,' said his mother.

'What does that mean?' said Melissa, turning to her mother, a sharp frown between her brows. She was like their father – tall and broad – the same wide forehead and indignant lips. 'This girl's about the same age as Rebecca, right?'

A febrile silence fell on the table. Nick felt Marina's fingers again on his thigh, offering support.

'That's not what I meant,' said Betty, defensive. 'I mean,

she's a teenager. It's that difficult couple of years, isn't it, all new hormones . . . that's all.'

'She's twelve,' said Nick, tensing his stomach muscles, daring to look up and see each face around the table. The skin on his mother's face sagged. He sighed as he mustered the strength to continue. 'And what she's accused me of couldn't really be misconstrued. She alleges that I put my hand over her mouth and then . . . ' he couldn't say the words, 'assaulted her.'

There was a hot silence, long enough for a bar of music, and then there was a rush to speak, to console, to fill the void.

'Do you mean . . . she's accused you of rape?' said Mark, his red face still somehow managing to look blanched, fearful of the reply.

Nick shook his head. 'I'm told she said that I . . . touched her sexually.' He swallowed and turned his palms up on the table. 'It couldn't be misinterpreted,' he couldn't look at his father, 'as Dad said.'

'That's just absurd,' said Graham, Melissa's husband. 'I mean, quite apart from the fact that you're one of the nicest guys I know – it's just ridiculous, makes no sense whatsoever – how could you do that while you were teaching a workshop?'

He was large and boyish and a good addition to the family. Graham was like a spirit level, tempering the emotions of each family member. Melissa was incisive and emotional, a sting in the tail like their father, but Graham could always be relied upon to steer arguments away from their molten core. The Christmas before last, Nick and his father had argued about his acting and the new business. Graham had smoothed things over when Tom had made the hurtful *those that can't do, teach* remark.

Nick shrugged. His neck ached from the build-up of tension. He reached to massage the muscle between his neck and his right shoulder.

'So what's the next step?' said Tom, arms folded on the table, as if this was a negotiation he was handling. He had done well for himself – left school at fourteen and after his national service had gone into haulage, worked his way up and then bought the company when he was in his forties. He was CEO now – board meetings on Friday mornings and business conducted over golf.

'Well, we just need to wait,' said Nick, quietly. 'I wish there was something else to do.' It wasn't an answer that his father liked. Tom Dean liked action, not waiting. 'My bail's for several weeks so I hope that by the end of that we'll have some good news.'

Mark cleared his throat. 'Yeah, Bob said the investigation can take quite a while. I guess we just need to sit tight.' He folded his arms and leaned on the table. Nick wondered if his elder brother did it deliberately – mirroring their father's body language.

'Well, then I suppose you need to try and put it out of your mind,' said Tom, corners of his mouth turned down. 'I assume the school have pulled your contract?'

Nick nodded, grateful for Marina's warm fingers in his. 'Yes, they emailed yesterday to say that pending the investigation the course would be cancelled.'

'So you can't work while this is going on?' his father said, frowning. 'I mean, most of your contracts are with schools, aren't they?'

'Tend to be.' Nick sighed heavily. 'There's a couple of media training sessions and I can still audition – actually there was a thing just a couple of days ago . . . ' Nick let his sentence fade.

Tom shifted his weight in the chair and wiped a hand over his mouth, as if to catch an unpalatable truth.

'Did the school pay upfront?' said Mark, eyes unblinking.

Nick shook his head. 'I invoice when the course is finished.'

'That's hardly the point,' said Melissa, 'I mean this . . . this is horrendous.'

Everyone turned to look at her. Silence fell on the table, each and every one of them acknowledging the truth in what she said but not knowing how to respond.

Betty began to stack the dishes, and Nick got to his feet to help. Action – any action – was absolving. 'Yes, it is,' he said to his sister as he took the plate from her place before following his mother into the kitchen. 'No doubt about that.'

Betty began to tidy up the kitchen and soak the pots, stacking the dishwasher with a swift, anxious focus.

The Sunday papers were unread on the kitchen table and Nick glanced at the headlines: professional footballers coming forward to say their coaches had groomed them, historical child abuse in the Catholic Church. It had been an onslaught for months, if not years. Savile. Cosby. Operation Yew Tree. Skeletons and confessions.

He glanced again at his mother, sensing the brittle energy in her. He put two hands on her shoulders. 'Leave it, I'll do it.'

'I'm best keeping busy. You go and sit down. I'll make the tea.'

Nick filled the kettle and put out the cups and saucers. There was a burning behind his eyes that was partly the wine and partly the strain of the dinner table confession. He didn't know if he felt worse or better now that everyone knew. He was grateful that he was in the kitchen. Hiding was solace.

The clatter of the dishes stopped for a moment and Betty said something Nick couldn't hear over the sound of the kettle. He turned and his mother was looking out of the window.

'What did you say?'

'I've got a bad feeling about this,' she said softly, eyes watering.

Betty opened the back door and snapped open a pink leather cigarette case, slipped a cigarette between her lips and took a long drag before exhaling towards the open door.

'Don't say that,' said Nick, moving towards her. 'I trust your intuition.'

'It'll be her word against yours.'

'Mum, I didn't do this.'

'I know that.' She reached out and squeezed his elbow. Her hands were icy cold against his bare skin. 'I know that, but it's like me with that bloody school.' Betty's cheeks hollowed as she inhaled again.

Nick pressed his teeth together. His mother rarely mentioned it. After decades of hard work as a maths teacher, she had been sacked a year before she was due to retire, for assaulting a pupil. She had escaped prosecution but lost her pension.

'Mud sticks sometimes,' she said, a column of fragile ash trembling on the top of her cigarette as she watched his face. 'Don't let this stick to you. You *fight* this.' Betty stubbed out her cigarette in a small crystal ashtray on the windowsill and then stood on her tiptoes to hug her youngest son. 'Don't let them say these things about you.'

Nick held his mother, feeling the bones of her spine through her silk blouse; the smell of her – perfume mingled with cigarette smoke – remembered from his childhood, kissing him goodnight. 'I'll do my best,' said Nick heavily. He wanted to fight, wanted to speak his mind, but the lawyer was only advising patience. And even if he was to fight, he didn't know how he would do that. How could he fight a twelve-year-old girl?

'You're a good boy,' said Betty, her eyes shining.

Nick dipped his head, feeling his throat tighten.

'Daddy,' Nick heard Luca call from the den.

He kissed his mother's cheek and walked upstairs slowly, hearing the sound of Ava crying. Luca met him at the top of the stairs and pulled him by the hand into the room. Rebecca was lying on the couch prodding her phone, while Jack was playing a video game. Ava was standing distraught, tears streaking down her face.

Luca pulled on Nick's arm to bring him down closer so that

he could whisper in his ear. 'Jennifer wouldn't let Ava play her flute and she freaked out.'

'She would have broken it,' said Jennifer sulkily, without looking up.

'I wouldn't *rompio*,' Ava choked, using the Spanish for 'break'.

Nick ruffled Luca's hair. 'She's just tired.' He lifted his daughter into his arms and almost immediately the cries stopped. He felt her head butt his neck and he rubbed her back, knowing that she would sleep in his arms if he let her.

'Stay and play this car game with us, Uncle Nick,' said Jack, agitating the joystick.

Nick stood in the middle of the room, swaying side to side to sooth Ava. A sick wave of realisation washed over him. He wasn't allowed to be here. He was in a room alone with his children, his nephew and nieces and that was now forbidden. He was breaching his bail. Breaking the law. He was no longer trusted with children.

'Please?' Jack urged, turning to look up at his uncle.

'Another time,' said Nick, turning and carrying Ava downstairs.

He pressed her small body into him for comfort. Marina was waiting for him at the bottom of the stairs. She reached up and rubbed Ava's back.

'Is she asleep?' he asked, turning so that Marina could see Ava's face on his shoulder.

'Close. She missed her nap today.'

He looked hard into Marina's eyes.

'Are you okay?' she asked.

'I don't know if I can take this,' he whispered.

Marina reached up and put a hand on the back of his neck. 'We are going to get through this together. You are the most wonderful man I know. I love you and I trust you. I know that we're going to be fine.'

Nick swallowed, feeling the heat of his daughter's sleeping body against his chest.

8

Angela

It was two o'clock. Her first day back at school since the suspension and the hospital and everything else and Angela was bunking off. She hadn't gone back after lunch.

She was on a swing in Ashburton Park, half way between school and home. She kicked the strange spongy tarmac with the heel of her Converse while Adam threw the other swings up and around so that no one else could play on them. It wasn't like little kids came here anyway – the place smelled of dog pee. Adam wasn't her boyfriend, but they had done this before.

The suspension had been cut from her record and she was no longer in trouble for bashing Jasmine, but she wasn't allowed out at playtime or lunch and had to eat in the classroom with a dumb support teacher. She felt at once forgiven and blamed. She had slipped outside after asking to go to the toilet.

Being at school was torture.

Everyone at school knew what had happened. Everyone was talking about her.

Angela wasn't sure how it had got out that she had accused Mr Dean, but the other children in her class were talking about her behind her back and sending messages about her. Jasmine's mother had even put it on Facebook, which would be hysterically funny if it wasn't pathetic.

When Adam was finished with the swings, Angela stood up.

He lunged at her and she flinched, but he was only reaching for the swing that she had vacated.

'No, leave just one. You have to leave just one,' she said, putting two hands and all of her weight onto the swing to protect it.

'How come?'

He had ridges shaved in one of his eyebrows and it made him seem asymmetric, although his face had a harsh proportion. Mean but good-looking, all flat brow and straight nose and defined jaw.

'Well, you've wound up the others, so leave the little kids one to swing on.'

'All right.'

She stood up and began to walk away. He took a cigarette from a packet in the pocket of his tracksuit bottoms and put it to his lips. Instead of lighting it, he slipped the cigarette behind his ear, ran and kicked the swing into the air.

Angela stood and watched him, resigned, not surprised but sad, because that was what boys were like.

Adam jumped up and caught the swing in two hands and

swung it away again before his feet even touched the ground. The athleticism in his body was mesmerising. He knifed into the air and spun the swing in mid-air before landing on one foot. He was just trying to be a vandal and yet he held such grace and poise. He was two years older than her: fourteen going on fifteen. He still looked like a boy but there was hardness about him.

Done, only just out of breath, Adam swaggered back to her, taking the cigarette from behind his ear.

'I'm a perfectionist,' he said in explanation, shaved eyebrow rising and a smirk on his lips.

She turned away from the swings. There was a derelict building in the middle of the park, with one wall painted bright pink and covered in graffiti underneath its caved-in, tiled roof. Adam headed towards the trees at the edge of the park along the railway line, and Angela followed.

It was an ash tree they were up against – one of the tallest trees in the park. A deep hollow ran up the trunk so that it looked like a vertical canoe or a coffin. Adam tried to wedge her into the space. The trunk was right between her shoulder blades when Adam pressed her. She smelled the wet leaves and smoke from his soft cotton shirt, the salt of his hair. They were hidden in a corridor of tall trees – a canopy blocked out the sky. There was graffiti on the trunks of the other trees, white and black swirls of spray paint.

He kneaded her and she stood with her chin up looking at the light filtering through the trees. There was a pain in her throat. She wanted to cry but couldn't. It was like a dream she often had, where she was trying to scream but no voice came out. Adam was touching himself and breathing hard. He was sucking her neck and it felt good and hurt at the same time. There was a shrill trill of songbirds high above, or was it in her head? It felt like that morning when she woke up and she wasn't dead – the same sickness and high-pitched throbbing in her ears.

He was inside her bra – that strange little vest bra that her mother had bought her. He breathed on her neck and her shoulder and Angela wondered if she was supposed to do something to help him, but she just stayed where she was – the rough bark of the ash at her back. She felt removed from herself, as if she was up in the sky above the dark canopy of the trees, with the invisible songbirds, or as if the tree trunk at her back was a control bar and she was a marionette dancing without will.

The ringing in her ears and the sharp scent of the leaves seemed to combine. The sound and the smell overcoming her, so that she thought she might pass out.

Adam suddenly pulled away from her and she watched him tugging at his jogging bottoms. He lost his balance on the uneven path that was threaded with tree roots and swayed for a second, before steadying himself on the wire fence and straightening his hoodie.

'You don't have any tits yet. It's just fat,' he said, smoke whispering from his mouth into the mature green of the trees.

Angela shrugged and turned to her right, looking through the branches of ash at the swings all wound up out of reach.

Life felt like that just now. Like the swings. Taken out of her control. Spiteful. A cruel joke. Unfair.

'Yeah, well you're a prick anyway,' said Angela, half-smiling, picking up her school bag and marching across the playground. 'See you.'

She was only fifteen minutes' walk from home and she headed towards the exit on the other side of the basketball courts. She didn't turn around to see his face, but she heard him spit.

9

Marina

Marina woke up ten minutes before her alarm sounded and turned towards Nick. She loved the smell between his shoulder blades first thing in the morning. He was still sound asleep. She threw an arm over him and discovered Ava curled into her father, thumb in her mouth. Sleep now submitted to consciousness. Marina embraced them both as anxious thoughts of the day ahead encroached on her mind. The last few weeks had been fraught. Nick's parents were helping out as much as they could, but all the flow had gone out of their lives since Nick had been unable to care for the children alone.

She shuddered and rested her cheek in the space between Nick's shoulder and ear, causing him to stir but not wake. She had a busy morning, a government presentation, but had taken the afternoon off so that she and Nick could meet the lawyer,

Faldane, together. Nick's police bail would be up in one week, and Marina hoped Faldane was going to tell them everything would soon return to normal.

Ten more minutes.

For ten minutes, she didn't need to wake and deal with this. She could fall asleep again. Almost immediately, she fell heavily into a hot, confused dream where she could hear screaming and taste blood.

It was a November day, overcast, a light misting of rain. She was seven years old and holding her father's hand. They were in Madrid, having left their home in Valencia behind just the day before. She was standing in clothes she had worn for two days because their belongings had been sent ahead and they had not yet been unpacked. They had travelled by train to be greeted by her paternal grandparents. Marina and her sister had been kissed and squeezed and pinched and passed from one relative to another. Cousins and aunts and uncles.

Now they were at the *matanza*. It was Marina's first slaughter and she was not sure what to expect, but she was hungry. A pig was going to be killed and then they were going to feast. There was an atmosphere of celebration but practicality – a strange utilitarian brutality – in the air, even before the pig was brought out.

It wasn't very warm, but her father was sweating – she could see from the stains on the armpits of his shirt when he raised his arm to gesticulate to his friends. Her mother was frowning as she had been since they left Valencia. They were in Madrid on her father's bidding – his promise. They were there for his dream – no other reason. They had mortgaged the farm and Marina and her sister had changed schools so that he could open a restaurant in the capital.

A wooden stool was set in the middle of the courtyard, and a length of rope placed on top.

The air was brisk but pungent with the smell of raw chopped onion and crushed garlic. Marina stood on her own as the pig was led out, a rope around its neck, pink snout tasting the air, keen eyes framed by long bleached lashes.

'What will happen?' Marina asked her mother, who said nothing, but smiled and put a warm hand on the top of her head.

Marina's Aunt Amelia, who had been busy making preparations, took her by the chin and planted a kiss on her forehead as she passed. Aunt Amelia smelled of garlic and the place where her fingers had touched Marina's cheek was sticky and burned, causing Marina to rub the sensation away.

The crowd gathered around the pig and Marina was pushed forward by her father as he moved closer to get a better view. The air throbbed. Everyone gathered, drawn like a seam around the violence to come.

Marina's father lifted her sister Pilar onto his shoulders. Marina stood between both her parents. She held her father's hand and slipped her other hand into her mother's back pocket.

Two men grappled the pig and forced its screaming body between their legs before it was hauled over the waiting bench.

One of the men held the pig with his thighs and his hands while the other man bound it. The rope caught the pig's ear and trapped it over its eye. Marina tapped her father's stomach, wanting to ask if the pig would be uncomfortable with the rope cutting across its ear, but her father only nodded and squeezed her shoulder, which meant he did not want to answer her questions just now.

The man who was straddling the pig punched it with something that looked to Marina like a large pen.

'Why did he do that? What's that?' she called up to her mother, tugging on her hip pocket.

'Electric shock, to stun it,' said her mother, not turning to her.

The pig screamed with such high-pitched human vigour that goose-pimples appeared on Marina's arms. She saw the pig struggle, watched the realisation of what was going to happen shine in its one uncovered eye. Even though her mother said it had been stunned, it kept screaming and Marina thought it sounded like a baby that needed to be comforted. Pilar had sounded like that just a few years before, her naked body rigid with temper.

Her cousin Pedro, who had a ponytail that fell to the middle of his back, came out carrying a large knife. The man who had roped the pig now lifted up its snout so that the animal's throat stretched out long and white, like her father when he visited the barber. The pig's white hooves clawed at the air.

Pedro stuck the knife into the pig's throat and cut right down to its heart. Marina squeezed her eyes shut and when she opened them, her Aunt Amelia was holding a blue bucket below the wound on the pig's throat, catching the blood. Her hands and her forearms were dark red, almost black with the blood. Splashes landed on her white, rolled-up sleeves and again Marina wanted to point this out to her mother, but said nothing, leaning into her instead. Her father was dancing around now, bouncing Pilar, who was giggling and holding onto his hair.

The first thing that Marina noticed was the silence. It felt unusual, furred, warm. The pig was no longer screaming and there was no other sound, although she could see people dancing and laughing and calling to each other.

It was as if the absence of the pig's screams had swallowed all other sound.

There was a flush of heat at the nape of her neck and she was falling, falling hard and heavy.

Marina woke up with a jolt of electricity in her limbs. She was still nuzzled into Nick and she jarred him awake.

'What time is it?' he said, turning onto his back and putting an arm over his eyes. 'What's the matter?'

'I was dreaming,' Marina said, still trying to find the stills of the dream but only remembering falling.

Ava woke up and curled into a ball, face down on the bed as was her habit. She resisted consciousness for the first few moments and then sprang into life, launching herself onto the bodies of both her parents as Marina's alarm sounded and seconds later Luca's feet pounded on the stairs.

Marina had held it at bay, but now, it was morning.

These days, they had to get up earlier so that Marina could accompany Nick on the drop-off to the childminder, but the morning routine before they left the house was unchanged: Marina got herself ready while Nick dressed the children, then Marina gave them breakfast while Nick walked Rusty.

After her shower, Marina sat before her dressing-table mirror, still partly asleep, thoughts hot and heavy in her mind. She didn't wear much make-up, but she liked to line her upper lids with soft kohl and dot her sunspots with concealer. She had liquid rouge that she swore made her look five years younger, and she now smudged this onto her cheekbones and temples and rubbed until she glowed.

She blasted her hair dry quickly and then tucked it into a messy French knot. She stood and glanced at herself quickly in the mirror on the wardrobe. Grey suit, white blouse. Today she was presenting to the Department for International Development before crossing town to meet Nick with the lawyer. She looked at her reflection, wondering what people would see in her today. She looked the same as ever: professional, approachable. The only sign of the chaos unfurling in their lives was the shadow of tiredness under her eyes.

Rusty came into the bedroom as Marina was putting on her jewellery. The little dog whined slightly.

'Don't cry to me. He'll take you out when he's ready.'

She smiled at herself in the mirror. It would have to do.

'Why's Daddy stopped taking us to school and nursery?' said Luca, jumping up and down in the hallway so that the pencils in his satchel rattled. 'It would be easier if he took us like before, so you could just go to work.'

Nick was taking Rusty quickly round the block.

Children were so routine-driven, Marina thought, and Luca was incisive. Nothing got past him and he was only six. She feared what he would be like as a teenager.

Ava lifted her denim skirt to hide her face. When she let it fall, *'Boo!'* Marina saw that she had banana smeared all over her face.

She grabbed a wipe from the kitchen and cleaned her daughter's chin and cheek, causing Ava to twist away.

'No! I want Daddy to do it, *not you,*' she cried in a voice of genuine outrage. Marina glanced at Luca, still waiting patiently for an answer to his question. As she was about to toss the soiled wipe into the bin, she noticed a coffee stain on the collar of her white blouse.

'*Mierda,*' she whispered under her breath, checking her watch. She had six minutes until they had to be out of the house.

'*Mami, eso no se dice!*' Luca called after her in righteous castigation of her bad language.

Marina had changed her working hours to allow for Nick's bail conditions. Since Nick was out of action as the main child carer and as no one else in the family had been available for the morning school run, Marina had to cover it. Betty now collected the children from nursery and school and looked after them until Marina was home from work. The perfect balance of their life had suddenly been knocked out of kilter.

'*Why* can't Daddy take us?' Luca asked again, this time in Spanish, as Marina walked downstairs buttoning a fresh shirt of a tone that did not quite match the grey of her suit.

'We explained already,' Marina replied in Spanish. 'We are a family and we all need to help each other out.' She checked the contents of her briefcase, making sure she had everything she needed: phone, presentation, wallet. 'Sometimes we need to share the load.'

'But he doesn't need help. *You* are the most busy.'

Marina felt a smile forced from her. She loved him. She grabbed his face with one hand and planted a kiss on his eyebrow. '*Precioso.*'

The key turned in the door and Nick and Rusty entered. The little dog paraded back and forth as if he had been gone for weeks, then streaked to the kitchen to lap water. Marina acknowledged a prickle of irritation that Nick had not dried the dog's feet. The hall carpet needed replacing because it had gathered the dirt of their lives, but it would last a year longer if the dog was dried after every walk. In the mornings, especially, Nick let it slip.

Still in his sweatpants, he hung up Rusty's lead and tried to squeeze Marina's waist as he passed – headed to the kitchen to put out Rusty's breakfast.

'Can you just get them in the car?' Marina said, brushing him off and tugging at the cuffs of her shirt. 'We're running late.' She was feeling stressed. Normally she would be reviewing her notes on the train just now, not worrying about mashed banana and coffee stains.

Swiping a nude lipstick over her lips in the hall mirror, Marina acknowledged she was annoyed with Nick for being dressed as if it was the weekend – as if he might go back to bed. She heard him mixing dog food in a bowl and pouring Rusty fresh water.

It was years now that she had been out-earning him, and sometimes she felt as if she was the *parent* in their relationship – the responsible one – but even although he had always earned less, and his job had been less *important*, she had taken heart that their rhythms had kept in synch: up at six, dressed and showered, out the door by 7.15.

She took a deep breath as she buttoned her jacket and checked herself in the mirror again. In the reflection she could see Nick on his knees talking to Luca. She knew he would be trying to provide a better explanation in answer to his question.

Once the kids were dropped off, Nick drove her to the station and then she had to run to catch her train to Waterloo – not even time to kiss him goodbye.

'See you at two,' she said, grabbing her briefcase.

On the train, she took her phone from her pocket and texted to Nick:

Have a good morning. See you later. Love you xx.

Since the police had taken his phone he had bought a strange, lightweight Nokia that had cost fifteen pounds. He had a new number. It wasn't even a smart phone.

After a few seconds, he texted back.

Love u more. Knock em dead. :)

She knew from the gentle eagerness of his tone that he had heard her irritation and was trying to make it up to her. She felt a brief twinge of guilt.

The train was crowded and she stood for most of the hour wondering how single parents managed. Her life had become so much harder because of Nick's bail conditions. Her bag was heavy and pulling on her shoulder and she shifted her weight in the cramped carriage.

As she was leaving the train at Waterloo, a man's umbrella tip caught her leg. On the platform, Marina discovered that she now had a ladder in her tights and no spare pair with her. There was no time to think about it. She walked as fast as she could to the Underground and caught the Circle line just before the doors closed. It was only a five-minute journey but she found herself jammed underneath a suited armpit. She had a flicker of panic and crouched down to check her briefcase again for the flash drive with her presentation on it.

The original file had been on her laptop that the police had taken away and so she had had to rewrite some of it at Betty and Tom's after lunch on Sunday. She didn't normally feel nervous before presentations – even one as important as this – but not having her own computer and one hour less sleep meant she had a ripple of anxiety in her stomach. She consoled herself that they would meet the lawyer at two. Her presentation would be done by then, and perhaps he would tell them that the police were calling off the whole investigation.

At work, she found a spare pair of tights in her desk drawer and asked Connie, her assistant, to load her presentation onto a laptop while she went to change. Coming out of the ladies' room, Marina noticed that Theresa was in the office. She was on the phone, pacing back and forth in the meeting room, looking out of the window onto Trafalgar Square. Theresa motioned at her through the glass and so Marina entered and waited, checking her watch. It would take her fifteen minutes to get to Whitehall, where she was to present.

Marina sat on the edge of the meeting table as her boss finished the call. 'Fine. Fine. Great. I've got to go, but I agree that we put it before the board.' Theresa hung up and turned, smiling. She had an off-putting wince of a smile. 'You all set for today?'

'Yes, I just . . .'

'Good luck.'

'Thank you.'

'I'm meeting with Bertha Spalding at two.' Theresa gave a dramatic facial expression – eyebrows high over wide eyes. 'You must join us.' Bertha was the newly appointed Secretary of State for Education.

'I can't. I've got that family thing. I emailed you about it last week, remember?'

Theresa's smile wavered. 'Right, I thought it was just one of Nick's plays or something? There's no way you can duck out of it? It's pretty essential that you're here, I think.'

Marina took a deep breath. 'Theresa, can I speak frankly and in confidence with you?'

'Of course.' Theresa faltered for a moment and then indicated a chair.

Marina sat and pushed back her shoulders. 'I need to be with Nick this afternoon. It's a legal thing.'

'A legal thing?' Theresa's head fell to one side in a gesture that Marina found confusing – empathy or scrutiny – she wasn't sure. 'He's an absolute darling; please tell me you're not divorcing him?'

Theresa was bright and dynamic, and as the head of the Board of Trustees, she was the kingpin at Child International, but Marina was never sure how to read her. She had been a top CEO in Human Resources before she took on this voluntary role, and now, it seemed, she was unable to take a step back. At times her boss was parental, almost motherly, and then at other times controlling and micromanaging.

Marina shook her head and swallowed. 'I meant to speak to you about it before now, but I think I hoped it would just disappear. I know we are obliged to declare any potential conflicts of interest . . .'

Theresa's eyes narrowed.

'The police are investigating Nick for an ... offence ... and it's a mistake – I don't mean he has made a mistake, *they* have ... they have the wrong person – but he's been put on police bail and he can't look after the children until that time

97

is up.' Marina looked up at the ceiling, at the strip lighting filtering through metallic grills. Her heart was fluttering in her chest. 'It's why I've been working from home so much. But I'm hopeful that we'll hear some good news today and this will all just go away . . . So I really want to be there, meet the lawyer with him, if that's okay?'

'Can't look after the children?' Theresa frowned. 'What on earth are they investigating him for, molestation?'

Marina pressed her lips together, considering her response. 'He's been accused of assaulting a child at a school he was working at.' It was a good answer, she decided. It sounded similar to what had happened to her mother-in-law – still traumatic but not shameful.

Theresa softened. Marina watched the realisation relax her face.

'Very well. Thank you for telling me. You're right, we do have to declare potential conflicts, but I don't see this as significant – certainly not right now. He hasn't been charged?'

Marina swallowed and shook her head.

'You work extremely hard, Marina. I'm behind you all the way, you know that. You get this sorted out. I'll try and arrange another time for you to meet Bertha.'

Marina wondered if she should say something more – clarify things – but Theresa had resumed her wincing smile.

'Thank you,' said Marina, standing up and smoothing her skirt, feeling genuinely grateful.

As she returned to her office, she realised that her face was burning.

10

Nick

Faldane's office was in Farringdon and Nick took Marina's hand as they left the Tube station and headed towards St John Street. It was bright but cold, the sky expansive and the sun a distant silver coin above London.

Faldane always seemed to be busy, on the hop between court and home, and Nick hadn't spoken to him in weeks. He seldom answered his mobile and when he did, he was perfunctory. Nick felt squeamish wondering what his lawyer would say. He only wanted to hear that the investigation was going to be dropped now that he was approaching his police bail date. But his stomach sensed a different outcome, the muscles in his midriff ached as if he was holding a crunch. In the lift in Faldane's office building, Marina squeezed his hand and Nick returned it. He held his breath waiting for the lift doors to open.

When Nick entered Faldane's office the handshake was warm but the smile slowly faded from his lawyer's face. 'I thought you were coming alone?' he said quietly to Nick before adding, 'Marina, hi,' and reaching to shake her hand.

'Is there a problem?' Nick raised his eyebrows.

Faldane clapped his hands with an awkward grin on his face. 'It's up to you. I've got some good news and some bad news. I thought we could discuss it and then you could share it with the family afterwards?'

Nick said nothing, but Marina was quick to react. 'It's fine, I can wait outside.'

'No,' Nick took her hand again. 'I'm glad you're with me. You took the afternoon off work. I need you here.'

Faldane was serious. 'If you're sure.'

Nick nodded at Marina and they sat before Faldane's desk, which was covered in files held together with elastic bands. The screensaver on his laptop was his daughter with a beach ball. Nick could see she had Faldane's eyes. After the outside chill, the office was too warm and Nick tweaked the neck of his shirt.

Faldane clasped his hands and offered another unsure smile. 'So what do you want first, the good news or the bad?'

'The bad,' said Nick, turning to Marina, who was nodding in agreement.

Faldane sighed, 'Okay,' allowing his eyes to focus on the telephone. 'Tell you what,' his gaze returned to them, smiling, 'I'll just tell you the good news first. The good news is that there is still insufficient evidence to charge you.'

'So when will this stop?' Marina was frowning, legs crossed, straight spine.

'We'll find that out when his bail is up, but at the moment, from what I have gathered, they do not have enough evidence at present to charge you with sexual assault.'

Nick pitched forward and breathed into pressed-together palms. For good news, it wasn't that good. It was just what they had been hearing for weeks. *Hang on. Wait and see. Bide time. Patience.* It was testing his sanity. 'All right then,' Nick sat back in his chair, rested an ankle over his knee in mock confidence, 'let's hear the bad news then.' He reached for Marina and let his hand rest on her thigh. A second later he felt her warm soft palm close over his.

The awkwardness in Faldane, that shy distant connection – freshers' week with his brother in Leeds – disappeared and the lawyer that he was suddenly took hold. His voice deepened and there was almost a physical change, which Nick ascribed to the lack of smile, but it was as if Faldane aged before them as his gravitas increased.

'It's hard to get disclosure at this stage in the investigation. The police like to keep what they have close to their chest, so to speak, but I have learned that they should soon be returning your laptop, Marina.'

Marina and Nick looked at each other and then back to Faldane. 'Good . . . ' Marina faltered.

'And what about my laptop?' Nick said faintly, 'And the kids' tablet?'

Faldane steepled his hands, pressing the fingertips together.

'Yours is being kept in evidence, as is your phone and the tablet. They have highlighted a number of pornographic websites visited.'

Bob paused and Nick felt the warm weight of it in the room. He became strangely conscious of his hand on Marina's knee and her hand on his. The heat of seconds seared. Nick wasn't sure if he was expected to respond or not. Of course he had looked at pornography, and yes it was awful that this had been discovered and that his wife was hearing about it, but he couldn't deny it, and part of him had expected it.

Bob rubbed a thumb over his chin, eyes to a piece of paper before him.

'It's not the existence of pornography on your devices, but the nature of the pornography that could cause us difficulty.'

'What do you mean?' said Nick quietly, almost holding his breath.

'Well,' Faldane half-smiled, 'none of the sites are illegal and all are freely available, but many feature non-consensual sexual violence . . . '

Nick felt the loss of Marina's hand on top of his.

'It's arguable these things are out of your control as a website visitor.' Faldane clasped his thick fingers and leaned forward on the desk. 'However, the police have highlighted searches that indicate you were actively seeking out violent content directed at women. One site in particular features restraints, face covered, hand over mouth, which could be argued is similar to the assault that the victim described.'

Nick swallowed, and took his hand from Marina's thigh.

Bob Faldane flicked open a file next to his computer and glanced at a note that had been handwritten on top.

Nick hunched his shoulders, as if expecting a blow.

'So, just an example of what they have ... *real rape* – it will be argued that you were specifically searching for images of women being violated.'

The room suddenly seemed smaller and the furniture loud and intrusive. Bob Faldane's small grey eyes did not leak any emotion or discomfort. He might have been describing the price and quality of silver teaspoons at an antique market, instead of laying bare Nick's furtive efforts at gratification.

Bob Faldane said nothing further but turned the piece of typed paper towards Nick and Marina. Nick put a hand on his forehead as he glanced down the list, but Marina was rigid by his side. Nevertheless, he was sure that she too read the searches they had uncovered: *red cherries, anal, real rape, brutal rape.*

Marina rose suddenly and strode out of the room.

Nick wiped a hand across his mouth. 'I'll be back in a minute.'

She was marching straight down St John Street, buttoning her trench coat as she walked, scarf trailing behind her. Nick jogged to catch up with her. He called on her but she didn't stop and he had to run in front of her and take her by the shoulders.

'I don't want to talk now,' she said, turning away from him. 'We can discuss it when we get home.'

Ava's face was so similar to her mother's. Since their daughter, Nick had begun to understand Marina on another level. He could see the deep imprint of pain he had caused her.

'I'm sorry,' he said instinctively. It was the first thing that came into his head but he soon realised it was the wrong thing to say.

'You're sorry? *Malparido*,' she spat at him.

She was disgusted by him, repulsed. Her shame for him chilled on his skin. She was frowning but her eyes were sad, reflective.

'It doesn't mean what you think. It doesn't mean anything.'

She unleashed a torrent of words at him suddenly, half English and half Spanish. 'What does it mean then? You told me *just now and then*, here we find that you are what – that you are addicted? And you want to watch violence.' Her eyes shone with tears. 'You want to watch a woman raped? A *girl* raped? You are a father. You have a daughter. You are my husband. Do you want to do these things to me?'

She stood before him, unmoving, defiant.

'No. You know what it's like – sometimes you click on things you don't mean to . . . ' He was trembling from his face down to his knees.

'No, I don't know what it's like. He said you searched for violence, searched for rape.' Her cheeks were now flushed with anger. She was out of breath, her eyes shining. 'Do you want to rape me? Is that what you fantasise about?'

'Please, I love you, and you and the kids are more important than anything in the world to me and I wouldn't ever *ever* hurt you. You have to know that. *Please.*' He considered dropping to his knees as he had done once when they had fought before they were married, and she had threatened to leave him and return to Spain. He sensed that falling to his knees would not be enough this time.

'Go! Go meet your lawyer. Deal with your business. I know now why he did not want me here. I'll get the children from your mother's.'

She spun on her heels and walked away from him. Nick thought about chasing her, burying his face into her stomach, begging for forgiveness. Instead he watched her go, the assertive swing of her hips, the vigour of her strides loosening the pinning of her hair.

Marina disappeared around the corner and he was filled with anger suddenly – at himself for being unable to stop her, frustration about the whole nightmare situation. He stood with his hands in fists at his side, feeling his stomach curdle with shame. She was right. He was a *malparido*. A creep. He took a long slow breath in, and then exhaled. The misty rain was turning heavy, wetting his hair and the shoulders of his shirt. Resolute, but sick to his stomach, he turned back to Faldane's office.

When he entered, Bob was engrossed in his computer, typing furiously with two forefingers. As Nick stood catching his breath in the doorway, the tapping of his fingers on the keys ceased.

'You're back.'

Nick approached the seat he had been sitting in before Marina's exit.

'Listen, I'm sorry I don't have much more time. I have to dash to court to meet a client in ten minutes.'

'It's all right.' Nick was dazed. 'I understand.'

'You know, maybe it was better she heard it now – here,' Bob pressed his full lips together, 'in the long run.'

Nick frowned, sitting down, 'What do you mean? I thought you said they don't have enough to charge me.'

'Right now, what they have shared with me is not enough to charge you but it's still too early to say that you won't be charged.'

Nick ran a hand through his hair. He was still shaking.

'Listen, they have to do a lot better than that if they want to press charges, but try to remember that as embarrassing as it is now, it's all part of a bigger picture. You've been accused of sexual assault and *that* is much more serious than your internet history,' said Faldane, zipping his briefcase and grabbing his overcoat from the hook. 'I'm sorry, I really have to rush. I realise this was a hard meeting and I'd love to stay with you and talk about it, but I only scheduled an hour and I need to get to my next appointment. Call me whenever you like.'

'I will, thank you,' said Nick, standing up, hooking a finger in his back pocket.

'I know it's difficult, but try to stay patient, and I'll let you know as soon as I have more.'

Nick nodded. 'Just tell me this. If it doesn't go my way, what could happen to me?'

'Are you asking about sentencing?' Bob's face was serious, jaw slack.

'Yes.' Nick swallowed.

'Well, if you are indicted and found guilty of non-penetrative sexual assault of an under-thirteen, you are looking at a maximum penalty of fourteen years.'

'Jesus.'

'That's the maximum penalty, of course – in reality you could serve a lot less, but you would certainly get a custodial sentence.'

Nick's mouth was suddenly very dry.

'But even with a lighter sentence, you would be put on the sex offenders register after release, which could last for ten years or more, and it would mean that even after serving your sentence it would be illegal for you to be alone with children, for example . . . even your own.'

Nick thought he had nodded in response. His heart was suddenly pounding in his chest.

'But, listen,' Bob slapped Nick's arm and then put on his jacket and overcoat, hanging a wine-coloured scarf around his neck, 'that's the absolute worst-case scenario. We're not looking at that yet. Right now, they don't have enough to charge you and they may *never* have enough to charge you.'

Nick exhaled, put his hands in his pockets, brought his shoulders up to his ears.

'You just need to focus on the here and now. Deal with what's in front of you.'

Nick nodded and followed Bob to the lifts. It felt as if he

was underwater. 'I'll let you go,' he said, putting on his jacket. 'Go on ahead if you're in a rush.'

He checked his watch. It was nearly four.

His mother would be picking up the children and Marina would get there soon after. Unless he hurried it would be prime time: homework; the assault of the day's stories; playground injustices; teacher's praise; skinned knees. In between it would be what was for dinner and who was making it. Then there would be no garlic or no peppers and someone would need to run out. He would arrive in the midst of this rapid current – food, bath time, pyjamas, stories, sleep.

And then it would be too late. He and Marina would both be exhausted and incapable of the emotional energy that it took to communicate as two loving adults.

He needed time with her to explain himself. He hoped that he could make her understand. Impatient, he pressed the button for the lift and then pressed it again, feeling a strange, controlled desperation, as if he was screaming on the inside.

11

Marina

When Marina got back to the house, it was empty. She had walked fast from the station at Farnham and her skin was moist with sweat. She stood for a moment, rubbing her temple, trying to remember what had happened. She had experienced it all so emotionally, so that it had been a blur – the office revelation, the fight in the street.

She looked at her watch. Betty would have collected the children already. She picked up the phone and began to dial her parents-in-law's number to tell them she was home early and would be right over, but then hung up, letting some of her weight lean on the receiver. She couldn't go right now. She needed time.

Upstairs, she ran a bath and then slipped under the surface, letting her head fall back to soak her hair. Water flooded her ears. Under the surface she heard the echo of the tap dripping. She raised her shoulders out of the water and wet her face, then took a deep breath in and out.

There were no bubbles, just salt, and her naked body wavered under the surface of the clear water.

Real rape.

Brutal rape.

It sickened her, but somehow it had not shocked her.

She knew he looked at pornography. There had been times in their marriage past – pregnancy, the pain of stitches – when she hadn't wanted him inside her. She knew he had used it then, but she had not known that he was still using it, and watching it on the iPad that they had bought only eight months ago for the children.

She hadn't wanted to know what he was watching; had not sought it out.

Steam and heat opened her pores and she swallowed, her throat clotting as she processed what she had heard today, what she *knew* about him and what she had *sensed*.

She sunk down deeper, lifting one leg to rest her foot near the tap. She felt suspended by the water, floating, open.

It had been in the flat in Balham, the first they had shared together. She remembered the bedroom almost exactly, the solid pine bed and the mismatched bedside tables, one in oak and one in mahogany; their old digital alarm clock with the faulty display so that the numbers five and eight were hard to distinguish. The worn, blood-red carpet and the cheap woven rug. A clothes rail instead of a wardrobe. An old-fashioned dressing table with a triptych mirror.

They had been together for two years.

The fingers of his palm spread between her shoulder blades. The gentle knock of the pine bed against the wall. Suddenly he reached for her hand, but as she was curling her fingers to receive his, he pulled her wrist back so that she pitched face down. At first it felt awkward and then uncomfortable. His weight was still on her, hand on her spine.

'Stop, let me up,' she had said, her voice muffled by the mattress.

He kept going. The faint pant of his breath.

'Stop,' she said, louder, trying to press up with her arms, but finding herself pinned.

She managed to get her left foot up against his body and kicked. She had strong legs. Not only did she succeed in getting him off her, but she pushed him right off the bed. He fell against the dressing table and then sat watching her, chest rising and falling. One leaf of the triptych mirror folded closed in the impact.

Marina sat on her heels. 'What the hell was that?'

'Sorry. Just got carried away. Sorry.'

He got back on the bed, smoothed her hair and kissed her shoulder, and then they continued.

Her wet toe touched the hot tap; it burned and she swiftly withdrew her foot back into the water that was already starting to cool. She sat up and washed her face and hair, then got out and roughly towelled herself dry. In their bedroom she was flushed and dizzy and sat down on the bed for a moment.

She had not lingered on it at the time, all those years ago, but somehow she had sensed that he had been acting out something violent that turned him on. There had been other times when he had held her throat when they were making love and she had told him she didn't like it; and once or maybe twice, when he was behind her and she couldn't see his eyes, it felt as if he had forgotten who she was.

The sound of the front door closing made her sit up. From downstairs, Nick called for her but she didn't reply. His feet on the stairs. She stayed where she was on the edge of the bed, wrapped in a towel, waiting for him to find her. She didn't know what it meant. She didn't have the words for it, in Spanish or in English, but it frightened her.

'There you are!'

His face was blanched with worry. He was holding a rolled-up newspaper that he tossed onto the bed, before falling to his knees and placing his hands on her hips.

'I am a *malparido*, okay? I'm not proud of any of that.'

She met his eyes, that tawny tiger's-eye glow. Despite everything, love for him flooded her. 'I can't talk about it. Not right now.'

'It sounded worse than it is, I promise. You just . . . click and get led places.'

She looked away from him and then stood up, brushing his hands away from her. It wasn't just what had been said in Faldane's office. She knew him deeply. Surely he knew that he couldn't hide anything from her. 'I need to go and get the kids from your mum's.'

She turned from him, but she could see his face in the mirror, strained.

'Marina, please? I'm sorry. I'm in real trouble here and I don't want to fight with you, too. I spoke to Bob after you left and he said I could get fourteen years.'

She turned to face him. He was shaking.

'And then this! Melissa texted me to say I was in the paper.' He handed the newspaper to her, opening it to the correct page. The photograph of Nick shown was a promotional still from *Scuttlers*.

Marina took the paper from him and read it quickly.

ACTOR BAILED AFTER SEXUAL ASSAULT
ON TWELVE-YEAR-OLD GIRL AT CROYDON
ACADEMY.

A twelve-year-old year eight pupil has been violently sexually assaulted at her school in Croydon.

Actor and drama teacher Nicholas Dean, who had a recurring role on the award-winning BBC drama series, *Scuttlers*, was arrested and questioned over the alleged assault before being released on police bail.

Dean runs a drama and media skills company called ACTUp and regularly tours schools delivering drama workshops. The actor's contract with the school in Croydon has now been terminated.

Dean's agent, Harriet Moore, of Artists United Agency, refused to comment. The victim cannot be named for legal reasons. The investigation continues.

Marina tossed the newspaper onto the bed. She was shaking, overwhelmed. She wanted to talk to him, but was afraid of the complex mix of emotions inside her and he wasn't her priority. She had children to look after.

'I need to get the kids from your mum's.'

She dropped her towel, turned her back to him and began to get dressed.

12

Angela

Angela sat in her father's car watching her parents talking on the doorstep. She was glad that she could only see their mouths opening and closing, her mother frowning and her father waving his hands in response. She didn't need to hear. They were talking about her.

As she waited, Angela dug into her backpack and found an opened packet of M&Ms and put one sweet after another into her mouth, watching avidly through the side window.

She took her phone out of her pocket. Adam had sent her a SnapChat picture of his stomach and hips, a slope of muscle and then hair:

Thinking uv u x

Angela drew the phone closer to look at his strange belly button. They had only fooled around outside. She had only seen him naked in parts, through the pictures he sent her, an electronic mosaic of his body.

There was another message from Jasmine and Angela shivered as she thumbed it to read:

Dean fingered u? Like fuck. Ur a liar and everyone knows it.

Angela put her phone in her pocket. Her father was making chopping motions with his hands to emphasise some point. It was like being at the movies, only this movie was her life.

She had not said a word to her father about Mr Dean, but her mother had told him. Her dad was a policeman and now the police were involved. Angela was worried. She didn't want to talk about it to him, but he was sure to say something when they were alone.

'What did he say?' Angela had asked her mother when she admitted she had told her father everything.

'He was hurt and angry,' Donna had replied, tapping a cigarette on the back of the packet to loosen the tobacco.

Angela had said nothing, keeping her face very still, but her mother said, 'Don't be stupid, he's not angry at you. He's angry at that bastard of a teacher.'

Angela wondered how her mother had read her thoughts. She wondered where they had leaked, her mouth or her eyes.

'He's not a teacher. He's an actor,' Angela replied.

'Whatever he is,' her mother lit her cigarette and her cheeks hollowed, 'he needs bloody castrating.'

Angela had had to Google *castrate*. Sometimes her mother told her that she was violent and would end up in prison. Clearly, Donna was one to talk.

'That's us, Angel, we can hit the road.' Her father slammed his door shut and sighed as he put two hands on the steering wheel.

He called her Angel, which was nearly her name. Her father had given her the name Angela because he said she had looked like an angel right from the start, yet it had never felt right for her. Sometimes her mum called her Ange and that was okay because it felt grown-up, but she hated Angela – all three syllables extended the way her mother said them – and Angel the most. She wasn't an angel. She was a bad person.

Stephen turned the key in the ignition and the radio came on gently in the background. They pulled out onto Shirley Road and then turned right onto Addiscombe Road. 'What do you want for tea? Do you wanna just get pizza? I could pick it up on the way.'

Angela heard strain in her father's voice. Usually on the drive to his they would chat about everything – music or some YouTube video she'd posted. Sometimes they even talked about school and her mum. She could talk to her dad about everything. Today he sounded funny. It was the voice he used when he was lying to her mum, or lying in general.

Stephen leaned over and turned the radio up a little, as if suggesting they didn't talk. Trees lined Addiscombe and Angela noticed how they were together in the distance, but grew apart as the car drew closer. It felt like her life, how she could never get to the point where she wanted to be. She decided that her father was uncomfortable because of what he had heard about Mr Dean.

'All right, pizza then.'

'That's what I thought. You've had a tough time. Don't want to force my cooking down you as well.'

Angela turned to him, but he was watching the road, taking the turn-off for South Croydon. He was chewing his lip and staring at the road ahead. She wondered if he was thinking about castrating Mr Dean.

Just after five, they pulled up outside her father's apartment. It was the kind of place that looked nicer from the outside. The exterior was swanky – clean and new with tan bricks and white plastic windows, but inside it was dark and claustrophobic. Angela had the pizza on her lap and the box warmed her thighs. She wanted to just stay in the car by herself and eat the pizza, but that wasn't an option.

Angela walked ahead of her father up the stairs to the front door then stopped, looking up at the CCTV camera he had installed to monitor people who came near the apartment. The scrutinising eye of the camera viewed her with detachment. She stood aside so that he could open the door and disable the burglar alarm. A rapid high-pitched beeping sounded as Angela lifted the lid of the pizza and smelled the cheese and salty pepperoni. The throbbing noise stopped and she stepped inside the flat.

Probably because he was a police officer, her dad liked a lot of security at home. *You can never be too careful.* There was still a burglar alarm at the other house, but Donna had disabled it as soon as her father moved out. *That's the last thing you need when you've got a headache, and what've we got worth stealing anyway?*

Better safe than sorry, her father had always said.

Inside, his flat was warm, almost hot because he left the heating on all the time. Angela liked it that way. Her mum was stingy with the heating. Since her father had left home the temperature had literally dropped – when her dad left he had taken the warmth with him.

Angela put the pizza on the counter in the tiny kitchen and went to her room to unpack, while her father opened a cupboard in the hall and reviewed the CCTV footage from the day. He did it every time he came home, fast rewinding through images of neighbours carrying shopping, and the postman smoking at the bottom of the stairs. He said there were too many people up to no good.

Her father had rented this flat since he left the family home. All the other rooms in the flat looked the same as they had when he moved in, but Angela's room was better. He had bought her a TV and a bedspread with love hearts on it, which Angela thought was too young for her.

The room had just one tiny window and the walls were a

pale apple green. There were three mirrors – one on the back of the door, one above the dresser and another full-length mirror that tilted in the corner. This meant that if Angela sat at a certain point on the bed, she could see herself from all angles.

Under normal circumstances, she didn't like looking at her reflection. She always looked away, particularly if she saw herself in profile or if she caught a view of herself from behind. The mirrors in her room in her dad's flat felt judgemental. They were like the eyes of girls at school who didn't like her, people like pretty, dark-eyed Jasmine.

Her room at home was full of her past: the pine furniture that she had written her name on with a school compass; old, worn stuffed toys that she had kept since she was little; the forget-me-not wallpaper she had chosen herself covered with all of her drawings and paintings; the photograph in a heart-shaped frame of her family five years ago when Angela was seven. In the picture she was grinning even though her two front teeth had just fallen out.

Like a hotel room, her bedroom at her father's was forever new. She could never quite make her mark on it. She had tried to hang a couple of sketches: portraits of pop stars and drawings of sweet peppers and a sheep's skull that she had done in art class – but the Blu-Tack wouldn't stick properly to the shiny walls.

Angela opened her bag and put her pyjamas underneath her pillow. She had brought a book with her: a hardback book of European oil paintings that her mother had given her. Angela liked looking at the pictures but hadn't read a word. Most of the paintings were of women without their clothes on and they were all looking out of the picture, as if they knew they were being viewed. Angela put the book on her bedside table and then emptied the rest of her backpack onto the bed. She noticed immediately that her tablet was missing. She had thought her bag felt too light when she left her mum's, but with everything else going on she had not double-checked. She realised she had probably left it in her bedroom at home.

She sighed, looking at the objects that had spilled onto the bedspread: her toothbrush and clothes and a Mars bar in case she got hungry in the night. Nestled against a sweater was her calligraphy pen. It was long and old-looking with a sharp gold nib. She held it in her hand as if she were about to write, then pressed the nib against the skin of her arm. Gently, so that it only scratched, she wrote ND. He had given the pen to her: Mr Dean. It wasn't just any old pen. It had been a prop on the set of his TV series, *Scuttlers*, and he'd given it to her after he saw the lettering she had done on a poster he'd asked her group to create.

It's one of a kind, just like you, he had said to her. *Don't tell anyone I gave it to you or they'll be jealous.*

Angela tucked the pen in the front pocket of her bag.

'Dad?' she called.

There was no answer. She opened the cupboard in the hall but did not find him there. The monitor showed an image split into four quarters reflecting different views of the front door. There was a safe in there too, which looked so heavy she didn't know how he had managed to get it in there. Angela sighed and looked for him in the lounge but he was not there either; nor was he in the kitchen, which was now filled with the sweet smell of warm pizza dough. She went towards his bedroom and the door was ajar.

'Dad?'

She nudged the door open, but the room was empty: the tight folds of the bed linen, all the surfaces clear – except for lamps and a clock. In the corner of the room was his Versa Climber pointed towards the window. He said the police had made him get fit and he wanted to stay that way. She had watched him use it several times: arms slick with sweat, T-shirt darkening down his spine, arms and legs pumping as if he were running fast although he was standing still, looking out onto Croydon. He had once described Donna as *sedentary*. Angela had had to look that up. It meant 'sitting down a lot' and, to be fair, her mum did.

On the chest of drawers there was a photograph of Angela when she was a baby, beside a picture of her grandmother, her dad's mum, whom Angela had never met because she had died before she was born. Her grandmother's eyes were like her father's – round and close together. Donna had told Angela that her grandmother had been an old bitch who was mean to her father, so Angela wasn't sure why the picture was in his bedroom. She presumed that Donna had been holding grudges and exaggerating.

She heard the toilet flush and turned. He was there, behind her.

'Ready for pizza, then?' he said, still with that strange strained expression on his face and the lying voice.

Angela looked at the floor and nodded, not wanting to look at him and see what she feared in his eyes: Mr Dean and all the things her mother had told him.

'Yeah, I'm hungry,' Angela said, skipping in the hall, trying to make herself seem happy. She wanted him to see her happy. She wanted him to be happy. She didn't want him to think about Mr Dean or her getting expelled or anything bad.

His smile was quick but cautious.

She paused at the top of the stairs as his expression changed: the worried face that meant he was going to say something important.

'Angel . . .'

Her hand was on the banister and he closed his palm over hers.

'I just wanted to say that your mum told me about what happened at school.'

She felt a sick feeling pressing upwards into her throat, reminding her of the time when she swallowed all the pills.

'I want you to know that . . .'

His breathing was funny. It sounded the way it did when he was on his Versa Climber, sweat darkening his T-shirt.

'Well, it wasn't easy for me to hear. Those things. I'm supposed to protect you. I know you might not want to talk to me about it, but I'm here anyway, if you want to talk . . . and don't worry, this . . . man . . . this actor, he's been caught and he's going to be punished.'

123

Angela looked at her arm. The pen scratches had reddened so that Mr Dean's initials were clear on her skin. She pulled her sleeves right down over her hands.

'I love you.' His eyes were shining and his lips were pressing together hard.

Angela nodded, not sure what to say. She really wanted to eat the pizza now, but was held in his gaze.

'Love you too,' she said finally, and then his grey eyes released her.

'You did the right thing to report it. I'm going to talk to the team that are dealing with it – make sure it's handled right.'

There was a pain in her throat that was so tight she wondered if she would be able to get words out. She had meant to ask him if he would drive back to her mum's and get her iPad, but instead she just said, 'Shall we have the pizza now, while it's still warm?'

Angela swallowed. She felt sick – the sensation increased by the sweet smell of dough spreading through the flat. Perspiration broke at her hairline.

'I won't let anyone lay a hand on you.' Her father ran his hand through her hair. 'All right?'

Angela smiled and let her head fall to his chest. Her father pressed her close. She dug her nails into her palm.

13

Donna

As Stephen's old Rover pulled away from the kerb, Donna opened the fridge and poured herself a large glass of Pinot Grigio. She sat in the chair in front of the television, not watching it but almost looking through it. She drank quickly, trying to process everything that had happened. It felt as if it was the first time she had been alone since Angela tried to commit suicide and confessed to being molested, and now they had had another fight. She drank deeply, remonstrating with herself as she tried to block out the argument from earlier.

'If you want, I could stay home this weekend.' Angela was slumped on the couch, feet akimbo before her and a bowl of crisps between her thighs.

Donna took a breath, about to reply, and then bit her lip. Stephen wouldn't like the change in routine and would blame Donna, particularly since she had delayed telling him about the assault. 'Your dad might be a bit upset. I know he wants to see you.'

Angela was sullen suddenly, sliding one crisp after another into her mouth, sitting so low on the couch that she had a double chin. 'I just want to stay home with you and watch crap TV,' she said, tugging on the cuffs of her sweater. 'We could get a takeaway.' Her eyes were furtive and hopeful. 'Please?'

Donna smiled at her. It had been a hard week for her at school. The newspapers had reported the assault, and although no one had printed her name, still the kids knew or else had narrowed it down to Angela, because she was being kept in at playtimes and lunchtimes. The Sexual Assault Referral Centre, who had conducted the examination, had offered Angela counselling, but she had so far refused.

'Well, you'd need to text your dad and explain.' She picked up some magazines that were lying on the floor and then one of Angela's crisps that had crushed on the carpet. 'You'll need to be sure and tell him it was your idea and not mine.'

'I did a new drawing last night. You could help me paint it?' Angela sucked her lower lip as she watched her mother's face.

'I don't like all that mess downstairs.'

'We could do it in my room.'

'I dunno, love. I'm tired.'

'Why are you cross?'

Donna looked at her daughter. She wasn't cross but she *did* want her to go to her father's. She needed time to herself, to think, to drink – just one night without the threat of an argument or name-calling. The assault had happened to Angela, but Donna had felt it in her bones. She needed time alone to recover.

'I'm not. I just think you need to consider his feelings.'

Her brows lowered; blue eyes darkening.

'You don't want me to stay.'

She kicked the floor with her heel and Donna pushed back her shoulders, preparing for a fight. 'Of course I want you to stay.'

Heart thumping in expectation of another row, Donna turned to Angela and saw her eyes shine with tears.

'Why do you take everything so personally? I just said that you need to call your dad and explain.'

'Fine.' Angela got up, spilling the crisps from the couch, and thumped upstairs.

As Donna knelt to pick up the crisps from the carpet, Angela returned and shouted from the living-room door. 'I don't want to stay here with you, either. My dad's better than you are.'

'Fine,' Donna said from her knees, stung. Anger suddenly reached up from her stomach and into her throat. 'I can't wait to see the back of you,' she shouted at the wall, feeling a vein throb at her temple.

Moments later, tipping the crisps into the kitchen bin,

Lisa Ballantyne

Donna heard the bedroom door slam. She put one hand over her face.

Donna refilled her glass and this time set the bottle on the coffee table. She had needed this time alone. She didn't know how to talk to her daughter, how to show she cared, how to help her through this. It was hard to give what she had never received.

A *little girl*, she kept telling herself. So young, but Donna found it hard to relate to her daughter in that way. Intellectually, of course, she knew that Angela was still a child – it was only a year since she'd got her first period. But whenever she looked at Angela, whenever she spoke to her, she didn't see a child on the cusp of puberty – she saw a disappointing version of herself, a lump of white clay that Donna just wished would mould itself into something better.

It had only been a few years since she had had the most precious little girl. Memories of good times hurt more because her daughter was now so unrecognisable from that gentle, good-natured child she had once been.

Angela was just four and they were hand in hand in Crystal Palace Park, going to see the dinosaurs. They sat in the grass picking daisies, which Angela piled onto her mother's knee. Donna split each stem with her thumbnail and then threaded them into a chain and tied it around Angela's neck.

She beamed – dimples in cheeks that were soft as the skin of mushrooms. Then hand in hand they went looking for the dinosaurs. Angela had a book about them and could name

128

most of them. But just around the corner a Tyrannosaurus Rex appeared between the trees. It loomed before them, life-sized, all scales and sharp teeth.

Angela screamed and Donna had to pick her up and hold her.

'It's all right. It's a model, see? It's not real.'

'It's a monster. I don't like it.' She was on the verge of tears.

'We'll go, then. Don't be scared.'

Donna carried her out of the park, the little hands tight around her neck. 'Don't worry, darling. Mummy wouldn't let anything happen to you. You're safe with me.'

She sat staring over the rim of her glass at the patio doors, which were becoming reflective as darkness fell on the back yard and the glow from the lamps shone brighter. Nearly thirteen and yet Donna had been unable to keep her safe. She remembered the taxi ride home from the Sexual Assault Referral Centre, after Angela had been subjected to what they called an *intimate examination*.

Intimate.

It was such a strange word, gentle but cold. It reminded Donna of an insect walking on her bare skin. It made her think about things she tried to forget.

Donna had held Angela's hand throughout. The examination had seemed an assault in itself, but Angela was silent, her eyes dark and flat, spreading her legs and turning her head to the side. Angela's pale hand limp in hers, Donna had felt empty, as if the sterility of the environment had swabbed away all of the normal, mothering responses.

Donna picked up her phone and opened up her browser. Nicholas Dean's Wikipedia page was already open because she had looked him up more than once in the past few days. The photograph had been taken a few years ago. He was a handsome man, smiling, all straight teeth and floppy blond hair and bright eyes. He was wearing a tuxedo and there was a hand on his arm, although the person the hand belonged to had been cropped out of the picture. He looked like one of those good-looking busy people you saw in central London – walking too fast in the crowd, looking at their watches, takeaway coffee in their hands. Donna stared at the photograph as her glass tilted in her hand. Paedophiles really did look like everyone else. There was no way to tell from the outside.

Donna stared at Nick's broad, white smile. She wondered what he got out of it. He looked so shiny and pretty. What could he want with Angela? How could he desire that sullen, chubby, immature little girl? It was sick, but not in the way people thought. Everyone thought it was about sex, a perversion. Donna knew that it was not about sex at all, but about dominance.

A thought shifted over her. She wasn't sure if her hand shook or if she was just distracted, but the wine slipped from her lips and rolled down her chin. She caught it with the back of her hand.

She had been older than Angela, but still naive. Sixteen, but didn't even know that she had been raped until she told the doctor her story, years later. All this time, she had never told anyone else. These things happened. She had been a waitress and he was the chef. He shouted and swore at everyone and Donna had been terrified of him. Even now she was sure that it was her fear that had attracted him to her, rather than her body. He had smelled her fear, like a dog.

Donna finished her cigarette and drained her glass, a morose heaviness settling on her. She shook her head twice, as if to shake the memory from her mind.

Her arms goose-pimpled as she remembered him holding her by the throat in the chill of the refrigerated larder. She hadn't screamed or even called out, although the door was ajar and someone might have heard her. She had frozen there and let it happen, cold and inert like all the other produce on the shelves. She had worked for three hours afterwards – finished her shift.

Donna flicked through the TV channels, finding nothing that would distract her from her thoughts. She muted the TV again and picked up her phone. She pressed the home button so that Nicholas Dean's Wikipedia page illuminated once again. Dean had two children, a boy and a girl.

He was beautiful.

He looked like a pop star.

The bastard.

She gulped her wine and poured another glass, feeling the buzz now, the gentle tingle in her brain. She let her head fall back against the armchair.

How had her life turned into this? How had she let it happen? It wasn't just the loss of Stephen. She wasn't sure she could cope with Angela on her own. She had friends who were single parents but they had good relationships with their daughters – they went on holiday together.

What had happened to them – the Furness family?

Suddenly everything had gone dark. It hadn't always been so.

She didn't normally smoke inside, but there was nobody home and she was just drunk enough not to care. Donna lit a cigarette and exhaled towards the ceiling, reeling in the pleasure of it, remembering better times.

Angela burst out of nursery and presented her latest effort. Donna bent to inspect it, hardly looking at it. 'Very nice.' She took Angela's hand and started for the door. They had to catch the number fifty-nine bus and were running late.

Outside drizzle had started. It was December and although it was only five o'clock, the sky was dark. Donna pulled Angela along the pavement, into the rain, walking so fast that Angela was running at her side. Donna kept the painting pressed onto her coat and the back of the paper became wet with the rain.

When they reached their bus stop, drenched, Donna realised that they had five minutes to spare. She bent and kissed Angela's forehead. Her daughter had a little pageboy cut that was now plastered against her head so that she looked like a porcelain doll.

A car splashed past. Donna lifted the painting that she had been holding.

'Mummy,' said Angela, pointing, 'you've got a heart on you.'

The red tissue-paper dye had soaked into the fabric of her pale grey coat, leaving a perfect love-heart stain.

Donna smiled, past caring, and held the artwork up as they huddled in the shelter. It was a giant heart rimmed by red tissue-paper flowers, and filled in by Angela's bright red handprints. At the top, it read, *Mummy I love you*, in black Sharpie teacher writing.

'That's my hand,' said Angela, reaching up to press her palm against one of the prints.

'I see that. So many of them. It's like a big flower.'

'No, no,' a frown suddenly underneath her wet hair, eyes insistent with impatience, 'it's *not* a flower. It's my big heart and all the hands are me giving you a cuddle.'

Donna bent and picked her up. She was heavy, four already and not long till she'd be in school. 'You're my precious girl,' she whispered, kissing her cheek.

She set her down. 'Look, that's our bus. Take my hand.'

Donna lit another cigarette and then let it hang, dangling her hand over the edge of the chair. That little girl had been amazing, the love of her life. Where was she now? She turned her head and let her eye settle on the school portraits on the mantelpiece. Six portraits cute as a button and then last year's picture – Angela swollen to a brute, her tie askew and the not-quite-smile.

Donna took another sip of her wine, wondering if she hated Angela because she was on the cusp of womanhood.

133

Did she dislike her daughter because she was becoming more like her?

Thinking would drive her crazy. Donna swallowed a burp and turned up the sound on the TV.

She missed Stephen, but had missed him before he left. He hadn't been unfaithful, but he had gradually stopped sleeping with her. When she asked him about it directly, he had been offhand, cold.

'I just don't fancy you anymore,' he had said. 'I think I still love you, but if I'm honest, I don't fancy you at all.'

No one needs the whole truth.

Donna took a long drag on her cigarette. She looked back on the woman who had heard those words with pity and shame.

They were in the bedroom. On the dresser was the picture of Stephen's dead mother, all pearls and set hair, smiling like a dog baring its teeth.

Donna was just out of the bathroom. She threw off her dressing gown, letting it hang from her shoulders. In the mirror she saw the reflection of the tattoo on her left shoulder: MUM in red letters below an eagle spreading its wings.

He was reading a book about international terrorism and didn't even look up as she turned awkwardly, trying to get his attention.

'You still reading?' she tried, biting her lip.

He glanced at her, but it was as if he didn't see her. Or if he did see the lingerie peeking from the top of her dressing gown, he didn't wish to acknowledge it.

'I'm about done,' he said, putting his book onto the dressing table.

She switched off the light before shrugging her dressing gown to the floor. She had bought new underwear – a lace body and knickers – yet still she only had the courage to show him in the dark. Her thighs wobbled too much and she thought she would feel better under the covers.

In the dark, under the weight of the duvet she reached for him, but he turned his back. She held onto his side for a moment, the skin of his abdomen and her fingers sticking together with warmth. Finally she peeled her hand from his body and turned her back on him, too.

On her side, in her new underwear, a hand under her cheek, she cried silently – tears leaving her right eye, rolling over the bridge of her nose and then splashing into her left.

She opened her eyes in the darkness. It felt like years since he had touched her unasked. Her body kept a diary of all the hurtful words he had said to her.

Her thighs were: *I don't want to make love to you because of the cellulite.* Her abdomen: *jelly belly – you never lost the baby weight, and Angela's nearly ten.* Her unpainted toenails and grey roots reproached her: *you don't make an effort.* Her crotch: *a bit of a forest,* and then her legs: *like a hedgehog – trying to give me a rash?*

Her breasts remembered: *sagging just a teeny bit;* her womb recalled: *you want another baby, but you're too fat now to get pregnant.* Her stomach kept the score from their rows, when she opted for peace at any price. Antacids in the bedside table drawer.

Lying on her side, the warmth of his body radiating onto the small of her back, she felt her body as a blank canvas that he had scrawled over again and again. It was her body, but she felt his marks, permanent as the tattoo on her shoulder.

She dried her eyes, inched away so that she no longer felt his heat, and tried to find sleep.

That had been nearly two years ago, and since then, Donna had been brimming with self-loathing. They were in a strange place now – not quite friends but not enemies either. Were it not for Angela – this difficult young person they had created together – she doubted they would speak at all.

Donna had no energy to make dinner and so put a slice of toast into the toaster. It was the last piece – the heel.

She staggered slightly as she left the kitchen, then went upstairs and changed out of her work clothes into a tracksuit. Habitually, absently, she picked up dirty laundry that was scattered in the hall outside Angela's room, stray socks and a vest-top. She sighed as she went into Angela's room to throw the clothes in the laundry bin. She would do washing tomorrow; tonight she was going to do her best to forget the past few weeks.

On top of Angela's bedspread was her tablet with the bright red cover. Donna cursed lightly. Not only would her daughter miss it but also there was a good chance they would come back for it. Donna sank down onto the bed and opened the iPad to reveal the familiar picture of Angela licking an ice-cream – white tongue and closed eyes. Unsure if she was dizzy from the drink or bending to pick up the laundry, Donna curled onto her daughter's bed with the iPad until her light-headedness passed. She opened up YouTube.

Nicholas Dean's face appeared on the screen. All of the suggested videos were clips of the TV series *Scuttlers*. Donna had not seen any of this. Head still resting on her daughter's pillow, Donna tapped on a video billed as 'Max's torture in Scuttlers season 3'.

It was a ten-minute video of Nicholas Dean, strapped into a chair, being repeatedly punched in the face until he was beyond recognition, then forced to sign a confession – the dark ink of the fountain pen mixing with his own blood as, blinded by eyes punched closed, he tried to sign his name.

Feeling thirsty, her head throbbing from the wine, Donna watched until the end. She saw the first blood and swelling, the nose crack and jaw dislocation, the blood trailing from Dean's mouth as he tried to sign his name with startled, unfamiliar hands. It turned Donna's stomach. She turned down the sound, but as she watched reminded herself that Angela must have seen this repeatedly for it to be recommended viewing.

When the video ended, Donna rolled the flap over her daughter's tablet and rocked herself off the bed. She looked down at her feet, still trying to steady herself. There was something sticking out from the frill of the valance around the bed – it looked like a scrapbook.

After two attempts because she was tipsy, Donna finally liberated the book. It was a sketchpad that Stephen had bought for Angela's Christmas the year before. She lay back on the bed, propped on an elbow.

Donna opened the book with nostalgia for the happy, creative little girl her daughter had once been. Angela had loved drawing since she'd been small and then it had turned into something more. The teachers had said she had a precocious talent. That was the word: precocious. True, Angela's pictures had looked different from the other kids' pictures, which were just stick figures and rainbows, but if Donna had been honest, she hadn't seen what was supposed to be special about them.

On the first page there was a sketch, which, although rudimentary and childish, was recognisable as a portrait of Stephen. Donna stared at the picture until the pencil marks started to distort. Stephen's brows began to lower and his mouth pinched – the expression Donna was most used to confronting.

Just then there was a sudden screaming noise; an undulating pulsing sound ripped through the house. Donna jolted and got to her feet.

At the top of the stairs she saw smoke in the hall and realised that the toast was burning.

She ran downstairs, knifed the thick charred toast from the toaster and binned it, then stood on a chair in the hall waving Angela's sketchpad in front of the smoke sensor until the noise relented.

Exhausted, fingers trembling, parched, Donna opened the windows in the kitchen to get rid of the smoke.

She coughed lightly, finding her empty wine glass and pouring another. As the smoke cleared, there on the kitchen tiles, she saw several pictures of Nicholas Dean.

The same picture from the Wikipedia page and then another picture of him and his wife attending a function. She was beautiful, too – as dark as he was blond – Italian or something. A still of Dean on the set of *Scuttlers* in Victorian dress. There were fifteen or more pictures, blown up, printed onto paper and cut out. There was a shiny real photograph of him, hand-signed in black marker.

Donna stood, fingertips chilling on her wine glass as she gazed at the pictures on the floor. She realised the pictures had fallen from the sketchbook, which she still had cast onto the floor. A strip of photographs protruded from the pad and so Donna bent and flipped it open, to reveal an old-fashioned photo booth strip, Nicholas Dean and Angela together, faces pressed up against each other. Donna pressed a hand to her mouth. She turned the photo strip over and on the back, in Angela's favourite purple glitter Sharpie, was:

A.F loves N.D

Donna squatted down and sifted among the pages that had spilled on the floor. There was a thick page from the sketchpad face down. Donna turned it over and held it up – a portrait of Nicholas Dean's face – obviously sketched from his Wikipedia profile, the same angle and smile. It was not a perfect likeness – Dean's eyes were far too large and his nose strangely misshaped, but Donna could tell that it was him and that Angela had spent some time on it.

The smoke from the toaster cleared and Donna stood staring at the photographs of her child with the man who had molested her. She wiped a hand over her mouth as sweat broke at her hairline. She wished she hadn't drunk the wine. Her brain was cloudy and she needed to understand what this meant.

14

Marina

Marina had cleared her calendar for the afternoon and so decided to go home early and work there. She thought about calling her mother-in-law to say she could pick up Luca and Ava from the childminder – save her the trip – but decided to do that from home.

She called Nick when she got on the train at Waterloo but he didn't pick up and so she left him a message:

Hey, I'm on my way home. Can u pick me up? I get in
at 14:38 xx

The fear that he would be charged had driven them both into avoidance tactics. Even when they were alone, the unspoken hung between them.

He didn't reply to her text, and when she arrived at Farnham,

Nick was not there so she walked home from the station, her bag straining the muscles on her shoulder: handbag stuffed with statistics on the vulnerability of child refugees, and the old-fashioned work laptop, heavy as a brick. As she walked, thoughts blizzarded in her mind.

Would her boss see the references to Nick in the press and consider it incompatible with her role as director of Child International? What did it *mean* that her husband, her lover, masturbated to images of women being tied up, choked and raped?

Sex between them was now was predictable, repetitive. Friday nights were almost a certainty, probably once during the week or maybe Sunday morning if the children had slept through and they woke up in time. Underneath the duvet, alert for tiny intruders. Quick and furtive. It was good sex, she thought. Marina loved him and his body. She had thought he felt the same.

After Luca was born, Nick had described her vagina as a familiar room with all the furniture taken out. She had always remembered that.

Had he always been secretly desiring something else? Something harsher, darker.

A French friend from university had once said to her: *one cannot desire what one already has.* That was it, she supposed. Desire was the chase, the ungraspable *now,* a craving and existence forever out of reach, glimpsed but never realised.

Luca had been a long but straightforward birth, but Ava had been quicker with more long-term consequences. Marina had needed stitches and the wound had granulated, creating a lump of flesh inside her that had made sex painful for them both. It was nearly two years after Ava was born before their sex life had got back to normal again.

Marina *knew* that the porn had started then. Had he become addicted because her own, real body was unavailable? Was it because they were having less sex, or had she by then ceased to be his object of desire? Object. She didn't want to be his object. She wanted to be his lover.

He had been at the delivery of both their children. He had cut the cords. He had left fingerprints of uterine blood on her abdomen.

These children were born of sex, but had procreation killed desire?

Despite the cold, Marina felt too warm. She walked faster and faster, as if to outrun her thoughts. Sex and love – how did the two come together?

She had been attracted to him from the minute they met, and the sex had been good right from the start, but they had fallen hard in love at the same time. After they'd been together for a year, she had gone back to Spain to visit her sick father. The separation had been brutal. She had lost weight and suffered insomnia just pining for him. Then they had got married and soon she was pregnant, but she had never felt him lose interest. She had always felt loved and desired. It had always felt real.

But he was an actor. Had he been pretending?

That time he pushed her down and pinned her – had he been acting out his fantasies of what he wanted to do, to her or other women? What would have happened if she had not managed to push him off the bed?

The clouds were pressing down on the red roofs of the houses along Firgrove Hill and Marina's head ached. With each footstep the right side of her skull seemed to throb. It wasn't just him. She had fantasies that she had not shared with him and had no need to – she didn't want to act them out. But they seemed so innocuous in comparison to the list that Faldane had produced in his office.

Was it the same for Nick? Was it possible to judge fantasies?

Rape and violence – did his fantasies have the same innocence at their core?

Fantasies were just that, after all, private dreams. In another time, they would have stayed private.

The car was in the drive when she arrived home. She turned the key in the lock, shook off her coat and put down her bags in the hall. She pressed the heel of her hand against her temple. She just needed a drink of water – she hadn't stopped since morning and had allowed herself to get dehydrated.

There was an unusual eerie silence. 'Nick?' she called, kicking off her shoes.

A sudden slam from the kitchen.

Marina frowned. Nick met her in the hall, still wearing his tracksuit bottoms as if he had not gone further all day than around the block with Rusty. There was something over-eager about his smile. She tilted her head to kiss his lips but he kissed her cheek instead.

'You're home early.'

'I left you a message.'

'Oh really? Dunno where my phone is.'

In the kitchen, he snapped the kettle on, avoiding her eyes. The room was cold despite the heating being on.

'I got a shitty email from Harriet.'

'Oh yeah, what?' Marina put her suit jacket over the back of one of the dining room chairs.

'She doesn't want me to go for the advert – or any advert – or any other job – until *this*,' he made sarcastic quotation marks with his fingers, 'is all cleared up. I'm officially grounded.'

'Oh sweetheart . . .'

'Yup. What kind of day did you have?' he said, his eyes lowered guiltily.

'It was all right. I had a meeting cancelled this afternoon and just took the chance to escape.' She leaned back against the kitchen table, rubbing her shoulder where the heavy bag had strained it. 'I've still got work to do, but I was going to call your mum and say I can pick up the kids. Save her the journey.'

He nodded, dropping a peppermint tea bag into a cup and adding water. When he handed the cup to her, their eyes met. The pupils of his dark eyes were dilated, eyelids thick and low.

'Are you . . . stoned?' said Marina, her voice sounding sharper than she had intended.

He ran a hand through his hair, caught out, embarrassed. Marina cast her eyes over the kitchen. The bag of grass was by the window, next to the new iPad that Melissa had donated for the children. It was cold because he had been smoking out of the window. Anger cut with disgust flashed through her.

'*Patetico*,' she said under her breath, tugging her blouse out from her waistband and leaving the room, walking upstairs as she undid the buttons.

She heard his feet behind her. 'Oh, come on, you're the one that's always suggesting we have a joint once the kids are in bed . . . '

'When was the last time I sat around all day and got stoned at two in the afternoon? I have a job, you know? I pay the mortgage.' In the bedroom she took off her blouse, tugging at the sleeves, and tossed it onto the bed. She unbuttoned her skirt and let it fall to the floor. As he came into the room she was sitting on the bed, taking off her tights. The anger had cleared her mind and the pain in her head was gone.

'I'm not stoned. It's just been a rough few days and every time I pick up a paper or turn on the TV there's some other celebrity being hauled over the coals.'

'So you're a celebrity now? Get a grip. You were in the *Evening Standard* and probably no one even noticed . . . ' She was bristling with temper now. She pulled on a sweater and her navy sweatpants.

'I didn't mean that,' he looked away, frustrated.

She noticed a sheen of tears in his eyes and it made her catch her breath for a moment, but she was tired and thirsty and still hurting from the revelations in Faldane's office. She still hadn't processed it – wasn't sure what to believe.

'You can't blame me for wanting to escape. I *can't* work. I'm stuck here.'

'So what?' Marina pulled on her woollen socks, 'I'm at work and your mother is looking after your children, and so you think you have nothing better to do than smoke a joint and what . . . maybe check out some porn?'

Nick exhaled, hands on his hips, chin down.

'Well what am I supposed to think? You were watching that stuff on our daughter's iPad. I have no idea any more how your decision-making works. I mean . . . on your *four-year-old daughter's* iPad.'

'I know how old she is.' The tawny flecks in his brown eyes now flashed with anger, as if lit from within.

They had been shouting and now Marina took a deep breath. 'I don't know what to think about this. I don't know what it means. I was trying to understand and be understanding, but I can't. I don't get it. I thought I turned you on and now I find out that violence turns you on.'

'Violence doesn't turn me on,' he said, lowering his voice.

'Rape is violence, you know that?'

'YOU turn me on, no one else, nothing else,' he said, taking a step towards her and putting his hands around her waist, letting his head fall to her shoulder. 'I told you already. You click on things and you get led places. I'm not proud of it.'

She pulled back from him a little, watching his face up close, the pupils still dilated from the drugs, but his eyes also earnest and full of pain.

'I'm ashamed of myself. I don't know what else to say to you.' He leaned in and kissed her cheek. He smelled of salt and smoke. 'Forgive me for this afternoon? I just needed ...' He pulled away from her gently and shrugged.

'What *did* you need?' she pressed.

'I dunno, to forget about it all. I can't do anything. I'm just stuck waiting and everywhere you look something reminds me of it. Pop stars, football coaches ... it's like every guy on the planet has to be Jimmy Savile.'

Marina straightened her shoulders. 'I don't think it's like that.'

'Well it feels like it. I didn't lay a finger on Angela Furness. But it seems like any girl can say whatever the hell she likes and the guy gets hauled over the coals without question. It's not fair. It's like the witch trials.'

'That's hysterical.'

'Is it? It's never the woman's fault.'

'It's *always* the woman's fault,' she said, her chest heaving as she tried to control her breath, trying not to feel polarised from him.

She turned to leave the room. There was a small stack of hardback books on the chest of drawers next to him. He swept them to the floor and when she turned round at the thud, he was wiping a tear from his cheek.

'Can we stop this? I said I was sorry. I can't get through this without you.'

His face had the wounded pique of Luca when he was upset.

'I know,' she said, smiling at him with closed lips. 'I just need time to think this through.' The sound of the toilet flushing caused Marina to open the bedroom door a little.

'Shit, your mum's here already,' she said, covering her eyes with her hand.

15

Betty

Betty parked her hatchback in the drive and turned off the engine. The grating, repetitive CD that the kids were singing along to suddenly cut out and Betty felt relief but then apprehension, glancing in the mirror at Ava, who had begun to pout as soon as the music stopped. Betty's head hurt and she needed a cigarette but she feared that there would be tears if she didn't get them into the house quickly. The children were both tired after long days at school and nursery.

'I'm too old for this,' she muttered, as she slid her aching hip out of the car, by which time both children had freed themselves from their car seats. She followed them into the house carrying a bag of groceries that she had noticed were missing from the kitchen. When she had called to pick up her grandchildren in the morning, the milk had been sour and there had been no coffee. It was as if, amid this crisis, Nick and Marina were putting all of their energy into the children and had lost sight of their own needs.

Betty called out to Nick as the kids tumbled into the living room. She put the groceries down on the table. There was no answer. She took the milk from the fridge and poured it down the sink before replacing it with the fresh milk she had just bought.

'Nick?' she called again, standing at the bottom of the stairs and looking upwards.

It was then that she noticed Marina's handbag and keys by the phone. Her daughter-in-law must have come home early and now they were upstairs together.

Betty sniffed in slight annoyance as she went into the kitchen and made herself a cup of tea. She checked on the children in the lounge. Ava was emptying toys from a box beside the sofa, her bottom lip protruding. 'I want the iPad,' she whined.

Betty knew that their own tablet had not yet been returned from the police but Melissa had loaned them another, knowing how much the children would miss it.

'I don't know, darling,' Betty said, turning on the television and scrolling to the children's channel in the hope that it would distract her. 'I'll have a look for it in a moment.'

Luca was in the corner, jacket still on, hovering over some cut-out paper sculptures that he had made earlier in the week.

'Luca, take your coat off, please,' said Betty. 'I'll make you both a snack.'

'Okay,' called Luca, without turning, still focussed on the paper tower.

'*Take your coat off.*'

As Betty turned to leave the room, Luca shrugged his anorak to the floor. The action was the only sign that he had heard her.

Betty took her cigarettes from her handbag and carried her cup of tea to the kitchen window. She opened the window and lit the cigarette, frowning and blinking as smoke drifted into her eyes.

She loved her grandchildren, all of them – perhaps Luca and Ava most because they were the youngest, and because they were Nick's – her baby's babies – but the extra childcare duties were draining. She was getting too old to carry little children around and deal with tantrums.

She took a mouthful of sweet milky tea and then a drag of her cigarette. Ever since that Sunday when Nick told them about his arrest she had had a sick feeling in the pit of her stomach and a pain up the back of her neck.

Tom often became frustrated with her because she took everything to heart. She felt what was happening to Nick in her own body, as if it was *she* who was facing prison. Her nerves had been shot since she had lost her own job in 1997.

She coughed a little – the rumbling, deep chest, ever-present cough that shamed her because it meant that she needed to stop smoking. Nick would always be her baby. Her firstborn, Mark, was like his dad, and liked to take his time about things; and so his birth had been the definition of labour – nearly three days until he appeared, weighing over ten pounds. Melissa, even though she was a middle child, had always been independent and high achieving, perhaps because she had been the only girl. Melissa liked to do everything her own way, and so her birth had also been difficult. She had been breech and then she seemed to right herself, before finally coming out bum first. Betty had needed ten stitches after Melissa.

Nick had slipped out like a seal. He was the best-looking of all her children and the sweetest. She remembered long afternoons looking at books or watching TV together with Nick snuggled into her. He had been the most affectionate child. It was wrong to have children thinking that they would give you something back, but Nicholas had always returned so much love.

She smiled, eyes watering, just remembering him, butter blond and huge brown eyes. Tom said that he was easily distracted, lacked discipline, but Betty knew that her son, Nicholas, was the best thing that she had ever done.

Feeling the chill from the window, Betty flicked the ash from her cigarette outside. It was then that she noticed the iPad and an opened sunglasses case with some cigarette papers sticking out of it. She frowned a little and flicked open the case. There was a polythene bag inside and Betty stubbed out her cigarette so that she could inspect the contents. It looked like dried herbs still on the stem. She sniffed it, then zipped the sunglasses case and put it to the side of the counter. She cleared her throat and closed the window, picking up the iPad for Ava.

Just then, she heard raised voices coming from the top of the stairs. Betty held onto the banister as she looked up towards the sound. It was Marina and Nick arguing.

For a few moments, Betty listened. Mostly it was Marina shouting at Nick, a tangle of Spanish and English. She didn't know how they could live that way. It was hard enough to communicate with her own husband in one language, let alone two.

Betty acknowledged a twinge of resentment: that her daughter-in-law had time to come home and fight with her son but didn't have time to collect her own children from the childminder. Worried that the children would hear them fighting, Betty went into the lounge.

'Do you want some toast, then?' she asked.

Luca was absorbed with the scissors and more paper. His grandpa had given him a ream of old fax paper and Luca seemed to have worked out a pattern where he could create a concertina of characters. Ava's face lit up at the sight of the iPad.

'And can I have some milk too, please Granny?' Ava said, the madam, all eyelashes.

'Those beautiful manners can certainly get some milk.'

Ava preened at the compliment, thudding her heel on the floor. Betty was grateful that there had been only English spoken since she had collected Luca and Ava from school. Her granddaughter sometimes spoke in Spanish to Betty – unaware that she couldn't understand. As a teacher, Betty felt this language experiment was too much to impose on the children, but Nick had been offhand. *They'll work it out in their own time.*

Betty's experience of children – and she had a lot: three of her own and a long teaching career – had taught her that children did not value adult agendas being imposed on them. But who was she? She was only the grandmother.

The children seemed oblivious to their parents' argument in the upstairs bedroom. Betty closed the lounge door behind her and crept upstairs. She meant to use the bathroom, although there was a toilet downstairs and going up hurt her hip. If her son and daughter-in-law came out, she would have no good excuse. They would know she was eavesdropping.

At the top of the stairs, Betty bristled and froze. Marina was losing it, shouting at Nick like she had never heard before.

'On our daughter's iPad? Who does that? On the iPad that your daughter uses to play games? What's wrong with you? It disgusts me.'

Betty frowned, confused as to what she meant.

There was the sound of Nick apologising. Betty stood at the top of the stairs, alert. Was he crying? A helpless pang of frustration drove her into the bathroom. She locked the door.

It felt as if her son was going through what she herself had suffered years before. She sat down on the toilet seat listening to the muffled sounds of the argument through the door. Nicholas was her son. She loved him. She believed in him. She would support him, no matter what. Whatever they said he had done, he was innocent. She knew his heart.

Betty knew what it was to have her integrity questioned.

Memories that she was accustomed to suppressing blistered in her mind.

She was a mother of sons.

That was all that was in her mind as Marshall Henderson stood, scraped his chair back and faced her. He was fifteen years old and bursting with swagger like the angry pimples on his cheek. He was a strange combination of child and man – emotional and petulant but ripped with anger – muscles new and hard on his still-growing frame. He was taller and wider than she was, but he seemed to take up an even larger metaphysical space, dominating the room, spreading out, like liquid turning to gas.

'What you going to do about it?' he challenged her, all thrust and tilt.

He was Nicholas's age, but even Mark would not have spoken to her in this way.

'Leave the classroom now.'

As the words left her mouth, she acknowledged her vulnerability. Teaching was all about performance. She had learned that early in her career – the first students she had stood before had taught her the need to *act* as if she was in control. The truth was projected; it didn't need to be real.

Marshall's challenge was absolute, and her guise fell around her ankles.

Betty had never been an authoritarian teacher. Most students were won over by her maternal nature, her love of the subject. Teaching was glorious to Betty: it was about giving inspiration, unlocking promise. It was passing on a secret. Her whole career, Betty had never lost that feeling. But in the last few years, the struggle to enforce discipline had worn her down. It seemed as if every lesson became a battleground, a few children becoming darkly empowered – knowing their rights, their dues, their scope.

Marshall stood his ground, pushing his shoulders back as his eyes narrowed. Betty repressed a flutter of panic behind her breastbone. She had to maintain authority. She had to seem unafraid but her fingertips were trembling.

'Leave the classroom, *now*,' said Betty, raising her chin, using all the air inside her to give her voice heft, yet heard inside her own head, her voice sounded as afraid as she felt.

He was so big, so intimidating.

'Go fuck yourself, Miss.'

She didn't even think about it. There was no moment of consideration, no cognition. It happened quick as a reflex. She hit him so hard it jarred her shoulder, and yet he didn't flinch. His height, his wall of muscle, was no match for her. He smiled.

She was aware of the silence in the class. Aware of the burn in her face, at the back of her throat, the sting on her palm. The whole class, each pupil whose face she recognised, was turned to her in shock and disbelief.

Betty almost had no breath, but she pushed back her shoulders. 'Did you hear me? Get out of this class,' she said in a voice that was so quiet but full of control.

It was a voice that even today Betty was still proud of – when everything shattered and smashed to the ground it was the shards that caught the light that she held dear. She may have been wrong that day, but she had held her ground.

Marshall just laughed at her. There was a faint pinking of his cheek where she had struck him.

'Well, I know one thing,' he had said, as quietly as she had just spoken to him, '*you're fucked now.*' No one else in the class claimed to hear him, but Betty heard every word.

He left the room, and she had felt satisfied and relieved, if only for the next twenty minutes. She was the mother of sons and she would not be spoken to in that way.

But Marshall had been true to his word.

As soon as he left the room he lodged an official complaint and then there had been parents, and the head teacher and social workers and the trade union.

She apologised, admitting that she was wrong, to the student, his parents, her union, the school and the local authority, but it had not been enough. Losing her temper meant that she lost her job and her pension, just months before she had been due to retire.

The truth had not mattered. Marshall had played an innocent victim, abused by her. For the school, justice being seen to be done had been more important than justice itself. It was this deeper violation that she feared for Nick.

Just then there was a thud from their bedroom and Betty put her fingers over her mouth.

'It's always the woman's fault,' she heard Marina shout.

16

Donna

'Did you have fun at your dad's then?'

It was Sunday night and Angela had just returned home.

Angela nodded once. She was curled in an armchair scrolling through her phone.

'Did you go out for dinner?'

'Pizza.' Angela didn't even look up.

Donna raised her eyes. 'What did you do on Saturday?'

'Dunno.'

Her sullen, pale face was turned from Donna, evading any communication, the light reflected from her phone lending her skin a bluish hue. Angela was receiving messages, one after another, but Donna didn't have the courage to ask who they were from, fearful of another fight. She needed to talk to Angela about what she had found in her sketchpad, but didn't know how to broach it.

Words came into being in her mind, then burst, quick as soap bubbles. It was hard to remember when they had last spoken civilly to each other. Every communication wounded. Donna reacted to what she imagined Angela was saying, while her daughter overreacted to everything. It was as if they were speaking two entirely different languages.

Donna stood in the middle of the room with her arms at her sides, knowing that she needed to try and reach her daughter.

'I was thinking your room needs decorating again.'

Angela met her eye and Donna took a step closer.

'We can go and you could choose some paint this week, if you like? Freshen it up a bit. Could be fun. Change the colour. Help to take your mind off things.'

'I suppose.'

A shrug.

'I just thought if we changed something it would help – a fresh start for you.'

Angela's eyes flashed violet, scrutinising.

'What colour do you think you might like?'

'I don't want one colour. I want to paint stuff, right on the wall. I want to do, like, a mural or something, right on the wall.'

Donna swallowed, and folded her arms. 'Well, what kind of mural? What would you paint?'

'Dunno, I'd do anything I liked, but right onto the wall.'

'But what would you paint?'

'Whatever I wanted.'

'Like what, though? Flowers or a rainbow?'

'I'm not six.' Angela's face crumpled in disgust.

'You could paint some big pictures instead and then we could put them up after we've painted.'

'No,' Angela's brow furrowed. 'I want to do a big mural right on the wall.'

'But what if you make a mess of it?'

'I can just paint over it.'

'I don't think it's such a good idea.' Images flashed in her mind of the portraits she had seen in the sketchpad. She imagined the face of Nicholas Dean on Angela's bedroom wall. 'It might end up looking like graffiti.'

'No, it won't.' A sulk taking hold.

Donna took a long slow breath in, knowing that Angela was challenging her, but aware that if she rose to it, there would be an explosion. 'Well, let's go to the shops tomorrow and you can look at paint anyway,' she decided as a compromise.

Angela's eyes flickered back to her phone.

'Have you thought any more about getting some counselling, love? Like the nurse said?'

'Uh?'

'You remember at the hospital? They want you to go and talk to someone about what happened?'

'Um, yeah,' Angela nodded, her face suddenly seeming younger. Spontaneously, but with a self-conscious effort, Donna leaned down and tousled her daughter's hair, which was greasy. Angela didn't pull away and so Donna felt encouraged.

'It would probably help, you know, talking to someone.'

'I don't want to.' Phone and thumbs held up to her face.

'Your birthday soon. Teenager, eh?'

Angela relinquished a small smile.

'What do you want to do? Go out for dinner, just the two of us?'

'Dad too,' Angela said, chin doubling, suddenly sulky.

'Whatever you want. It's your birthday, after all. Can't believe you'll be thirteen already. Where did the time go?'

Donna sighed then reached out to touch Angela's hair again, smoothing it with her fingers. It clung in clumps, the strands not separating, and it distracted Donna from her comforting task.

'You need to wash your hair.'

'Later.' Almost inaudible.

'It feels like you haven't washed it all weekend. You need to shower a lot more now, you know.' Donna withdrew her hand. 'You're not a little girl any longer. Every morning. Or else you'll smell.'

Angela launched herself up from the armchair, her pale face twisted into anger and hate. '*You* smell, you stupid old cow. You stink.'

Donna stood back, hand on her chest from fright as Angela charged past her and up the stairs.

She started to follow, then turned back into the living room. Her fingers trembling, Donna took a cigarette and lit it, swinging open the patio door. She sucked hard on it, castigating herself for failing again. It would be hard to ask about the photographs now and Donna wasn't sure if she should show them to the police or not. She would ask Stephen's advice.

Her cigarette was smoked halfway already, and Donna had stopped shaking. There was an ominous silence from upstairs. Donna crushed the butt against the side of the house and dropped it into the ashtray. She felt trapped. It reminded her of a video she had watched of an ant on a piece of white paper unable to escape a circle drawn around it in black marker pen – a perceived barrier that could not be crossed.

What had happened to her and Angela? The breach between them was palpable, and yet they had once been close.

She closed the patio door and shivered. There was no other choice. She knew she had to go upstairs and face her.

17

Angela

Angela slammed her bedroom door and rested her head against the wood, making a face as if she was about to cry, but she couldn't. When she had been little, she had cried all the time, so she didn't understand where her tears had gone. In the bedside table she kept a secret supply of chocolate. She opened the cabinet and reached through a shiny mess of empty wrappers until she found a Twix. She sat on the bed, breathing heavily down her nose as she ate with concentration. No other thoughts crossed her mind until the crunch of the biscuit had ended and the last sweet melt of chocolate passed over her tongue. She sat with her hands at her sides, looking down at her feet, buffeted by the swarm of feelings inside her. It was hard to sit still. Just then she noticed that her sketchpad was poking out from underneath the hem of the bed sheet. Angela's heart began to pound and she dropped down onto all fours on the carpet and pulled the pad out. Right away, she could tell something was wrong. The drawings were sticking out at angles like badly shuffled playing cards. With trepidation, Angela opened the first page.

Drawing one should have been her father, then the autographed photograph that Mr Dean had given her – a still from *Scuttlers* – then it should have been the rough pencil sketches she had made of Mr Dean on his first week at Croydon High. They were bad because they had been sketched in class – his nose too pointy, his eyes too large. The next picture should have been her favourite, the painted drawing of him – a life-sized portrait that was a likeness. It had taken her three evenings to finish it. Instead she found the printouts from the internet that she had used to trace his face.

It was completely obvious what had happened. Her mother had been snooping in her room, looked at her private drawings and then put them back in the wrong order. Angela lay down on her belly and peered under her bed. The jewellery box was still there and she reached under and pulled it towards her. She sat up, queasy with worry that the ring, too, would be gone or in a different position.

The diamond ring was still there, still strung on its chain and pressed into the ring cushion just as Angela had left it the night she took the aspirin. Donna hadn't found it. Angela kissed the cold sparkling stone. There would have been trouble if her mother had found that. Girls her age didn't own two-carat diamond rings, although Donna was probably too stupid to know exactly what it was.

But Donna had found the drawings. Angela wanted to go down right now and kick her in the face. The snooping bitch. Instead she knelt and carefully sorted the drawings back into the order she liked them. She ran a hand over the pores of the paper, smoothing the pastel outlines of Nicholas Dean. She stopped when she found her favourite portrait. It was quite good, she decided. It didn't look like she had painted it. It looked professional. She hadn't shown it to anyone, except Jasmine, but they both agreed it looked like him. It was a real likeness. The watercolour had bled through the sketch lines, but other than that it looked like a real artist's portrait. His cute smile that made him seem shy – she had almost captured it – and the light in his brown eyes that she had recreated with a tiny spot of white paint. Angela stood up, holding the picture in her hands, a flush of indignation coming to her cheeks.

She laid the painting on her desk and picked up the calligraphy pen that Dean had given her. *Don't tell anyone I gave it to you*, she remembered. The weight of it in her palm felt special. It had a long gold nib, about four millimetres in diameter. She had bought a bottle of ink to go with it, just like in the olden times, but she had only tried to write with it a few times. Angela took the dip pen and pressed the nib into a piece of thick drawing paper on her desk, scoring an invisible signature and a heart with its hard metal edge.

She carefully slid the sketchbook under her bed, then threw open her bedroom door and ran downstairs. She was only wearing socks and she slid off the bottom step and had to catch herself on the banister to stop herself from falling. Her mother hung up the phone and turned towards her, cigarette pointed at the ceiling.

'You were in my room, *Donna*. You're not allowed to touch my stuff.'

'You'd left dirty laundry all over the hall, as usual. I was just putting it in the basket where it belongs.' Her eyes were too wide, not blinking, attempting innocence.

'Didn't mean you had to riffle through my stuff.' Angela's face flushed, squeezing the pen in her fist. Sweat broke along the crease of her palms.

'I didn't riffle through your stuff. I was putting the dirty laundry where it belongs and I saw the photos sticking out from under the bed.' Donna crushed her cigarette into an ashtray on the table.

'That's a lie. You were snooping on me, 'cause you're a nosy bitch.'

Donna's face was blotchy and afraid and Angela had never hated her so much in her whole life. She wanted to rip out her hair and stamp on her face.

Her mother did a strange thing with her body, as if she was trying to straighten up and put her nose in the air, but her spine was still hunching over, like the coward she was. It made her seem awkward and uncoordinated. 'Angela . . . I was going to come and talk to you about this anyway. I wanted to give you time. I wasn't spying on you,' she folded her arms, 'but I was very concerned by what I saw. You need to be honest with me about what's been going on with that teacher. Has he touched you more than once? Have you been out together?'

Angela's rage was quelled for a moment, like the tide sucking back before its rush towards the shore. She stared at her mother, breath heaving inside her.

'This is the man you said assaulted you, and you have ...' Donna's hand swirled upwards in a strange spasm, as she tried to find the words, 'love notes to him, hidden in your bedroom? Drawings of him, love hearts ...'

'What do you mean, I *said* he assaulted me? Don't you believe me?'

Her mother folded her arms tighter over her body. Her face was ugly and cross. 'I didn't mean that. But you need to be honest with me.'

'I hate you,' Angela said, tears making her mother's face blur. The rage was still in her arms. It was as if all the blood in her body had drained into her fists.

'I need you to talk to me. What's this all about? You need to tell me what happened with you and Mr Dean. You need to tell me *all of it*. I need to understand how you were hurt.'

'I *told* you,' Angela howled.

Her mother was standing very close now. She was looking right into Angela's eyes and when Angela glanced at her it was as if her mother's face had expanded. Suddenly her face was huge and her murky green eyes enormous. Angela heard the thump of her own heart in her ears.

She squeezed her fist and felt the pen in her grasp. In a single motion, without moving her body, she drew up her arm and stabbed the calligraphy pen into her mother's cheekbone, just below the eye.

Donna screamed and stepped back, a hand covering her cheek. Blood flowed through her fingers and she took her hand away and looked astounded at the red on her palm. The wound was already starting to swell.

Angela felt a brief flood of relief, exhilaration, at the sight. It had felt the same when she pulled out Jasmine's hair, but then a sickness washed over her. She was so bad. She was the worst girl in the world. She deserved to die. She wanted to die. Her arms were now heavy at her sides. The pen, nib inked in her mother's blood, fell to the floor.

'Oh, oh, oh,' her mother was saying, over and over, fingertips touching the wound which was swelling so fast that it made her left eye see wrong, pulled out of shape. 'Oh no, oh, no, oh.'

Angela rubbed her fist with her left hand, as if she had hurt it stabbing her mother. It did hurt, but not in her hand. It hurt somewhere else. She couldn't find the hurt with her fingers.

'Sorry,' she said.

She turned and left the room as her mother propped herself on the table, then turned away and leaned against the wall.

Angela closed her bedroom door and stood with her back against it, shoulder blades against the wood. She looked down at her white soft knuckles. She flexed her hand and watched the dimples form.

One, two, three, four, five ... she counted.

Angela made a fist and punched herself in the cheek.

It hurt, but not too much. It was easier to hurt other people than it was to hurt herself. She rubbed her cheekbone, then tightened her fist and raised her chin, clenching her teeth and pressing her tongue against the roof of her mouth.

Once.

Twice. She hit herself again and it brought tears to her eyes.

Three times.

She went to the mirror and looked at the swell. She pressed a palm against her cheek. She hadn't broken the skin but the bone was tender and she thought it might bruise.

On her knees, she retrieved her drawings of Dean and laid her favourite picture on her desk, smoothed a hand over his face. He had a beautiful face. She still remembered that first day when he came to Croydon Academy. She had been embarrassed because of his strange drama games, feeling stupid in front of the class, but he had squeezed her shoulder and said, *well done, Angela, that was a really good job.* He remembered names quickly. He knew *everyone's* name after five minutes, yet still she had felt special.

Nick.

They were allowed to call him that.

Nicholas.

It was a nice name. Angela thought that she might call her baby that, if she had one and it was a boy.

Angela opened a drawer in her desk and took out a strip of matches. She had pinched them from her mum a few months ago, when she had been trying to start smoking. It was hard to take up a habit that one of your parents excelled in – Angela had only been reminded of her mum's stinking breath and the sweet, dirty smell of her clothes. The first puff had made her sick.

She had only tried smoking to see if it would make her lose weight. That was why models smoked, but Angela had given up after striking only one match.

Now she opened the flap of the book of matches. She ran her thumb along the smart, red heads. Nine matches left. Nine like a cat's lives.

Angela opened the window and then climbed up on her desk so that she could peer through. Outside smelled oily and cold: cars and dirt and houses. It had just started to get dark and the sky was navy blue. The air was already smoky from chimneys that sent grey streaks into the night. The red-tiled roof was below Angela's window and she leaned out onto it, to test the breeze. The tiles were slippery against the palms of her hands.

She opened her sketchpad and lifted up her favourite painting of Nicholas Dean. She struck a match and lit the corner of the page, holding the painting up so that it burned and smoked out of the window. The flames were quick and hungry, a dark line drawing closer to the centre of the paper and vanishing Dean's hair and ear. As the picture burned, Angela leaned out of the window further and kissed his lips. She liked the flames. She turned the paper in her hands and watched the flames turn and consume another part of the paper. She liked the heat and the danger, liked controlling it but knew that it was ultimately uncontrollable. Fire was the ultimate creation. It brought warmth and love and life, yet it also brought destruction. It was fed by the air, just like people. It brought light, and heat and community; it burned and ravaged and destroyed.

More than any of that, it was the fire's beauty that captivated Angela: that seductive flame, the bold glow, the taunting, tantalising tongues. Nicholas Dean's face was consumed by it and disappeared. Suddenly the flames raced along the paper, towards Angela's finger and thumb holding the painting to the air. She had been in a trance and the heat near her skin made her yelp. She drew back and let go of the paper and a twisting, turning flame floated into the bedroom and landed on the duvet.

Angela turned from the window as the bed caught fire, a tiny crown of flames and then a strange slow fire that smelled strange. She didn't know what to do, and she was just about to call out to her mother when her bedroom door slammed open, and Donna stood there, her right eye swollen and almost completely closed over, blood on her cheek and her neck.

Standing on the desk, looking down at her mother, who now began to shout and then run down the stairs, Angela felt nothing but detached. It was as if she was surrounded by a hard, transparent shell and she was suspended inside, floating like a yolk, looking out, dumb and deaf.

Angela climbed down from the desk. She stood with her hands at her sides and her stomach sticking out, watching the flames eat her bed. The smell was horrible, like microwaved plastic.

Her mother appeared at the bedroom door brandishing an extinguisher. She squinted with her one good eye at the label, pointed the nozzle and pressed on the lever. White foam burst onto Angela's bed. The flames died.

There was an eerie silence. Even though the window was open, the air was blue with smoke and Angela couldn't see her mother clearly. Donna dropped the extinguisher and it thudded onto the bedroom floor. The air was thick and hurt the back of her throat.

'That's it, Angela, we're done.'

Angela frowned in the smoke, not sure what her mother meant. She put the tip of her thumb into her mouth.

'I can't do this anymore.' Her mother's voice wasn't angry, but tired. 'I've had enough. You win. I'll call your dad tonight. You can go live with him.'

Looking at her mother through the transparent shell Angela felt tears at the back of her throat. The tears tasted of smoke.

'I don't care,' she said.

Part Two

'The rape of a young person is tragic . . .
the person goes from knowing nothing
to believing nothing.'

Maya Angelou

18

Nick

It was after lunch and Nick was in the study hunched over Marina's work laptop. His parents were downstairs because they were going to pick up the children from the childminder and bring them home. He sat in his running clothes with Rusty at his feet.

He opened his inbox and frowned. It was mainly junk mail – no new job requests since he had been fired from Croydon Academy. There was nothing from his agent, Harriet, although he had not expected it. *Let's take a fresh look at things once your crisis is over,* she had said, and Nick had wondered if that meant that she was letting him go. She was right, of course. Getting parts was hard enough without police bail that restricted his contact with children and press coverage that implied he was a paedophile.

His crisis. A good way of putting it. When would it ever be over?

Email done, he opened Facebook and Twitter and Google. Marina's work laptop was so slow that each window took minutes to open. He looked out at the paper bark maple tree; its fine autumn colour now gone, leaves curling in on themselves before falling. He was trying to stay strong but he felt as if he was corroding on the inside. He ran his fingers through his hair as he waited for the websites to open, then, unable to restrain himself, he typed his name into Google.

Sweat breaking at his temples as if he had already started his run, he found a Facebook page called 'Croydon Parents Against Paedophiles' set up just one week ago. One of the recent posts carried a link to the *Evening Standard* story about him. The post, by 'Admin' read, 'Check out what happened at Croydon Academy. Parents Against Paedophiles need to act. Stop child abusers hurting our kids.'

Nick read compulsively, thumbnail between his teeth. There were links on the page to his business website, ACTUp, his Wikipedia page, and also his agent's website as well as more innocuous links to Childline and the local police station. Below a photograph of him, beaming at the premiere of *Scuttlers*, a number of comments had been posted, and Nick expanded the tab to read.

I hear the police have let him out. That poor girl will be scarred for life and he's free out there – wandering around ready to molest another of our kids.

Paedophiles are worse than terrorists.

It makes me sick that people like Dean actually seek out jobs with children.

Trembling, Nick closed the laptop and sat back in his chair. It had been nearly two months and his bail was soon up. He was close to the end of this. The police still didn't have enough evidence to charge him and they were running out of time.

He got up and went downstairs, Rusty scampering at his heels, then sat on the chair in the hall to put on his trainers.

'Are you going out?' his father said, standing before him with his arms folded.

'I'm just going for a quick run round the park. I'll be back before the kids get home.'

'Your mum's just going for them now.'

'I said I'd be back.' Nick looked up at his father, whose face was forbidding, unspoken words crowding into his eyes. 'I just need to loosen up.'

His father straightened, inhaled and said, 'How are you doing for money?'

'What do you mean?' Nick said, tying his laces and raising an eyebrow as he looked up at his father.

'I know lawyers aren't cheap.' His face had aged and the skin now hung around his predominant emotions, so that his neutral expression was one of anger and disappointment.

'We're okay, thanks though.' Nick pulled down the cuffs of his running shirt and flexed his toes, suddenly desperate to be outside.

'It must be a burden on Marina, though. I just wanted to offer – give you a few grand towards the lawyer.'

Nick shrugged, feeling suddenly shorn. 'Lawyer's not asked for any money yet . . . ' Nick whispered, not wanting his mother to hear, although he was sure they had discussed the offer of money. 'Thanks anyway,' he managed, despite his humiliation.

'Well . . . you just let me know if you need anything.'

Craving the cold air against his face and the rhythm of his feet on the pavement, as if he could somehow outrun all of this, Nick turned for the door.

Just then, as he was sliding ear buds into his ears, his phone rang. Instead of talking through the microphone on his headphones, he unplugged the jack and the speakerphone projected, 'Mr Dean, this is Detective Sergeant Brookes . . . '

Nick quickly took the phone off speaker and turned slightly away from his father, although he knew he had heard. Thomas Dean frowned.

'Hello,' said Nick, trying to keep the hope from his voice. *This could be it* – the moment when the nightmare stopped.

Brookes cleared her throat. 'I was just calling to advise you that your bail is being extended a further three months to give us more time to gather evidence . . . '

Nick squeezed his left fist, cleaving inside.

'But, what do you mean? How can it take this long? I'm innocent.' He was whispering but the emotion in his voice brought his mother to the door of the living room. 'How can you just,' he punched his thigh with his fist, 'just . . . extend it, back to square one, start all over again?'

'We need more time to complete our investigation.'

Nick hung up, closed his eyes for a couple of seconds to

compose himself, then held up a palm to delay the questions from his parents as he called Faldane. Fingers rubbing his mouth and the stubble on his chin, Nick listening to the ring, expecting that Faldane's phone would go to answerphone, but just then, he picked up.

Nick talked and Bob interrupted. 'Don't worry. It's to be expected. I told you this would take months, perhaps longer.'

'Don't worry? I can't even pick up my own kids from nursery. I can't work. Just because someone made an unfounded allegation—' Nick stopped, hearing his voice cracking.

'Listen, what we can do is request a change of bail conditions.'

'What do you mean?'

'We can request a change in the bail conditions so that you can be unsupervised with your own children.'

'Will they allow that?'

'We can try. I had meant to call you. I suspected they would extend bail, because they have new evidence passed by Angela's mother. Probably that has meant them needing more time.'

'Angela's mother?'

His parents' anxious eyes pursued him like bees.

'Listen, I don't have all the details. Why don't we talk once I've spoken to my contact at the station?'

Nick hung up. His mother and father loomed.

'Well?'

'I'm sorry,' he said, opening the door. 'I just need to go for a run. I'll be back soon as I can.'

He ran down the drive and onto Firgrove Hill, their unasked questions chasing him. He ran too hard, too quickly, and by the time he reached the park, he was near hyperventilating. He pitched forward, hands on his knees, until his breathing steadied. The path stank of fox, a sulking musky whiff in the long grasses below the trees.

He stood up, hands on his hips, half-smiling. He was the fox now: hunted, but by two different kinds of hound – the police and the unseen parents and community who had already tried and judged him.

Nick took a deep breath and resumed his run, jogging at an easy pace, enjoying the feel in his thighs and his stomach as his muscles propelled him forward. All the stagnation that had been around him this last couple of months released and he started to feel more positive. He had done nothing wrong; he had to be proved innocent in time.

His feet splashed in the mud, spattering his calves. It was all absurd. The fact that *Angela Furness* had accused him was almost laughable. He would never admit it to anyone, but there *were* young girls he had worked with – not as young as Angela but not much older – whom Nick had felt attracted to. Thirteen-year-olds often looked a lot older than they were and sometimes they were confident, mature, flirtatious. But *Angela?* Even if he had been a paedophile, Nick couldn't have imagined he would have gone for her – shiny alabaster skin and body like a Rubens cherub. Her angry petted mouth.

Yet Angela's truth was held higher than his. She could

accuse him and be protected, be given anonymity, while his life was destroyed. There was no physical evidence, yet she was believed. It was as if everything had become distorted. There was no such thing as the truth anymore.

Sweat streaking down his spine, Nick looked at his watch. He had been out too long – nearly an hour. The children would be back. He cursed lightly under his breath. He had almost outrun his anger but now he was late.

He sprinted back home. As his feet crunched on the ash drive, he saw Ava standing up in the bay window, held up by his father, slapping her palm against the window at him.

Nick smiled and went to the front window then pursed his lips and put them against the glass. Ava bent down and put her lips opposite his, leaving a wet, open-mouthed smudge on the windowpane.

Nick opened the front door, wiping his forehead with the crook of his elbow.

'Daddy, Daddy,' he heard from the living room. Rusty breathed in Nick's face and whacked his forehead with his tail as he bent to undo his laces. He smiled despite his troubles, shaking the sweat from his hair as he kicked off his shoes. Endorphins pumped through him and he felt better than he had in weeks. He might be a suspected paedophile, but at least his family and his dog loved him.

Feet liberated from his dirty trainers, Nick bent and rubbed Rusty's bristly face. Just then, an explosive sound came from the living room. Still squatting over Rusty, Nick looked up, confused. The dog bolted from his grasp into the living room and began barking. Over the sound of Rusty, there was a long cry that Nick recognised immediately as Luca's.

In the front room there was a hole in the centre of the bay window, and Luca was in a foetal position on the floor amid a mosaic of glass. Betty hunched over him, pulling him to his feet before Nick got to him. He was clutching his head, which was bleeding slightly behind his ear. Nick dropped down onto his knees and pushed back Luca's hair to check the wound. Broken glass on the carpet cut into Nick's knee but he barely noticed.

Tom squatted amid the broken glass and picked up a dirty brick wrapped in plastic secured by elastic bands.

Luca had been hit on the left of his head and it was bleeding slightly and swelling. Nick picked him up and swayed him gently from side to side. 'Little man, I need you to stop crying so you can tell me how your head is.'

Luca didn't cry easily. Marina had shut the tip of his finger in a car door once, but freed him quickly. He had been just five yet had held the broken tip of his finger in his other hand and said, calmly, 'It's quite sore, *Mama*.'

Now Luca sobbed in Nick's arms. Betty rubbed her grandson's back and picked up Ava, who was also crying out of fright.

'What the hell happened?'

Luca gulped for breath and Nick sat him on his knee on the couch.

'This came through the window,' said Tom, holding up the brick. 'Must have thrown it bloody hard to get through the double glazing. I never saw anyone. We were round at the side waving at you and then we all turned when we heard you come in.'

Nick turned Luca's head to the side and felt again the bump that was visible underneath his hair, like a growth behind his ear. 'We need to take him to A&E – get him checked out.' Nick rushed his hands over the rest of Luca's body, making sure there were no other injuries. Luca sniffed and pressed his small hand to his head.

Ava was still crying and Nick stood and took her from his mother. With both children in his arms, he walked to the broken bay window. Traffic sounds and the cold drizzle of the day reached in through the jagged hole.

'Who did this?' said Betty. 'The vandals!'

Tom unwrapped the brick from its cellophane, which was an A4 polythene pocket containing an envelope. He put on his reading glasses and held the envelope at arm's length.

'What is it, Dad?'

'It's addressed to Marina.'

'Wait,' said Nick, putting the children down on the couch.

It was too late. Tom opened the envelope and took out a sheet of white paper. Tom's brows lowered as he looked at the page in front of him.

'What is it?'

'It's a picture of you and Marina,' his father said, almost whispering.

'What the hell . . .' Nick took the edge of the paper his father was holding.

It was a black and white photocopy of a picture of him and Marina from a premiere a few years ago. Nick recognised it instantly, but his own face had been carefully cut out, so that Marina was looking up at a hole in the page. Printed underneath were the words: 'YOU MARRIED A PAEDO. YOUR HUSBAND LIKES LITTLE GIRLS.'

Nick took the paper from his father and stared at it, trembling. He ran a hand over his face and felt the rough salt on his skin, dried into his pores after his run.

'Why would they do this?' he whispered, his throat suddenly dry. Facebook was one thing, but now the abuse was literally coming into his home.

19

Marina

Marina opened the door to Sergeant Brookes and Constable Watson.

Brookes stepped inside and unbuttoned her trench coat. 'Mm, that smells nice.'

'We're just making dinner,' said Marina, hearing her voice as apologetic. She assumed that Brookes was just trying to be friendly, but the comment sounded out of place, as if the officers wanted to join them. It was Saturday and she was exhausted after a long week, and the police were the last people she wanted to see.

Nick was cooking in the kitchen and now came out, dishtowel over one shoulder, his face ashen with worry and tiredness.

Marina felt exposed, standing in the hall with her husband before the police officers. She felt their relationship scrutinised. For years she and Nick had felt as one, in tandem, but now they were off kilter. He was too eager to please her and she was consciously swallowing her qualms. It was too much strain – every day another trauma. She had come home on Friday to find her son in hospital getting X-rays for a potentially fractured skull.

'It was just a courtesy call, really; we've just interviewed your parents about the window incident and we wanted to check you were all okay – see if there was anything you wanted to add.'

Nick nodded and motioned for everyone to come into the kitchen. The table was set at one end, as it had been the night when Brookes and Weston had first taken Nick to the police station. Ava was playing on the floor with Rusty, stroking him with gentle clumsy thumps, talking to herself. Luca, head bandaged, was leaning on a beanbag in the corner, playing Lego. His face was still pale and Marina tousled his hair as she passed.

'We heard the hospital gave the little one the all-clear?' said Brookes, taking a seat at the table and removing her notebook.

Luca looked up from his tablet, sensing that he was being talked about.

'He was very lucky,' said Marina. 'They thought he might have a haematoma. He was just in the wrong place at the wrong time, but I think most of the velocity was taken up by the window.'

'There was no concussion or internal bleed so that was the main thing. It gave us all quite a scare,' said Nick.

'I can imagine,' said Brookes, finger in her notebook.

She and Weston both declined the tea that Nick offered. 'Unfortunately there was no forensic evidence on the brick or the paper. We did speak to Angela's parents about the incident, but to be honest, they are not suspects. News of your arrest was publicly available and sometimes with this kind of offence—'

'I didn't do anything. I'm innocent! And how did they find us?' Nick spurted. 'I feel like a marked man.'

Marina sat down beside him and put a hand around his waist. He had lost weight and she felt the bone of his lower ribcage jutting into her wrist. He seemed to relax as soon as she put her hands on him, lowering his voice. The children were playing in the alcove by the stairs. 'We wondered if there's too much information about Nick online. He's been in the Farnham local paper a few times, and I did a search online and his company is registered at Company House with our home address. Should we change that? Is that how they found us?'

Brookes' cold blue eyes sparkled with something akin to reassurance. 'It would be a good idea to do that, as a precaution, and you can remove your address and phone number from public phone books that are now available online. And let us know if you see anything at all that is remotely suspicious.'

Nick straightened his shoulders, frowning.

'But who would do this?' said Marina.

'I can tell you that the criminal damage and common

assault on your son is being treated as a separate case to the sexual assault charges.'

'But surely they are linked?' said Marina. 'This was a message – a message for me – and specifically mentions the allegation.'

'We are dealing with both investigations and will you let you know anything that becomes apparent.'

Nick exhaled, elbows on the table, letting his head fall into his hands.

'Thank you,' said Weston, standing up.

Brookes closed her notebook.

'But what I don't understand,' Marina's cheeks pinked in anger as she spoke, 'is why someone would do this. Should we expect another attack? They *really did* smash our front window, and they *really did* hurt my son, something that could have been much, much more serious . . . Should we be afraid?'

'This was probably meant to shock, and does not necessarily mean that further violence will follow. But if you see anything suspicious, please let us know and we will follow it up.'

Nick closed the front door and rested his head against the frame. Marina pressed her face into his back and crossed her arms across his chest. He turned to her, kissing her brow bone and then her lips.

Marina still felt so much love for him, but sex and touching had changed. Sometimes, when she woke at night, his presence was so heavy in the room: the heat of him, the handsome repose of his face. She would find herself wide-awake trying to fit this man she loved with the fears that came unbidden in the dark. She would swing her legs out of bed and retreat to Ava's bed, or to Luca's – just to find peace, and sleep. She and Nick still performed their old rites of affection, hands squeezed, backs rubbed, but they were effortful, as if the meaning behind them had changed. Now, even in touch, they spoke different tongues. It felt like the *matanza* – that day when she was a child and the pig was led out to slaughter – her aunt's arms red with blood, her father dancing with joy while the pig was tied down and slaughtered. She had grown up a little that day. She had seen things as they were, rather than as she had expected. Now she felt the same way about Nick. Seven years married and now she wondered if she was only just starting to get to know him.

'Daddy, I'm hungry,' Ava called.

'Just ten more minutes, sweetie,' Nick called through Marina's hair, reluctant to release her. He clasped his hands around her hips.

'What are you thinking?' she asked, leaning back to look up into his face.

'I dunno. I feel like someone's out to get me, and now I'm scared my family's going to be hurt as well. I don't care about me, but ...' he leaned forward and inhaled the smell of her scalp, 'it would kill me if anything happened to you, or the kids, Mum and Dad.'

Marina looked up into his face, his brown eyes flashing with worry. '*I* care about you.'

191

'I didn't tell you but if you look at Facebook there's a whole local campaign going on – Croydon Against Paedophiles – or some bullshit, and it seems like I'm the only one being talked about so far.'

Marina took her hands off his waist and went to her laptop, which was sitting on the kitchen table. Ava crawled over, put a hand up her trouser leg and began to tickle her calf. It was a game they played but Marina did not react. Nick leaned over her shoulder to help her find the page.

'Did you tell the police?'

'I told them, but apparently as there are no specific threats against me it doesn't constitute a criminal offence.'

'But who is it? Who made this page?'

'They said they'd look into it.'

'Maybe the same person who threw the brick through the window.' Marina felt heat rising in her face.

'I'm *hungry*,' Ava cried again, tiring of trying to distract her mother and lying prostrate on the floor.

'Ten minutes, *bonita*, ah?' Nick called, resuming his position by the stove. 'Chicken'll be ready before you know it.'

Marina frowned deeply and logged out of Facebook. She noticed that she had two email messages and opened them.

Corvus Corone is now following you.

Corvus Corone mentioned you in a Tweet.

Marina opened Twitter to find she had three notifications. She used Twitter seldom, just when she was bored on the train, or when she had an exciting project at work. She opened up her page, which was headlined:

Marina Alvarez, Mother of two, Maker of awesome paella,
Director Child International. All tweets my own.

The icon for Corvus was a black crow, its beak wide open.
That made sense – Corvus Corone was Latin, meaning carrion
crow. Her throat closed.

There was no identifying information on 'crow's' account,
but there was a pin indicating that the owner was located in
Iceland, and had joined Twitter only one week ago. Crow was
only following Marina, and had no other followers. There
was only one tweet, and she sank into her seat as she read it,
a chill on her skin.

@marina_alvarez ur husband is a paedo, yet u work @
childinternationallondon @theresa_long How can u
protect any child? #EndChildAbuse.

'Nick,' she said, quietly, still staring at the screen.

At first he didn't hear her over the sound of the extractor.
She reached over and grabbed the back of his T-shirt. He
turned to her and she waved him over.

'Gimme a minute?' he said, shaking a tray of frozen chips
before closing the oven and appearing at her shoulder. 'What
is it?'

'*Mierda.*' Elbows on the table, both of them staring at the
screen, she pressed her knuckles against her lips. 'Who the hell
is this and look . . . ' she pointed at Theresa's name on the tweet.

'They've copied in my boss.'

20

Stephen

Stephen put the last of Angela's bags into the boot of the car and closed it. She shuffled out of the house with the hood of her grey sweatshirt up over her head and her chin down. Donna stood at the door with one hand tucked under her elbow and another pointing a lit cigarette at the sky.

Angela didn't say goodbye to her mother. She got into her father's car and closed the door.

'That's us then,' he said, walking up to Donna, tapping his car key against the palm of his hand, a weal of words in his mouth, but he held his tongue.

Donna's cheeks hollowed as she sucked on the cigarette. The exhaled smoke blew in his direction, but he conceded that it was the wind and not a deliberate attempt to slight him. The ugly cut and blue swelling underneath her eye made her face seem bitter and harsh.

'You win, eh?' she said, avoiding his eye, yet smiling.

'I didn't want it like this.'

'Yeah, well, you have her now, don't you?'

Stephen rocked on his heels, tapping his car key against his palm. 'I'll try and get some information from CID about when we should hear. New evidence will hopefully mean a charge.'

Donna nodded and put the cigarette to her mouth.

'I appreciate you asking my advice about that,' he said, meaning it. 'It was the right thing to do.'

After arrangements had been made for Angela, Donna had told him about the photographs she had found of Angela with the teacher, presumably out alone together. Stephen had told her to go straight to the police, who had taken the photographs and also Angela's mobile phone into evidence.

'We'll see,' she shrugged, turning from him so that the dark swelling under her eye was exaggerated, the side of her face pulled out of shape.

'There's a chance the school will report those bruises on Angel's face, you know. She's not exactly flying under the radar there – her every step is monitored. They will ask questions. You should prepare yourself for that.'

'I told you, she did it to herself.' Her mouth drew together, like a pinched seam.

'I'm not saying you weren't provoked. I believe she did that to you.' He could feel the anger rumbling inside him, but he kept his voice low, checking his breathing.

Donna half-laughed, and took another drag, then shook her head. 'Oh, thank you *so much*.'

'There's no need for that.'

'For what?' Her blue eyes suddenly focussed on him, the fury in them exposing the whites round the irises. 'You need to know that there's something seriously wrong with her head.'

'For God's sake.' Stephen took a step closer, the whiff of her perfume sullied with smoke clawed in his memory. 'Her teacher attacked her!'

'Before that – she was angry *before that* – and you know it.'

'I think *you're* angry, and perhaps that's understandable.'

'She's out of control. I could have lost an eye.'

'You're her mother. You're supposed to teach her, protect her—'

She stubbed out her cigarette on the brick wall of the house and turned to go back inside. 'Well, if you're parent of the year see if you can get her to go to that counsellor that the sexual assault team recommended. God knows she needs her head read.'

Stephen inhaled, a rebuff on his lips, but Donna went inside and closed the door behind her.

There was no point in pursuing it. He whistled as he made his way to the car, trying to change his mood for Angela.

In the car, Stephen didn't say a word until they had pulled out onto Shirley Road.

'So,' he said, turning to smile at her, 'I thought we could go get you a new mobile?'

'Yes, please,' said Angela, a strange hurt smile on her face.

'And it's your birthday soon. Thirteen is a big birthday. Thirteen is special. If you see something ...'

As they approached the shopping centre, Stephen turned the steering wheel, letting it slide easily between his fingers. 'Once we've got your phone, we can maybe go to a café and get some ice-cream while we set it up?'

Angela nodded and her hood fell down onto her shoulders. The bruise on her cheek looked bad – so bad, he almost regretted his words and wondered if they should go home for ice-cream – or if he should ask her to wait in the car while he went to get the phone. Out with her on his own, it would seem to strangers that *he* had hurt her. It was pointless even considering asking her to stay in the car; she would want to choose her phone, and she would want to eat her ice-cream right away, before it melted.

Hands at ten and two on the wheel, Stephen took a deep breath and exhaled down his nose. He had prepared what he was about to say.

'Angel, I heard from your mum about what happened the other night. I know you probably don't want to talk about it, but if you do, I'm here and ready to listen.'

She turned and nodded once, pulling her hood back up over her head.

Her hands were pressed between her knees and he laid his hand on top of them, then turned off the engine. 'You know I'm always on your side?'

She nodded quickly. He tapped her knee and got out of the car.

Stephen walked backwards away from his car and pressed the lock button. The lights flashed in recognition. Angela was at his side, hands in the pockets of her hoodie, hunched over and scuffing her feet. He had got in trouble once before for suggesting that she be more ladylike, and now kept his mouth shut. At least her hoodie meant that her bruised face was less visible.

Angela chose a large-screened Android phone that she said was better than the one she had before. Stephen paid in cash. Then she chose chocolate ice-cream with M&Ms and granola sprinkles.

Back at the flat, he had put flowers in her room: sunflowers and irises. The irises had blue throats matching the colour of her eyes. He had put a chocolate on her pillow next to a new stuffed animal – a koala.

'Well, what do you think?' he said, turning on the light and pointing to his efforts.

'I'm too old for stuffed animals,' she said, putting her bag down on the bed.

Stephen smiled. 'Fair enough. Now you're going to be here all the time, we can change it. We can make it more grown-up – proper teenager's room.'

'It's fine,' she said. Her face was blotchy and red, as if she was about to cry, but Stephen decided it was just the swelling on her face.

'Do you want me to get some ice to put on your face?'

'No.'

'It's probably too late, anyway. The worst is out already.'

Angela sat down on the bed. 'Yeah, the worst is out,' she said faintly, looking at the floor.

'I'll run you a bath then . . .'

Stephen didn't fully close her bedroom door behind him. He listened to hear if she was crying.

He turned on the taps, and then ducked into the hall cupboard. He bit his lip as he clicked the mouse, opening files he had saved on Nicholas Dean: his police interview but also internet files on his acting career and articles on him for magazines and newspapers, pictures of his wife and children.

When the bath was ready, he knocked on Angela's door. She was wearing a polka-dot towelling dressing gown that her mother had bought her a couple of years ago. It was tight on her hips and chest. Her hair was greasy, strands clumped together.

'I put bubbles in it for you, and I have some posh shampoo and things.'

She nodded and walked ahead of him down the hall, towards the steam and the warm, synthetic strawberry smell of the bubble bath. At the door, he stopped and took her by the shoulders, turning her around to face him. She was looking down at her white chubby feet. Stephen smiled. Her eyelashes were so long. Even with her bruised face and her greasy hair, she was so beautiful to him.

'Listen to me. Are you okay about this? Staying with me all the time? I know it's not easy with your mum and I apart.'

'It's okay.'

'We'll make your room here even better than your one at home.'

'Okay.'

'I think it'll be better for you and your mum, too. Gives you both some space, and then you can spend quality time together. You can go shopping and things . . .'

'Mum only goes shopping to Tesco.'

Stephen smiled, trying not to laugh. It was true. 'Well, I'm sure that'll change. You can do fun things together, mother and daughter . . .'

'She hates me.'

'She doesn't hate you.'

Angela looked up into his eyes. 'She does. She said she did. She said I was a monster.'

'You mother drinks too much. I'm sure she says a lot of things she doesn't mean. It's another reason why I'm happy you're here with me . . . Safe.'

'She wasn't drinking when she said that.'

'Well,' Stephen took a deep breath, not sure how to counsel Angela. He tried his best not to criticise Donna but he found it hard to conceal his contempt for her. 'It's clear you both need some time apart. I needed to be away from her, too. You're here now, and I'm going to look after you properly. I love you, more than anything else in the world.'

Angela lowered her eyes, long black lashes brushing her pale cheeks. Stephen wrapped his arms around her and squeezed her tight.

'All right, Angel, you jump in and I'll get started on dinner.'

'Love you too,' Angela whispered, into his chest.

*

Downstairs, Stephen triple-locked the main door then began to prepare dinner. He had bought two different ready meals: a curry for him and a bolognaise for Angela. In the fridge was a chocolate fudge cake that he had bought specially for her. He would heat it after dinner, so that the sauce was warm.

He pierced the film of the packaging and then stood watching the meal turn in the microwave as he thought about Nicholas Dean laying hands on his little girl.

The smell of hot plastic and garlic reminded him of human sweat. The smell of a man changed when he was frightened, Stephen had observed early in his training, when he had been involved in interrogations.

He wanted to hurt that actor, Nicholas Dean, for what he had done to Angela. It would be deserved. Donna even expected it. She had said as much: *What are you going to do?*

It was more than his job was worth, and what if Angela was lying? There would be no saving him this time if he was caught taking the law into his own hands. He would have to trust justice.

The microwave pinged and Stephen set Angela's dinner aside before beginning his own. He bought these meals often, yet still he checked the label to remind him of the different stages of cooking.

Donna was so stupid; so deeply fearful. She had asked his advice about the drawings and the photographs of Angela with Dean. Stephen had told her to take it straight to the police. Sometimes he wondered what he had ever seen in Donna – how he could ever have married her. After just one meeting, his mother had told him that Donna was not worthy of him.

An image, unbidden, appeared in his mind. He was accustomed to it, and he watched it impassively as the screen of the microwave hummed before him: Donna with a strong hand around her throat being raped in a freezer.

She had told him the story early in their relationship and he had never been able to think about her for long without that image being placed, like a piece of coloured Perspex, over the way he saw her. It explained Donna, the way she was now: like the pit of a peach, all scars and deep grooves.

'How you getting on, Angel?' Stephen called out.

'I'm out.'

He put cutlery on the waiting plates, then carefully peeled back the burning hot plastic film.

'Three minutes, on the table,' he called to Angela.

Stephen set up two trays with the plates, cutlery and napkins, so that they could eat in the living room with the television.

A few minutes to spare, he slipped back into the cupboard under the stairs to watch the CCTV footage from the day. He watched it at the fastest speed, yet it seemed that he never had enough hours to catch up with what he had missed. Most of the footage was blank, just his doorstep and the railing, but occasionally a neighbour would pass, the post woman, an elderly lady, the European guy renting the flat below that Stephen had always been suspicious about.

Better safe than sorry, his mother had always said.

*

When he had caught up on the CCTV, and Angela was still not downstairs, Stephen opened his laptop and clicked on the file named 'Dean'. He had taken copies of the artwork and photographs that Donna had just passed to the police. He selected the photo booth shot of Angela and Dean together, and opened it out to full-screen.

The man looked like a choirboy, younger than his years but lecherous at the same time. Stephen had already found out where he lived, but so long as justice prevailed, he would do nothing apart from watch. He swallowed, and closed the file down and then the computer.

He would keep his mouth shut and watch, but if the police delayed or failed to charge Dean, then Stephen would act.

21

Nick

It was late afternoon. Nick was alone in the house with his own children. It didn't feel as much of a relief as he had anticipated.

Faldane had managed to get the bail conditions changed but everything else was still in limbo. Nick watched the television feeling bleak, bitter.

Ava and Luca had not long returned from day care and Ava was napping on the couch in the kitchen alcove, while Luca was sitting on one of his sister's brightly coloured miniature chairs, turning the pages of a book about dinosaurs. He still had a large lump, which made his little head seem strangely cuboid.

'Dad?' said Luca, peering over the top of his book.

'Mm?'

'Are you going to get put in jail?'

Nick sat up two inches and his half-closed eyes flashed open. 'No. What makes you say that?'

Luca put the book down on his lap. 'I heard Granny and Grandpa talking and then last week the police came here.'

'That was because a bad person threw a brick through our window and hurt your head.'

Luca nodded twice and raised his book a little, the workings of his mind reflected in his large brown eyes.

'Yes, but Grandma told Grandpa she was worried *you* were going to jail.'

'Did she?' Nick felt heat spreading from his neck upwards.

'Yes, and she told Grandpa to offer you money because good lawyers cost a lot.'

Nick sighed and put his hands on his head. 'C'mere.'

Luca closed his book, put it down at his side and went to his father. Nick pulled him onto his knee, ran a hand through his hair and kissed his cheek.

'You're a good boy, you know that?'

Luca nodded, his face gravely serious.

'I'm going to tell you something, but I don't want you to say anything to Ava – this is just for big boys, okay?'

Eyes even larger, Luca nodded again.

'Do you know what it feels like when someone says you did something wrong, but you know you didn't do it and that they're telling lies about you?'

'Yes.'

'Well, that's what happened to Daddy, but don't worry, the

police are very good and they're investigating and I'm sure that the truth will come out.'

Luca's face was suddenly pale with worry. His lower lip, wet with spit, quivered.

'Has anyone ever told lies about you?'

'Yes, when I was in primary one, Bernard said I had put milk in the sandpit but it was really him.'

'And what did the teacher do?'

'I told her I had already drank my milk and put it in the bin and she believed me.'

'Right. So that's like the police. They're looking in the bin for my milk carton and when they find it, they'll know I didn't put it in the sand.'

'But . . .'

'But what?' Nick smiled and kissed Luca's warm hair, breathing in the smell of him. His son had a different smell from his daughter – saltier.

'You must have done something else. They must think you did something really bad. Only then can you go to jail.'

Nick breathed down his nose. He had forgotten whom he was dealing with – Luca was as incisive and persistent as Marina.

'Someone said I . . . hurt them, but I never touched them.'

'Did they say that because they don't like you?'

'I don't know. I didn't think about the person. I never knew they thought about me.'

'Daddy?' said Luca, half-smiling and frowning, a confusing expression only his son and wife shared.

'What?' Nick put a hand on his son's warm hair.

'Your face is all red.'

'Is it?' Nick swept Luca off his knee. 'It's just hot in here.' He stood up and switched the television off.

'Go wake your sister. We'll take Rusty out before Mum comes home.'

Luca tucked his hardback book under his arm and left the room, back straight, head so much bigger than his small thin body.

Nick sank back into the couch and pressed the heels of his hands into his eyes.

Marina was working late. Nick had the children bathed and in bed before she got home – order restored. He was in the middle of cooking an asparagus risotto when he heard her key turn in the lock.

The rice was fattening and he was about to add the parmigiano when she came in and put her laptop onto the table. She went to him and he turned his lips up to meet hers, finding instead her cheek.

'Something smells good,' she said. Her tone was still distant. He wanted to get back to that place they had been at, before the police walked into their home. They were brittle now. She denied it, but he could feel it. He would never have believed it – their relationship had been the strong foundation in his life – but now it felt as if they could break at any moment. It was the mundane that was saving them right now: the kids' schedules, the laundry, bills to be paid, the fucking risotto. The real *them*, the people that met in between, felt shaken.

He turned, hoping to coax a smile from her, but then saw her face. She looked worn, dark circles under her eyes.

'You all right?'

'Better now I'm home. How long's dinner? I want a shower.'

'However long you need it to be.'

She took a beer from the fridge and smiled at him before leaving the kitchen. Nick turned his focus back to the frying pan, a knot of anxiety in his stomach. They had always been so open with each other, but now he didn't know what she was thinking. They were still having sex, but it felt different, as if she were detaching from him, studying him. When he touched her now, he thought about it before it happened.

He finished the risotto and pushed it to the back of the stove. It was easy to reheat. He took a beer and drank it waiting on her, looking out of the window at the late January night. There were no more leaves on the trees. It was already dark and he had to squint near the glass to see outside; standing back there was only his reflection. There was no one he wanted to look at less than himself. Nick took a deep swill of beer. The malt and bubbles on his tongue reminded him of happy times but did not cheer him.

His parents were right. He was going to jail. At the very least he was looking at an expensive jury trial – just another piece of entertainment-industry flotsam accused of horrific acts of sexual abuse. Even if he didn't end up in jail, in solitary confinement to protect him from the other inmates who wanted to rape him, he would never work again. He would end up driving his father's lorries. He took another swig, watching his dark reflection in the window.

He gulped his beer imagining prison: violent assaults and disinterest from the guards. Anyone who had a daughter would think he was fair game. But that wasn't his worst fear. His worst fear was Marina doubting him, and he felt it now.

She came into the room, popped the caps on two more beers and put them on the table as he spooned out their risotto. She found the unopened mail set on the counter and sat down at the table to open it: bank statements, and a letter marked 'Patrick, Wiseman & Faldane'.

She turned it over. 'From the lawyer?'

'Really?'

Marina inserted her thumbnail and ripped open the letter. It was a bill for three thousand pounds. 'Legal services to date ... ' she read, 'we trust you find this in order and look forward to receiving payment shortly.'

Their eyes met. 'And you've not even got to court yet.' Marina put the bill back into the envelope.

He gave her the best portion and placed it before her. She opened the cutlery drawer. 'You want a spoon or a fork?'

'Spoon.'

'Me too.'

They ate in silence for a few minutes.

'You all right?' he said, looking at her tired eyes.

'Yeah, fine, why?'

'I dunno. You seem ...'

Marina let her fork drop against the porcelain. 'Theresa called me into her office about the Twitter thing. Didn't go unnoticed.'

Nick also put down his spoon, washing the mouthful down with beer. 'What did you say?'

'What do you think? I said the police were being completely unhelpful – failing or refusing to connect the dots and that we were now victims ... from every angle.' A single tear left her eye and she nudged it away with the heel of her hand when it reached her cheekbone.

Nick held his breath at the sight, shocked, and then, feeling a curl of responsibility, shame, he reached out, took the hand away from her face and held it.

'Today, Luca asked me if I was going to jail.'

'Who told him that?'

'I think he overheard my parents talking. I tried to explain, but you know Luca ...'

'That's why he's been wetting the bed.'

For the past month, even before the brick incident, Luca had wet the bed at least twice a week. He had been dry at night since he was three.

'We don't know that. It could be a phase.'

She smiled and withdrew her hand, 'Yeah, the phase where his dad might go to prison.'

Nick hung his head. 'Tell me what Theresa said.' He needed to change the subject.

'Well, you know what she's like, all . . . ' she waved her hand in the air, a gesture when she was trying to find an English word, 'all double. Duplicitous. She said that she is behind me – that she has my back, but I don't believe her, and she asked for details and I . . . told her everything.'

'Was that wise?'

'You know that I'm obliged to declare any potential conflicts of interest. I had no choice. Before I told her that it was just "assault" but now I had to admit that you were being investigated for a sexual offence. I told her about the brick through our window and the Facebook page. It's on the news . . . on the web anyway. But I couldn't tell what she was thinking.'

She was picking at her food, making little holes in the rice with her spoon, like Luca. Nick ate quickly, big mouthfuls to take away his words.

She sat back in her seat and her spoon sounded against the plate. 'I know this is happening to you, but a lot of it is directed at me. My job is at stake here. They're targeting *my* Twitter account and throwing a brick through the window with *my* *name* on it.'

'I'm sorry,' he said, not knowing what else to say. 'I can't control any of that.'

'I know that,' she was angered suddenly, 'but you can *react*. You could feel the way I feel, completely . . . outraged.'

'That *is* how I feel.'

'So show it! I don't see that. I don't see you going mad, losing your mind.'

'Do you want me to?'

'No, but I want some kind of normal reaction to being accused of ... of ...'

'You tell me how you want me to react, all right?' Anger flared through him. 'Tell me how you want me to be, and then I'll be that, okay?'

Her cheeks flushed. 'Not only are you being accused of this ... this ... terrible crime but they are attacking me, attacking your children. If it was me I would be fighting it. I would want to protect us. I would be going crazy.' Her eyes shone, anger or hurt, he couldn't tell.

'How can I fight it?' he raised his voice. 'Of course I want to protect you, but *how can I* fight it?'

'You can fight it by being normal, by being upset, by getting angry at this ...' She went on and on, telling him how he should feel and how he should behave. He closed his eyes for a second, wanting to just take her by the throat and squeeze, just to get her to shut up.

'Of course I'm angry,' he said, feeling heat flush his face from hurt at her words.

'You act like you don't care.' Marina began to cry. The tears were like a smashed glass, recalibrating. Nick reached out and took her hands and pressed his forehead against hers.

His chest heaved. They stayed like that for a moment, breathing in and exhaling each other's breath, as they did after making love. 'I was trying to keep it inside. I'm trying to stay strong – for you, for the kids. It's not that I don't care.'

'I'm sorry,' she whispered, 'I just don't know how much more

I can take. I'm trying to be supportive,' she gulped air, 'but this is not just all about you. This is affecting us all.'

It was true. Guilt knuckled under his ribcage.

'C'mon.' He thumbed a tear from her cheekbone and attempted a smile. 'I know my risotto sucks and is not even worthy of sharing fridge space with your paella, but at least it has one of your five a day.'

She cocked her head to one side and laughed a single syllable, then sighed, picking up her fork.

'We're going to be okay,' he said to her, as much to reassure himself as her.

She nodded, a brave smile on her lips, as if trying to convince him she believed him.

When they were both finished he kissed her oily lips before she had a chance to lick them.

22

Angela

'I don't want to see her,' said Angela.

It was late morning and she was lying on her stomach on her bed, sketching the back of her left hand. Her art teacher at Croydon Academy had told her that hands were the most difficult part of the human anatomy to draw, and that was why Leonardo de Vinci sketched them so many times. Angela's hand on the page was slimmer and longer than her real hand, and she had added the diamond ring to the ring finger, even though the ring was still safely in her music box. There wasn't room for her music box under her bed at her father's flat, so she had tucked it to the back of the bedside cabinet.

'You have to. You wouldn't see her on your birthday and I think she really misses you. She said she'd wait for you outside the cinema. I'll drop you just outside, and I can come back and collect you, or your mum said she would bring you back. See how things go.'

'I don't want to.' Angela picked up her pencil and continued to sketch. Her mother had sent her a birthday card that was so big it didn't fit through her father's letterbox. Inside had been a fifty-pound note. She hadn't seen her mother since she left home. Every time she thought of Donna, she imagined the stab wound under her eye and the black and blue swelling, and self-hatred welled up in her like pus.

'Well, you told her you would go last night. She might be on her way already. C'mon, let's go. Get it over with and then I'll get us something nice for tea.'

'What will you get?' Angela closed her sketchpad and swung her legs over the bed.

'What do you want?'

'KFC.'

'Your wish is my command.'

As they pulled into the retail park, Angela could see Donna standing outside the cinema, dressed all in black – jeans and a short duffel coat. The sight of her mother after so long brought a sharp pain to the back of her throat. She missed her, but was also frightened, of her mother and of herself. She was scared that she would behave like a monster again, or be called a monster.

Her father pulled into the kerb and Angela got out. It was freezing outside and the wind rushed at her from all sides in the vast space of the retail park. Angela tucked her hands into her pockets and watched the grey paving stones as she walked towards Donna.

'Hello.'

Angela shrugged, the wind buffeting her, and then slowly met her eye. There was now only a tiny red mark on her mother's cheekbone and her face looked normal, healed.

'You won't believe it, but I missed you,' said Donna, hugging Angela with one arm and turning her towards the cinema. 'C'mon, let's get out of the cold.'

Inside was warm and smelled of sweet popcorn. The movie they were going to see was not on for another half hour.

'Do you want something to eat then? Get a hot dog or some ice-cream just now and we can get popcorn to go in?'

Angela nodded and they joined the queue together. Her mother was different – she never offered to buy Angela sweets. It had been a long time since they had gone to the cinema together, and on previous occasions, Donna had said that food and drink was too expensive. Angela had the feeling that Donna was trying to make it up to her after their fight. She chose a hot dog and they found a seat near the fast-food stall. It had been quiet before, but now more children were coming in, laughing and running back and forth.

'Happy birthday.'

Angela looked at the table.

'It's the first time I've not been with you on your birthday.'

'Didn't you want something?' Angela asked, keen to change the subject, hot dog near her lips.

'I'm all right. It's so expensive, it puts me off.'

Angela smiled, grateful for the familiarity of the remark.

'I have money from Dad. I could buy you something.'

'Thanks, love. I'm all right.'

There was a long pause, and Angela looked down at her hot dog, sensing the words unspoken between them.

'So, it is okay at your dad's?' Donna said finally.

Angela was relieved, not wanting to talk about what had happened the last time they saw each other.

'Yeah, it's good. He says I can redecorate my room.'

Her mother's face pinched and Angela remembered the argument about painting a mural on her bedroom wall. She bit deeply into her hot dog.

'You're further from school. Harder to see your friends, but I suppose with all that's happened ... that's not such a bad thing.'

Angela swallowed, her mouth full. 'Yeah, I'm still kept in at playtimes and lunch.'

'That'll stop soon.'

Angela brushed a hand over her stomach, then focussed again on her hot dog, but her mother noticed.

'What's the matter?'

'Nothing, it's just a bit sore.'

'Really? What's the matter?'

'It's nothing.'

'Is it your period?'

Angela tried not to roll her eyes but couldn't help it. 'Stop it.'

Donna pressed her lips together and her cheeks creased. It made her face look old. Angela rustled the paper of her hot dog. She could tell that her mother was about to say something she found uncomfortable, and worried again that she was going to mention the fountain pen.

'Did your dad speak to you about talking to the counsellor?'

Angela shook her head and picked up her hot dog, but felt a sudden wave of fatigue. She wished she had asked for ice-cream instead.

'They called me again and I told them you were living with your dad. I want you to think about it. I can get some time off work to take you.'

'I don't want to talk about it, I told you that.' Angela felt her cheeks flushing with anger. She looked at the table and her now-cold food.

'I would sit outside. I wouldn't need to hear anything. You could speak to her by yourself. But, I dunno ... I think it's important to talk about what happened to you.'

'Noooo,' Angela said again, this time pushing her hot dog away with such force that it slid off the table.

Donna sighed and bent to pick it up, placing it back on the table. Her face was grey with disappointment and Angela felt another flash of sheer hatred for herself that was almost painful. Donna opened her mouth to speak and Angela raised her shoulders in anticipation of the criticism. It didn't come. Instead, her mother pressed her lips together and stood up.

'Let's just go and watch the film, eh? Try and have a nice time.'

As they passed the popcorn, Donna said, 'Do you want some then? Even though you didn't eat much of your hot dog.'

'No, my stomach's still sore,' Angela said again, this time nudging her belly with her wrist.

'Have you been eating rubbish?'

'No,' Angela whined.

'Your dad doesn't think twice about giving you that stuff, but it's not good for you. I can tell you've put on weight.'

'*You've* put on weight, you fat cow,' Angela said, scowling, yet still following her mother as she handed over their tickets and made her way towards Screen Eight.

'Come on,' said Donna, coaxing, but Angela stopped and put her hand flat onto the wall.

'Let's just go in, shall we? We don't need to talk to each other. Just sit and enjoy the film.'

Angela bent over suddenly, back of her hand to her lips.

'What is it?' Donna's hand on her back, rubbing.

'I think I'm gonna . . .' Angela retched, but only a thin stream of brown water came out. She hadn't had anything to eat since breakfast and that was only a bowl of Rice Krispies, as she had been nervous about seeing Donna again.

'Oh dear God.' Her mother took her by the elbow and led her towards the toilets, steering Angela into the disabled cubicle.

Angela lifted up the toilet lid and retched again, but this time nothing came out; the pain in her stomach was becoming worse. She crouched over, arm over her belly.

Suddenly she felt herself spun around.

Donna took her by the shoulders and held her right up to her face, wide eyes and pale, dry lips. 'Listen to me. You didn't take something again, did you? Did you take anything at your Dad's – pills?'

'No, I promise. My stomach's just sore.'

Donna lifted up Angela's sweatshirt and T-shirt, placed a hand on her bare stomach. 'Where does it hurt – left, right, or in the centre?'

'Here,' Angela whimpered, forefingers pressed to her side.

'It could be your appendix. Does it hurt that much? Shall we go to hospital?'

Angela nodded, then blew her nose on the tissue paper in the cubicle.

A few minutes later they were in a taxi, once again on their way to Croydon University Hospital. The car swung out onto Purley Way and Angela fell gently against her mother. She had not meant to, it was just gravity, but now she chose to stay there, head resting on her mother's shoulder.

Donna seemed to tense, but patted Angela's knee. 'Not long now.'

Angela waited on a plastic chair while her mother checked them in at the reception desk. The waiting room was quiet: a man holding his hand in a tea towel, a couple who seemed bored, a young man with a baby in a pushchair. The man who had hurt his hand was taken first, then a young man in blue came forward, holding a clipboard.

'Angela Furness?'

Angela and her mother followed him into a white room with a desk and a chair and a bed covered in tissue paper.

'Hello, I'm Ahmed the triage nurse. You say you've been sick and have a sore stomach?'

Angela nodded.

'She was only barely sick, but she's been complaining of sharp pains in the middle to the right of her tummy.' Donna leaned over and raised Angela's sweatshirt. Angela pulled it back down and hugged her stomach. 'I was worried it's her appendix.'

'Okay, let's take your temperature then, Angela.' He raised a machine that looked like a small gun. 'I'm just going to pop this into your ear. Sit still for me. It won't hurt.'

Angela sat very still. It tickled when the nurse brushed away her hair from her neck.

'All right.' Nurse Patel sat back in his chair. 'Your temperature is very slightly raised. I would have expected it to be higher if you had appendicitis, but if you wait a few minutes, I'll get a doctor to see you.'

Back in the waiting room, Donna sat forward in her seat, straight-backed. The tension in her body made Angela think that her mother was still angry with her. She was staring straight ahead, at the corridor leading to the examination rooms. If her mother had relaxed and sat back in her seat, their shoulders would have touched. Angela imagined that her mother didn't want to touch her or see her.

'You *promise me* you didn't take any pills.' Donna turned

suddenly and faced Angela. 'If you did, we have to tell the doctor right now.'

'No.' Angela was sitting deep into the plastic chair, her shoulders rounded and her stomach sticking out. 'No.' She returned her mother's gaze, unblinking, mouth open.

'You promise?'

'I promise.'

Donna straightened again. Angela watched her mother's foot tap impatiently on the floor. 'You don't want to live with me, that's fine,' Donna said, very quietly, but loud enough that Angela could hear her, 'but you absolutely must not try to hurt yourself again.'

Her mother spoke looking straight down the corridor, so that it seemed as if she was talking to herself.

'I'm sorry,' Angela mumbled.

'What?' Donna turned to her. Her nose and eyes were very sharp, and made her look like a bird.

'Sorry,' she said again, chin to her chest.

There was another long pause with her mother looking at her and Angela felt suddenly ashamed. She expected that Donna would ask her *what for*? She wanted to cover her face, but stayed where she was, avoiding her eyes and staring at her black Converse shoes.

'Angela Furness?' A young doctor with red hair pulled back into a knot stood at the edge of the waiting room.

Angela and her mother followed her down the corridor. 'Just over here. Hope you weren't waiting long.'

'Not at all,' said Donna, already putting on her fake nice polite voice.

The doctor asked Angela to get up onto the bed. She lay back with one hand over her stomach.

'All right Angela, I'm just going to press on your tummy now, and I want you to tell me if it is sore at any point.'

'Okay.'

The doctor lifted Angela's sweatshirt and T-shirt and pressed all over her stomach from the top to the sides and down at the bottom, near her thighs. Twice Angela said, 'It hurts,' but she wasn't sure if it was because of the doctor's hands, or if it just hurt anyway.

The doctor pulled down Angela's T-shirt and looked at the notes on the clipboard. 'You're what? Twelve?'

Angela smiled. 'I just turned thirteen.'

'Oh. Teenager. That's exciting.' She smiled, showing all her teeth, looking first at Angela and then at her mother.

'You were feeling sick earlier. Did you actually vomit?'

'A little bit.'

'She threw up at the cinema, but it was mostly dry retching. She hadn't eaten much, and she said she had stomach pains.'

The doctor's face was suddenly very serious. 'I see you were admitted a few months ago after an aspirin overdose?'

Angela and her mother nodded. Suddenly Angela felt Donna take her hand. Angela squeezed it.

'All right, well, I'd like to test your urine. The nurse will come and take a sample from you.'

Angela nodded.

Soon the curtain was drawn back and a large nurse with a

huge smile appeared. 'Hello, Angela. I have something for you.'

The badge on her uniform said Akwa and she had strong black arms and smelled of fresh flowers. She held out a cardboard vial and asked Angela to go into the toilet and pee into it. Angela did as she was asked, then waited with her mother behind the curtain.

'Maybe you've got food poisoning. Have you eaten anything strange at your Dad's?'

Angela shook her head. Donna rubbed the back of her hand.

After a few minutes, the curtain was drawn noisily back and the doctor stood before them, one hand in her pocket and another resting on the bed. Angela stared at her and the pens sticking out of the pocket of her white coat. Her name badge was obscured by the clipboard.

The doctor looked at her mother. 'I'd like a quick word with Angela, and then I'll ask you to come back in.'

Donna started, her eyes becoming very round. 'But—'

'Just a few minutes, if that's all right.'

'I'll just be out here,' said Donna as she left them alone.

The doctor lowered her chin and met Angela's eyes.

'Angela, your urine test shows that you are pregnant. Did you know that?'

Angela shook her head.

'Do you know how it happened?'

Angela said nothing, looking at the doctor, but not moving at all, not even blinking her eyes.

'I'm going to have to tell your mum, okay? I'll ask her to come back in.'

When her mother returned, Angela looked down at her hands. She didn't want to see Donna's face when the doctor told her.

Donna sat down in a plastic chair, handbag resting on her lap.

'The urine test shows that Angela is pregnant.'

Donna's handbag thudded onto the floor. 'What do you mean? That . . . that's impossible.'

The doctor's face was without expression. 'I need to ask you both to wait here for a few minutes. I've contacted social services.'

Angela lay back on the pillow and began picking her nail. She didn't want to be pregnant. She felt as if she was sinking down backwards into the bed. It felt like falling.

23

Donna

Donna's hand shook as she slipped a cigarette from the packet. She was outside the hospital, a grim, side-less shelter designated for smokers. Most of the other smokers were patients, coats over pyjamas. It had just turned dark, the moon lurking unseen behind the Croydon skyline.

Donna turned away from the others, the cigarette unlit but poised an inch from her lips. *Angela*, she whispered, eyes stinging with startled tears. Donna put four fingers over her mouth and breathed through the fleshy grille of them.

Pregnant.

The horror of that word now. It was wrong, sick, depraved. It didn't feel so very long since Angela had been growing inside her. She remembered stretching her palm over her abdomen and feeling the baby move, feeling the muscular shudder of her inside.

She had been such a good baby. Hungry for milk and waking with a smile. Love for her had consumed Donna, utter and absolute. Her smell, her softness, the sound of her laugh, intoxicating. The lazy blue eye contact when she latched onto the breast. The silky feel of her hair, her chubby knees. Gums clamping down on the knuckle of her forefinger.

It had been her duty to protect her.

Still a little girl. A little girl.

Donna's fingers trembled and she pinched her nose between finger and thumb. The cigarette fell from her knuckles to the ground and she stooped to retrieve it but then stayed like that, hunched over, watching the cigarette dampen on the wet slabs. Images she tried to refuse assaulted her mind.

What had been done to Angela?

Croydon towered above her, crowded her, like a gang – all concrete and reflective glass and growling overpasses. The swabbed and disinfected hospital offered no solace.

She felt her face chill in the wind and only then realised she had been crying. She wiped her cheeks with her right hand.

What had been done to her?

Donna turned to look at the entrance to the hospital, knowing that she had to go back inside and face it. The weight of the news pressed on her. Her hands were leaden at her sides, pulling down on her shoulder blades. She began to walk back in, her imagination a storm of images that she blinked away with the unremitting tears. Goose-pimples prickled her skin, an unshakeable chill.

She remembered the freezer and a hand around her throat

and the deep pain inside her. It had felt as if she had been severed, like a tree. The deafening crack and splitting before the fall.

In the lift, Donna caught her breath. Angela was felled, broken. She was her mother and she had to protect her.

She expected that she looked awful. She rummaged in her handbag for some make-up, but found nothing but an old lipstick. She rubbed a little on her lower lip and smudged her lips together. The police were on their way to the Sexual Assault Referral Centre at the hospital.

It was Detective Sergeant Brookes – the same woman they had spoken to last time Angela was in hospital. The detective looked tired, red hair pulled back at the nape of her neck, her grey suit hanging on her thin body.

Her breathing uneven after the tears, Donna followed the officer into a small room near the nurses' station. There was only one chair – an office swivel with a ripped plastic seat.

'You sit,' said Brookes, propping herself against the desk.

Donna put her handbag on the floor and sat facing the detective, hands clasped before her. There was a salt taste in her mouth from the tears. The room was very bright, lit by a large strip light along the false ceiling, and Donna felt self-conscious, thinking her skin would be red and blotchy. She pulled on her fringe as if it would help to cover her face.

'We will need another statement from Angela. I'll be very gentle with her.'

Donna breathed into her palms.

'I'd like to talk to her about whether the alleged sexual assault at her school is related to her pregnancy. It's very difficult, I know, so we'll go slow . . .'

Donna nodded, swallowing.

'Has she told you who the father is?'

'I don't think she knew she was pregnant.' Donna felt her eyes stinging, as if she were about to cry again. 'Can't you tell, anyway?'

'What do you mean?'

'Well,' Donna wiped her nose with her knuckle, 'she's pregnant – can't you just do a test to see who the father is?'

'It's not that easy. The first thing would be to determine whether or not Angela wishes to proceed with the pregnancy. If she does, then any of the tests would be deemed invasive . . . taking samples of the placental cells, for example.'

'Invasive?'

'Tests such as an amniocentesis would endanger her pregnancy and that would be unethical, however keen we are to discover paternity.'

'Unethical? What do you mean? We could find out her teacher raped her, that he didn't just . . . didn't just . . . and then she'd have an abortion? Well, of course. She has to have an abortion anyway. She's only thirteen years old!' Donna's breathing was shallow and spots of light appeared at the sides of her vision, as if she might faint. She put a hand on her chest and felt her heart thudding inside her. 'Can't you take a sample of her blood and check that against the teacher's?'

'It's not quite so simple. We took a DNA sample from Mr

Dean when he was questioned, but the techniques used to determine paternity mean either conducting an amniocentesis, or else, if there is an abortion, collecting the ... ' Brookes cleared her throat in apology, 'products of conception, for forensic examination, to be cross-checked with suspects.'

'She's only a little girl. She can't have a baby of her own.'

Brookes handed Donna a tissue from a box on the nurse's desk.

'She *has* to have an abortion. She has to.'

'It is her decision. Angela needs time to come to terms with what is happening and then talk through her options with her doctor and the social worker, as well as you and her father. If she does decide to have the pregnancy terminated, we will work with the medical staff to collect the products for examination.'

Donna blew her nose hard, her mind turning with frantic thoughts.

'It *has to be* that teacher. I could tell something else was going on – that she hadn't told me everything.'

'You know we took Angela's phone into evidence after you found the paintings and photographs?'

Donna nodded.

'There is another suspect.'

'Another?'

'Were you aware that Angela had a boyfriend at school?'

'A boyfriend? No. Who?'

'Her phone showed texts to and from a boy we were able to confirm is in year ten at Croydon Academy. His name is Adam Chance – do you know him?'

'Definitely not.' Donna raked her hands through her hair. 'How do you know it's a boyfriend? It could just be a friend.'

'Forgive my characterisation. The nature of the messages suggested that there had been some physical contact between your daughter and this boy.'

'Her father's going to go insane.'

'We will need to speak to Mr Furness about this too, just in case he has information.'

Donna nodded and looked at the floor, and Brookes' brown leather shoes. 'Angela's been living with her dad for nearly a month. We had a fight. We were having a day out together today when this happened – first time I've seen her since she left home. I'm supposed to have her back at her dad's by nine.' She felt her pocket for her phone.

'We would like to talk to her first. We could do it at the station or at home, but I wonder if it would be easier if we just did it now?'

'She won't be good at the station.'

'As I thought. I'll find us a room and we can take her statement here.'

'I'll call him. Stephen's expecting her home.'

Brookes was silent, her eyes visibly working through implications and scenarios.

'We will need one of you – your husband or you – present when we question her, but perhaps it is best if it's you, because of the nature of the questions. Let's see what Angela says about the venue and we'll take it from there.'

*

Brookes left the office and Donna let her thumb hover over Stephen's number. How to tell him this? She decided to wait. The door was ajar and through the blinds Donna could hear the nurses laughing. *You'll need a glass of wine after that, love.*

Donna needed a glass now. Her eyes were hot and her head ached. She followed Brookes down the hospital corridor. She hated hospitals – always too warm, the sterile smell, the sound-less rubber floors. It was like entering a trap, and all around you could see its victims: people with needles in their arms and masks on their faces. Donna didn't ever want to end up here.

Angela was ready to go – shoes and hoodie back on. She looked happy. She looked just like she had yesterday: normal, pale, chubby.

Brookes was standing a few feet from Angela, awkwardly staring at a device in her hands. It was clear that she was waiting on Donna.

'Hey, love.' Donna approached and squeezed Angela's shoul-der. 'Sergeant Brookes has a few more questions for you. Do you want to go down the station or talk to her here?'

Angela looked ominously at Brookes, who smiled. 'You're not in any trouble, but it would be good to talk to you. I know you've had a hard day.'

'Here then,' Angela said, lower lip protruding, shiny with spit.

'Shouldn't take too long,' Donna tried to console, but Angela tugged her shoulder from her mother's grasp.

Brookes led them into a clinical room, with a bed in it and

plastic chairs stacked. As Brookes set out chairs for them, Donna motioned that she was going to make a call and stepped outside.

She pressed the call button and prayed that Stephen's phone would go to answerphone. Through the window, she could see Brookes arranging the seats in a small circle and then asking Angela to sit.

After only three rings, he answered.

'What's the matter?' he said right away, without even a 'hello'. 'You guys at each other's throats already?' He laughed lightly.

Donna swallowed.

'Hello? Hello?' he said, mistaking her pause for a misconnection.

'I'm here. I'm at the hospital.'

'Hospital?'

'Angela felt unwell at the cinema. I thought it was her appendix.'

'Is she all right?'

'She's fine, but . . . the police are here and about to talk to her again. It wasn't her appendix. She's . . . '

'Dear God, what now? Is she all right?'

'Stephen, she's pregnant.' Repeating it now, Donna was surprised that her voice did not quaver. As throughout her marriage, she waited for Stephen's reaction before allowing her own.

'How is that possible?'

'I don't know. She needs to decide what to do, but if there's a termination – I want a termination – they can test for the father. They have Dean's DNA, but . . . ' Donna caught her breath, her heart thumping in her chest, 'they also said she might have a boyfriend at school.'

'What?'

'I didn't know anything, I swear.'

'I'm coming down.'

'Don't, Stephen, the police officer said she only needs one of us and it's best if it's me.'

'*I'm* her guardian now.'

'I'm here already.'

'I'm coming down anyway.'

'The police—' Donna began, but Stephen had hung up. She put her phone back into her pocket and joined Angela and Sergeant Brookes, taking her seat between the two.

Angela was slumped in her chair, hands in the pockets of her hoodie.

Brookes spoke. 'I want to ask you a few questions again and I'd like your mum to stay with us while I talk to you, is that all right?'

Angela nodded, face blank as a bun.

'Mrs Furness, I know you've been through this before. I would ask you not to speak for Angela but feel free to interject if you think anything is unclear and . . . Angela . . . if you don't understand anything I ask you, please let me or your mum know. I will record this interview, take notes on your statement and read it back to you to make sure I have recorded what you said correctly. All right?'

Angela and Donna nodded.

Angela swung her legs underneath the plastic chair, back

and forth, back and forth. Donna heard the creak of the chair against the linoleum floor.

'Hopefully this won't take very long. Obviously we're still working very hard on our current investigation – what you told us before, about Mr Dean touching you in class. Tonight I just want to ask you a few extra questions. Okay?'

Angela nodded.

'Did the doctor explain to you that you are pregnant?'

Angela nodded, her face devoid of any emotion.

'Do you know how you got pregnant?'

'I'm not fucking stupid,' Angela sneered suddenly, folding her arms over her stomach.

'Angela!' Donna interjected.

Brookes held up a hand then turned smiling again to Angela, 'I'm sure that you know that pregnancy can happen after having sex.'

Angela splayed her legs and looked out of the window onto the ward. Her stomach rose up, a gravid rebellious mound.

'Can you tell me how you got pregnant? Pregnancy can happen when you choose to have sex with someone, or if you are forced to have sex, or ...'

Angela's eyes were still focussed on the window, unblinking, their blue seeming to darken, absorb the light.

'Who might have got you pregnant?'

'I don't know.' She fidgeted now, eyes on the floor and then inspecting her clothes, a stain on her cuff.

Donna folded her arms, still reeling, but trying to maintain her carriage even though she was caving in on the inside. She swallowed and tried to concentrate. She wanted the officer to ask about the boy from school. She needed to know the answers now.

'You recently gave a statement about your drama teacher sexually assaulting you?'

Angela nodded.

'Did you and Mr Dean have sex? You said he covered your mouth, and touched you between your legs, but did he put his penis inside you – that time, or another time? Or did he show you his penis?'

There was a long pause. Angela was hunched now, hands between her knees. She shook her head once. It wasn't clear what she meant.

'I need you to talk to me, Angela.' Brookes pitched forward, elbows on her knees and hands stretched out, mirroring Angela's body language. 'I saw you shake your head to that question I asked you about Mr Dean. Can you answer yes or no? I want to make sure I understand what you're saying.'

'Don't know. Leave me alone. I don't want to talk about it. I want to go home.'

'Angela?' Brookes pressed her lips together.

Boom!

A fist at the window.

'Dad!'

Angela jumped up and opened the door. Brookes whispered into her recording device that the interview was paused.

Angela threw herself into Stephen's arms and he kissed the top of her head. He wore a checked shirt with sharp, ironed creases down the sleeve, and immaculate jeans and trainers. Donna braced herself for his reproach.

'I came as soon as I could,' he said, smiling, reaching out a hand to Brookes.

Brookes smiled at him and Angela, who was still pressed into her father, arms around his waist. 'We're in the middle of taking a statement from Angela just now. I wonder if you would mind waiting outside until we finish?'

Donna opened her eyes wide, knowing that Stephen would not relish being excluded.

'Surely we can both be with her.'

'We only need one parent or guardian present and we have already begun with Donna.'

Stephen put his hands in his pockets – matching Brookes' smile. 'I am Angela's father, and she's living with me full time. I'm also on the police force and—'

'I understand that you are a police officer, but right now you are a parent, that's all, and a parent that I need to stay outside, while I continue with Angela and her mother. We've already started and so I'd be grateful if you could just wait here until we're finished.'

Stephen gave Brookes a closed-lipped smile. Perhaps to Brookes and the passing nurses he seemed agreeable, consenting, but Donna knew he was seething. He patted Angela's shoulder to release her.

Stephen sat just outside on a chair opposite the window and Donna watched him through the glass, waiting with folded arms, his gunmetal eyes glinting with subdued anger.

Angela was sullen now, sliding down in her chair as Brookes glanced over her notes.

'I know you're tired but it won't take much longer. We were talking about Mr Dean. Do you think he could have made you pregnant?'

Angela looked through the window at her father, then down at her small, bitten nails. 'Maybe.'

'Maybe. Can you tell me what you mean by that?'

Angela shrugged, her mouth pinched. Donna reached out and took her hand, hoping to urge her to speak, but Angela withdrew from her mother's touch.

'It's hard to remember. He hurt me and I couldn't see what he did because his hand was over my face.' Suddenly Angela opened her palm and placed it over her face. She kept it there for ten long seconds, looking at Brookes and her mother through the gaps in her fingers.

'Was this behind the stage at school, or another time?'

'Behind the stage.'

'Can you describe what happened for me?'

'I told you already.'

Brookes smiled. 'Do you want me to read back to you the statement you gave us a few months ago?'

'No.'

'You just said that Mr Dean hurt you. Do you think that he might have put his penis inside you, or his fingers?'

'I think so,' her voice was faint.

Brookes leaned forward and clasped her hands on her lap, so that she was looking up into Angela's face. 'Remember you've

238

done nothing wrong. My job is to protect you and make sure that no one hurts you.'

Angela's pale face nodded.

'Have you had sex with anyone else, either because you wanted to, or because they forced you?'

Angela shook her head vigorously and took a fist of her hair into her hand. 'I don't want to talk about this anymore. I want to go home.'

Brookes inhaled and sat up in her chair, nodding at Donna. 'All right. Let's leave it there. We can speak again.'

Angela burst out of the chair, opened the door and threw herself into her father's arms. Donna looked into Brookes' tired face. 'Well then?'

'We might need to try again in a day or so. I'll speak to her father. Should I speak to Stephen about scheduling another visit?'

'That's probably best.'

In the corridor, Brookes put one hand in her pocket. 'Thanks for waiting,' she said to Stephen, who seemed inflated with impatience. Addressing them both, she said, 'You will make an appointment for Angela with your GP, for prenatal care and ... discuss your options?'

Stephen and Donna nodded.

'Very well, good evening.'

As they watched Brookes make her way to the end of the ward, Stephen rubbed Angela's back. 'Give me a minute with your mum, sweetheart?'

Stephen took Donna's elbow and led her a few feet away.

The action felt controlling, dominant, and she eased her arm from his grasp. 'Pregnant? There has to be some mistake, surely.'

'I wish there was, believe me.'

'I mean ... we knew she'd been assaulted but ... she's still a child ... it isn't possible ... she's barely even got her first period.'

Donna blinked. 'It's been about a year. It's possible.' She wiped a hand over her mouth. 'More than possible. It's real.'

'God help her.'

Donna looked up into his face, forgetting her own self-consciousness and feeling a rare flush of tenderness for him. 'Take care of her tonight,' she said, as she picked up her handbag.

'I'll see you soon, love,' Donna said to Angela, who was still sitting on a plastic chair in the corridor, picking at a stain on her leggings.

Angela didn't look up or acknowledge her mother in any way, so Donna bent and kissed her cheek, which was clammy and cold, like clay. 'Call me if you need me.'

Donna left before them both, getting a cigarette ready in the lift as she descended.

24

Marina

'Shall we go to bed?' Nick asked.

He had been watching television while she had been doing work emails on her phone. 'You go ahead. I'm going to have to look at this on the laptop. Theresa just forwarded me something.'

In the study, Marina opened up her laptop and turned on the desk light. She heard him in the kitchen cleaning up, and then brushing his teeth. It was nearly eleven. In truth, she didn't need to look at the report that Theresa had sent: there would be time in the morning. She had been stalling; no energy tonight for the wordless embraces and kissing of shoulders that were meant to show that everything was all right; each of them always facing the same way so that there was no danger of eye contact. They weren't communicating well, but touch meant

241

they were still together. If they stopped making love they were in trouble, but tonight Marina couldn't face it.

Now, in the study, waiting for the laptop to power up, Marina put two hands over her face. It was a relief to be alone, away from him. As soon as the children were in bed, she and Nick loomed in the house and she had to deal with him and what had happened.

The laptop chimed its readiness.

In her email, she opened the report and then looked at it in her browser. She was too tired to read, rubbing her eyes. Along the corridor, Nick switched off the bedside light and the far end of the hall darkened.

Marina blinked, distracted from the report by another email from Theresa about a promotional video. Child International had recently paid for the video, and this was the first rough edit.

She heard the soft purr of Nick snoring, which meant he was on his back. When she was in bed, he slept on his side, holding her. Often he would wake himself up snoring when she was not by his side.

Marina downloaded the file for the promotional video, then scrolled to the downloads menu to view it. A video opened in a window of the screen. It was a woman with a belt around her throat, and black mascara tears running down her cheeks.

Marina sat back in her chair, a hand clasped fast over her mouth. There was a counter on the video that showed Nick had watched it twelve times. Shaking, she closed everything down then stood up, the back of her hand to her mouth, breathing onto her knuckles.

After everything, this was still what he needed to do every day. This was not clicking and being led somewhere – this was addictively seeking out videos of sexual violence. When? While Ava was napping? When he dropped them off in the morning? He was under investigation and but still he seemed to need it. Marina had not wanted to know what he watched when she was pregnant, but now she wondered if that had been wilful ignorance. Had there long been a side to Nick that she had known but not been willing to confront?

And Angela – could it be that Nick had hurt her? Were children easier because they couldn't fight back? What else was he hiding from her?

Trembling, Marina went into the bathroom and closed the door. She washed and then looked at her dripping face in the mirror. Just *wondering* if he was capable of hurting Angela felt like a betrayal. She washed her face again, washed her hands and scrubbed her nails, the image of the crying woman still dark in her mind. It was a betrayal of her – it made their marriage, their love, *wrong* somehow.

She dried her face. Her head hurt – she needed to cry but was unable to. She had to talk to him again but felt so fatigued by explanations and her own relentless quest to understand him. She brushed her teeth, disgust thick in her mouth. She brushed until her gums bled, spitting red into the sink.

Still asleep, he turned and his arm fell over her waist as soon as she got into bed. The heat from him blazed at her back. In the darkness, she waited for sleep, hearing only her heart and the sound of his breathing, the weight of his arm pinning her to the bed.

The next day, Marina had the afternoon off and they collected the children together and then went to Brickfields Country Park for a picnic. Marina carried a bag of egg sandwiches and homemade brownies that Ava and Luca had helped to bake at the weekend. The brownies contained Smarties, at Luca's behest. It was cold but dry and the air smelled of new pine and fox. As they walked along the woodland path, the children charged ahead, stomping on the wet leaves.

It had been Nick's idea to have a picnic and Marina had jumped at it, instead of being trapped in the house with their fears and suspicions. She had not spoken to him about the internet history but it was all she could think about. He had woken up depressed and now was sullen at her side, walking with his hands in his pockets.

He had called Faldane first thing but the lawyer had still not returned his call. Nick had hung up, his face reddening with emotion. 'I know what's going to happen. I'm going to be charged and then found guilty. It's a farce. Every day walking around with a fucking noose around my neck.'

The children had been in the next room. 'Nick, watch your language.'

He had walked away from her.

The trees were stark; stripped of their leaves they looked like lungs bared against the sky. Marina was grateful to be walking, following the children who were running towards the pond, screaming with laughter. She was trembling so hard it felt as if she was shivering, although it was nothing to do with the cold.

There were ducks at the pond and Ava and Luca were running straight towards them. Marina trotted after them to make sure they were safe, picnic bag whacking against her calf. It would have been easier for Nick to run, but he was lost in his thoughts.

At the pond, Marina opened the bag and gave the children a slice of bread each, which they broke up and threw into the water for the ducks. In summer, the pond was framed by a beautiful, bright green weeping willow. Now the bare branches seemed to skulk over the children, a giant witch's hand.

'Daddy, do you want to feed the ducks?' said Ava, eyes bright as she held out her slice of bread towards her father.

Nick kicked at a patch of mud with his toe and did not look up.

'Nick?' Marina said, trying not to sound cross.

He looked at her blankly.

'Ava's talking to you.'

'What, *bonita*?'

'Do you want to feed the ducks? I can give you some of my bread, if you want.'

'Thanks, I'll be all right – you feed them.' He turned away, thumbing his phone.

Marina rolled her eyes and squatted between the children,

watching the ripples in the water as the ducks swam for the sodden bread. Nick's phone rang and she turned to watch him answer it with a frown, one hand pressed against his ear. She felt a complex flush of emotion for him: a blur of anger and love. She gave Ava an overly enthusiastic smile as a duck gobbled the bread she had thrown.

The duck climbed out of the water and flapped towards Ava, eager for more. Marina wrapped her arms around her daughter, tucking her safe in the space between her legs. Ava huddled there, not usually one for cuddles but startled by the duck. Marina kissed her, smelling the cold park in her hair.

Squatting like that on the edge of the pond, Marina heard Luca say, 'Daddy, why are you crying?'

Nick stood just out of reach of the willow's claw, hand on his forehead. Marina stood up quickly and moved Ava from the water's edge. Nick suddenly slumped down against the base of a tree. He was completely breaking down, phone on the grass beside him. Luca stood straight-backed before him, a hand on each of his father's knees.

'Daddy? Why are you crying?'

Nick reached out and pulled Luca into him, wetting his hair with his tears.

'What's the matter?' said Marina. 'Who was on the phone?'

'I can't take this anymore,' Nick whispered, tears coursing down his cheeks. Luca was nestled into him, young face anxious against his father's chest.

Ava began to cry.

Nick stood up and lifted Luca into his arms, breathing into

the little boy's shoulder for a moment before setting him down.

'Nick, talk to me.'

Marina ran a hand through Ava's hair as she looked up into his eyes. She had never seen him like this.

'It was Faldane,' Nick breathed, wiping his eyes with thumb and forefinger.

'Oh God, what?'

'They say Angela's pregnant.' He looked up at the sky, hands on his hips. He wiped the tears from his cheeks yet still they came. 'If she has an abortion, they can check my DNA against the foetal matter to see if I'm the father of Angela's child. There you go . . . ' he smiled at her, an awful contortion of grief, 'happy?'

Marina reached out for him, caught between needing to comfort him and the children.

'DNA is on genes,' Luca said authoritatively.

'I'm sorry,' Nick said, searching his pockets until he found the car keys. He tossed them towards her and they landed in the grass at her feet. 'I'll see you later.'

'Nick . . . ?'

He turned and ran away from them – back the way they had come. Luca ran after him but was unable to catch his father. Marina watched her son's pace slow, and then his defeated slump as he turned back.

'Nick!' Marina shouted, watching his figure decrease in size and then disappear into the woods.

Ava was crying against Marina's knees. She beckoned Luca back, letting a hand rest on the crown of her daughter's head.

Now Marina felt like crying, but it wouldn't do to have the whole family in tears.

'What did Daddy mean?' said Luca, out of breath, unzipping his jacket and throwing it to the ground. 'About not being Angela's father?'

'That's not what he said, darling,' Marina said to him in Spanish, not looking at him, but opening the picnic bag and thrusting a roll into his hand. Luca looked down at the roll.

'It *is* what he said,' Luca replied, in English, his face obstinate, looking at his roll with suspicion. 'I heard him.'

Marina tore a roll in half and gave it to Ava, setting her against the tree to eat it. She turned to Luca in exasperation. 'You didn't hear him correctly,' she said in Spanish.

'He said, "I'm not Angela's father".' Luca stood with his arms at his sides, stubbornly speaking English. He had heard the words in English and so he reported them in English. Marina turned to him. He was unwilling to change languages because translation would alter the truth of what he had heard.

Marina sighed in defeat and ran her fingers through his hair. She was angry at Nick for being so unguarded but she knew from her own childhood that children had a way of understanding their parents' worries whether you told them or not. In English Marina said, 'He didn't say that. You misheard. He said "the father of Angela's child". It is different to being the father of Angela.'

'Okay,' said Luca, taking a small bite of his roll.

Marina bent and kissed him.

Another child would forget such a remark in an instant, but

she knew her son would now be committing what she had said to memory, realising his mistake and unpicking it – finding another question.

As the children finished their rolls, Marina called Nick three times but he didn't answer. She left no message.

When they walked back to the car, she saw him at the far side of the car park, tossing stones into the trees. She put the children into their car seats and then walked towards him.

'Are you coming home with us?' She put her hands into the hip pockets of her jeans, raising up her shoulders.

It was pine cones he was throwing, not stones. He came to her, holding one in his hand, tan and spiky. She glanced back at the car.

He leaned down and put his forehead on the top of her head. 'Sorry.'

'Are you all right?' she asked, looking into his brown eyes, which were conflicted, flints of guilt and fear.

He tossed the pine cone away and sighed. 'I dunno. I shouldn't have lost it in front of the kids.'

'I've never seen you like that.'

He wrapped his arms around her, squeezed her so tight that she smiled, despite herself. 'Now you have three babies, huh?'

They both tried to laugh.

Marina broke free and looked up into his face.

'This could be a good thing. If she gets an abortion, they can do the test and then discount you.'

Nick shrugged and took her hand as they walked back to

the car. 'For the pregnancy, yes, but Faldane was very clear: I'm still being investigated for the sexual assault. They are linked but separate. Just like the brick through the window.'

At the car, Nick threw his jacket into the boot. His face had changed again, resolute, distant. Marina sighed, getting juice for Ava from the picnic bag in the boot, a knuckle of guilt under her ribs. Just last night she had wondered if he had wanted to rape Angela, and now here she was pregnant. The night always cast her thoughts in a negative – a reversal of tones, so that light was dark, and vice versa.

Not long ago she had castigated Nick for not showing emotion, but now he had broken down when he heard his DNA would be compared with the DNA of the foetus. Were the tears fear or guilt, or both?

Marina buckled her seatbelt as Nick reversed out of the car park. She took her phone out of her bag and flicked back and forth between messages and her Facebook page. Twitter showed three notifications and she opened it up.

A slick lick of panic closed her throat. It was three posts from the crow. Keeping silent, Marina read each one as Nick turned on the radio and adjusted the air conditioning. This time her boss had not been copied, nor Child International. This time it was personal to Marina.

@marina_alvarez you are married to a rapist creep. I will violently rape u – see how u like it.

@marina_alvarez u don't protect children. Ur gonna get raped till u scream.

@marina_alvarez I know u like it. Ur gonna get raped over and over.

Marina let her phone slide into her bag, her fingers trembling. Luca was talking to Nick about the difference between petrol and diesel and her husband was floundering again. She looked out of the side window, then felt Nick's hand on her thigh.

She swallowed, turning to him.

'You all right?' he said, looking at her, one eyebrow raised.

25

Stephen

Stephen was at work, filing a report on a drunk driver but distracted by the interview video of Adam Chance, who might have raped his daughter.

Might have raped. *Might.* The word seared. Stephen needed certainty. He felt like fighting – needed to beat someone for this, beat them with his bare hands – yet he stayed completely still, watching the cursor flash on the computer screen. Thoughts swarmed in his mind.

What are you going to do about it? Donna's words.

He still remembered the feeling in his fist when it had smashed into the boy's skull. It had felt as if the riot was inside his own body. The boy's skull had cracked so easily. Stephen hung his head, sweat breaking at his hairline.

He had watched the CID interview with Adam Chance when he had been brought in for questioning and cautioned, after correspondence had been found on Angela's phone suggesting that she and the boy were engaged in some sort of sexual relationship.

Chance! That was really his name. Adam was gangly, red-faced and pimply, visibly frightened despite his swagger, even in the poor picture quality that the interview-room camera afforded. He was just fifteen. Throughout the course of the interview he denied intercourse with Angela, repeatedly.

'Yeah, I fought about it, but she's only year eight an' she's too fat, like. I wouldn't shag her.'

It seemed to Stephen, and he was sure it had occurred to the officers conducting the interview, that Adam was all bravado. The text of his interview was frank and explicit, but the camera found him picking his spots and biting his nails. When the officers pressed him, his face flushed scarlet and his eyes shone with tears. Although he didn't like to admit it, Stephen thought that Adam was probably a virgin.

What have you done?

Done to her.

Stephen still believed the actor must be guilty. He felt it in his bones. That man had violated his daughter and deserved to be put away. Stephen knew how the system worked. Adam was just a boy fooling around with a girl below him at school – unless it was proved he was the father, and even then, he might not be prosecuted. Both he and Angela were underage and both could be considered consenting. Angela had not accused Adam of sexually assaulting her.

Stephen went to the bathroom, washed his face in the sink

and looked at his eyes in the mirror, lashes wet and separate. He felt desperate, unable to stay here another moment. Doctors made bad patients and police officers made bad victims.

That was how he felt – a victim. She was his only child. He felt everything she felt. If Adam was let go, and then Dean was not charged, Stephen knew that he would have to act. The abortion would confirm that he was right about Dean. He was going to speak to Angela about that today. He didn't like having to discuss such things with her, but she absolutely had to have an abortion. Even Donna agreed.

He looked down into his wet palms. It would be such gratification to take justice for Angela with his bare hands. He imagined breaking Dean's skull, cracking it like a fresh egg.

But was she lying about Dean? If Angela had been more attractive he might have believed she had made it up – flirting with an actor at school. But a little girl like Angela? It had to be real, because it was so incredible.

Stephen shook the excess water from his face and then put his hands under the dryer. No matter that he was a father wronged, another violent incident would end his career. He would be left doing night-shift work as a security guard, working for less than minimum wage alongside ex-squaddies with shell shock.

Back at his desk, Stephen opened up the criminal database. He bit his lip, then began a search for 'violence against the person' offences in the south-east, and cross-checked the results with those recently released from prison. The search resulted in a large sample, but when Stephen discounted crimes of violence directed at a female partner, there were only three names remaining, two of which were older career criminals. Stephen stared at the mug shots: dark, emotionless eyes and slack mouths, chins tilted upwards in defiance. He committed the names and faces to memory. He had never come in contact with these men and that was best.

When finally his shift finished, Stephen stripped out of his uniform. His handcuffs clunked onto the bottom of the metal locker. On the inside door, there was a faded photograph of Angela, aged eight, gap-toothed smile and hair in braids. He smiled at her as he stepped out of his uniform trousers. She had been a stunner at that age, small as a bird with huge eyes. The separation had affected her badly: first the weight gain and then her behaviour.

Stephen sat down and fed one socked foot into his jeans and then the other.

A memory came to him, unasked for: Donna standing before him in the bedroom, her eyes watery and her eyeliner smudged. He had been pulling away from her for years, first emotionally and then physically, and now he could barely look at her.

'But why?' she had whined.

'I just don't fancy you anymore,' he had said quietly, smoothing the left side of his hair with one hand. It was brutal, he knew that, but she had asked. 'I've stayed here because of Angela, but I don't think I can do it any longer. It's not fair on any of us.'

He met her eyes, blurring with the impact of his rejection. The skin sagged and pulled on her face, like unrisen dough. Her thin, pale lips with the tiny lines around them.

'Please,' she had said, 'I need you.' She was beyond shame and he felt for her, but still couldn't bring himself to hold her, to forgive.

He put his hands on his hips. 'I'll rent somewhere. It might take a while. We can just take it slow, but I don't think we should sleep in the same bed from now on. I'll move into the box room.'

The queasy smell of her: salty musky hollows, the stale hot stink of alcohol.

'The box room's full of stuff,' she said, voice cracking.

'I'll clear it out.'

The nights were the hardest for him, her head on his shoulder, pinned in their accustomed embrace with her curled towards him, taking her own comfort.

Way back, when they had been young, before Angela or the mortgage, when his feelings for her had still been tender, she had told him she had been raped. She had told him in bed, and he had not known what to say or do. She didn't want to report it to the police; she didn't want him to find the man (although Stephen had secretly tried and could not). Donna didn't even know his full name.

He had held her and apologised, for what he was never sure, but the knowledge had always made him overthink sex with her, careful not to accidentally hurt or demean, although sex itself was demeaning – or so it seemed to Stephen.

Stephen closed his locker and felt in his pocket for his car keys. Outside the day was cool but bright. He headed towards

Croydon Academy. He had changed his shifts so that he could collect Angela from school each day. He drove at exactly two miles under the speed limit, always indicating when he pulled out and never running an amber traffic light. He passed his old house on the Portland Road, where he had lived with Angela and her mother, and then at the school pulled into a waiting bay and turned up the heating in case Angela was cold.

Just then, Adam Chance wandered out of the school, followed by a pack of boys, all skinny, school bags slung low on their shoulders. Stephen let his foot rest heavily on the accelerator and the car revved audibly. Adam turned but did not seem to see Stephen slouched behind the wheel of his car.

Angela was still nowhere to be seen. She was often late, coming out last with her school shirt untucked, trailing her bag an inch off the ground.

Unable to stop himself, Stephen turned the car around and followed Adam out of the school car park. The boy turned up a side street off the Portland Road. He had bad posture, stooping over his phone before returning it to his pocket, then scuffing his feet as he walked towards home.

Adam stopped and looked over his shoulder, as if sensing he was being watched, but he did not see Stephen sitting back in his seat, sun visor down.

Adam pushed open the wire mesh gate, smiling and prodding at the phone in his hand. The curtains were drawn in the front window. The small front garden was overgrown, full of dandelions and daisies, and littered with odd items: plastic toys, a bathroom sink.

He watched through half-closed eyes until Adam opened his front door and stepped inside, then turned the car around and went back to the school. Adam was nothing more than a boy and Stephen was convinced he was a virgin. Dean was another matter.

In the distance, Stephen saw Angela walking down the school steps. She looked so small from a distance.

He tightened his fists so that the knuckles pinked, the tendons white. He was prepared to get justice for her, even if he couldn't do it himself. If the law failed, he would see that Dean got what he deserved.

On the way home, she was sullen, staring out of the window. He smiled, trying to coax her into talking. He felt better now he had thought of a way of cracking the actor's skull, without having to skin his own knuckles.

'Are you tired, Angel?'

'Bit.'

'Was today okay?'

'Suppose.'

Normally it was easier to discuss things in the car, watching the road, without the glare of eye contact, but today she felt especially closed to him. His words seemed to bounce off her, as if repelled.

'Listen, I wanted to talk to you, sweetheart.'

'What?'

'It's not a nice subject, but it's important.'

She didn't look at him, but he sensed she was waiting for more.

'I've made an appointment for the doctor for you – to see about an . . . abortion as soon as possible, you know?' She was silent.

'You know what I'm talking about, yes?'

'Will it hurt?'

'I think if we go soon, it won't hurt so much. You can just take some medicine and then it will just come out. I think that's how it works. I'm sure the doctor will tell us all about it.'

Angela said nothing. She sunk down further in her seat.

'Darling?'

'But it's a baby, right?'

'Sweetheart, no it's not.' He turned to her, but she looked out of the window. 'It's just a bunch of cells.'

Angela shrugged her shoulders.

'You're *my* baby – you can't have a baby yourself. Can you? You're too young. Even you know that.'

She was silent again, although he thought he saw her nod. She stared out of the side window at the terraces and the trees and the heavy grey sky.

'I made an appointment for tomorrow morning. I'm off work and I can go with you, but if you prefer your mum we can call her tonight.'

He turned into the drive and Angela got out and slammed the door shut. She knew he hated that.

'Hey,' he called, locking the car and following her to the front door. 'There's no need for that.'

She ignored him, opened the door to his apartment with her own key and walked straight to her bedroom.

The alarm system beeped and Stephen disarmed it, and then bent to take off his shoes. He followed Angela to her room. She was sitting on her bed, backpack still on her shoulders, biting into a chocolate bar.

Stephen took a deep breath.

'Look, I know you don't want to talk about it. It's not something a girl your age should have to deal with, but it's here whether we like it or not, and I'm afraid we have to make that decision and sort it out.'

'Why do you want to kill it?'

'I don't want to kill it. I just think that you are a young girl.'

'I'm thirteen.'

Stephen smiled. 'I know. My teenager. But thirteen is still too young to have a baby and the longer we leave it, the harder it will be. Let's get it done tomorrow and then you can leave this all behind you.'

'You don't care about me.' Her large eyes, still so reminiscent of the baby she had once been, glassed with tears.

'That's not true. You know I love you more than anyone else in the world.'

Angela hung her head, staring intently at the milk chocolate bar in her hands.

Stephen ran his hands through his hair.

'You had Adam arrested. They told him he might go to jail for raping me, but he didn't.'

All the air left Stephen's body. 'I didn't have him arrested. The hospital called the police and then the CID had your phone and found your chats with him. It had nothing to do with me, I swear.'

'You told the CID to take him in.' Her mouth was full of chocolate, her tongue and teeth black.

'I didn't.'

She turned away from him, jaws working, face pale and contorted, as if in pain.

'Did you have sex with him?'

'What?'

'Don't talk with your mouth full.'

'You just asked me a fucking question.'

He raised his finger. 'Don't talk to me like that.'

She spoke to Donna like that, but had never been disrespectful towards him.

'Noooooo!' she screamed. Suddenly she rushed past him. He was quick to react and grabbed the hood of her hoodie, but she slipped out of it and he was left with the top in his hands as he heard the front door slam. By the time he got to the front door she was running down the street. It seemed like years since he had seen her run. He chased her, in his socks, not even taking the time to put his shoes on at the door, but she was gone. He thought she might have run into one of the back yards but he couldn't see her anywhere.

'Angela!' he called, not caring that he sounded like a lunatic. 'Angela!'

He had lost her. The shock and humiliation jarred him. He would have to phone Donna and admit it. He decided to wait until dark. Kids always come home when they're hungry.

26

Angela

She knew where he lived.

Even before the stories in the press she had known where he lived. She and Jasmine had looked him up online and a magazine article had mentioned Firgrove Hill in Farnham and then they had found his exact address in the online phone directory. They had looked at satellite images of his house with its grey-red roof and imagined that they saw him in the driveway.

Now, walking down Firgrove Hill, Angela wished that Jasmine could see her. All the houses looked beautiful with white, criss-cross windows like when you drew a house as a little kid. It was like a fairy-tale and he was the prince. She changed to walk on the opposite pavement where the house numbers were odds and not evens – she knew he was number fifty-nine. The hedges were wet and she could smell leaves and countryside as she walked to his house. It was different from Croydon. She put a hand on her belly, thinking about the baby growing inside her. She smiled. It would be blond with brown eyes, just like him. She let her arms fall to her sides.

The numbers five and nine were white against the wrought-iron gate and also on the door at the top of the drive. The house had bright red bricks and white window frames and there was a little hedge dividing it from the house it was attached to next door. An awning over the second-floor bedroom windows had also been painted white. Angela waited at the gate for a moment, staring at the house. She felt excited to be here. It was just after five o'clock. The little garden was lovely, a tree and daffodils and a plastic slide for the little kids. Angela knew he had two children – a boy and a girl. He would be a good dad. His life was perfect. It was the kind of life you were supposed to have when you grew up.

Carefully, Angela opened the gate and walked up the drive. The gravel crunched under her feet. The sky was high, blue and cold and she felt small beneath it.

She liked being in his drive. It was smart, *all in order*, as her dad would have said. There was a silver car in the drive and Angela noticed that there were two children's car seats in the back.

She stepped onto the red-tiled doorstep, a flutter of nerves, but then stood on her tiptoes to press the doorbell.

As soon as the bell sounded there was barking. Angela didn't like dogs and she frowned, but did not turn away. She straightened the waistband of her jogging bottoms.

The door flew open and a small bristly dog dashed out and started to sniff at her trainers. She was glad it wasn't a big dog. Angela looked up. It was Mr Dean. He was wearing jeans and a T-shirt and he looked tired and then cross. He looked more normal than she remembered, but she hadn't seen him in a while and had been looking at his internet photos. He had a dishtowel in his hands. His face fell when he recognised her.

'Hi,' she said, swallowing.

'What the hell are you doing here?'

'I dunno. I wanted to see you.'

'Angela. Are you kidding? What the f— You could get me into real trouble. You have to get out of here. How did you get here?'

'I came on the train. It was all right. I had to change at Clapham Junction was all.'

'How did you find me?'

Angela shrugged. She felt shy.

'Well you need to go home. Jesus Christ, what do you think you're doing?'

'I wanted to see you.'

Mr Dean put his face in his hands. He stood like that for a few seconds and Angela wondered if he was crying, but then he took his hands away and he wasn't crying at all, but his face was red.

'You can't just come and see me.' He stepped outside and looked up and down the street.

'You're on your own?'

She nodded.

'I can call you a taxi to take you back home.'

'I want to talk to you.'

'You can't. Don't you understand that what you're doing right now means I'm breaking the law? It's illegal for me to be near you, because of what you said about me.'

'I didn't mean for anything bad to happen to you.'

Suddenly there was the sound of feet on floorboards and a little girl stood in the hallway. 'Daddy?'

Nick turned and shouted at her. 'Get back in there. Luca?' He picked up the little girl and carried her into the living room. Angela heard Nick talking to his son. 'Look after your sister and stay in here.'

Angela stepped into the hallway.

Nick shut the living-room door. There was the sound of crying from inside, perhaps because he had raised his voice. Angela was disappointed in him.

He was frowning, but barely looked at her. He picked up the phone in the hall and began to dial, but made a mistake or forgot the number and hung up again and began to redial.

'I don't have enough cash in the house for the taxi.' His neck was red. 'Can you get the train back again? Can you do that?'

'I think so. I mean, I got here, so . . . yeah.'

He turned to her, hands on hips and face angry, desperate. It reminded her of his face in the YouTube video where his character was about to be tortured. He opened his wallet and flicked through it, counting notes. Angela felt her arms heavy at her sides, panicked that he was going to just give her a tenner and push her out of the door.

'What do you want?' He was still flicking through his wallet, counting money.

'I wanted to see you is all. I wanted to tell you that I miss you being at our school.'

His chest was heaving, as if he had stopped running suddenly.

'I drew a portrait of you. I didn't bring it with me.' She wouldn't say anything about the baby. She wondered if he knew.

He swallowed and she watched the Adam's apple on his neck bob up and down. The little girl was still crying inside the living room. The noise was distracting and made Angela feel embarrassed. In her imagination, Nick would have invited her in. She might have played with his kids while he got her a Coke.

'Listen, you really *need to leave*. I'm serious.'

Angela looked at the carpet. It was dark red. It made her think about the blood that had come after she had sex for the first time. Her mum had thought it was her period, but it hadn't come yet. It wasn't time. She blinked because she felt her eyes burning. She didn't want to cry, but she felt sad that he was asking her to go.

'I'm sorry,' she said, quietly.

The tears from the living room had stopped and now Angela heard the clock ticking in the hall. She kept staring at her trainers against the red carpet. She hated herself suddenly, fully, from the inside out. She was stupid and ugly and no one would ever love her. She couldn't remember why she had come all this way, but she wanted Mr Dean to put his arm around her again. She wanted him to touch her. Maybe if he touched her, she would feel as if she were real.

'Angela, stop doing that . . .'

She looked down. She hadn't been aware of doing anything but now saw that she had been scratching her left wrist with her long nails. She hadn't felt a thing but she had drawn blood. She looked at her wrist, red like the carpet.

The living-room door opened and a little boy appeared. He was dark like the little girl but seemed very like Mr Dean – the same mouth.

'Dad, what is it?'

Nick pointed at the little boy, 'Stay in there, like I told you.'

The little boy hesitated, staring at Angela with enormous brown eyes, then turned back into the living room and closed the door.

'I didn't think you'd be like this.'

'Like what?' he said, throwing the dishtowel over the banister.

'I thought you'd be a nice dad, not shouting.'

His shoulders sagged. 'Why did you have to come here?'

'I missed you.' She felt a lump in her throat.

His face looked hurt and angry, hands on his hips, his chest still heaving.

'I still have that thing you gave me.'

'What thing?'

'The pen. I didn't tell. I didn't tell anyone you gave it to me, but I like it a lot. I used it to draw a picture of you – the outline anyway – before I painted it.'

'Are you trying to get me in trouble?' he snarled. 'Is this another deliberate ploy?'

She felt afraid of him for the first time.

'I don't know what's going on with you, Angela ... you tell the police that I, that I ...' it hung in the air, unspoken, 'and then you turn up here. But let me tell you, what you're doing right now is worse than saying that I ... This could really finish me, and I don't know if you're naive or if this is all part of the game, but it's not funny. It's not funny at all.'

'I had a fight with my dad. I can't stay with my mum anymore because I stabbed her, with your pen.' He was looking at her, unblinking. 'I stabbed her in the face with your pen and then she didn't want me to live with her anymore.'

Nick covered his face with one hand. 'What?'

'My mum was being horrible to me. I didn't mean it but I was really angry with her. But she's okay now.'

Nick sighed.

'So what ... now you're living with your dad?'

'Yeah, I'm with my dad but I fell out with him, too. He wants to take me for an abortion but I think my mum should go with me for that. Only she hates me.' Angela caught her breath. She had mentioned the baby. She hoped he knew.

He said something under his breath, which she thought was a swear word, and walked away from her, towards the kitchen. Angela waited for him to return, looking at the family photographs that were set in white frames and placed on the wall by the stairs. There were shoes by the door in different sizes.

Mr Dean came back with a cotton pad soaked in disinfect-
ant and a large plaster.

'Give me your wrist,' he said, quickly.

She placed her hand in his. He didn't look at her, and her
wrist stung when he pressed the cotton onto it. She felt his
anger in his brisk movements. Her eyes flooded with tears
and she bit her lip. She hung her head and tears rolled down
her cheek. She was crying because of the warmth of his hand
beneath hers.

He saw her tears as he was preparing to stick the plaster and
frowned but became more gentle as he pressed the dressing
against her wrist.

'Ever since that first day, I worried about you. I thought you
needed someone to listen to you, someone to care.'

Angela's throat closed, and she took small gasps, trying to
compose herself, trying hard not to embarrass herself by really
crying in front of him. She had liked him too on that first day.
He wasn't like a teacher. He was a like a real person and she
liked the way he touched her, squeezing her shoulder when she
did something he liked. She tried to talk now, to respond, to
tell him that she had felt the same, but it was impossible. She
could talk and then feel the shame of bursting into tears, or
she could stay quiet and calm. She nodded at him, and sniffed,
salt at the back of her throat.

'That's all I was ever trying to do,' he continued. 'Care for
you. Everyone told me you were a nightmare, a problem child,
but I thought that you just needed ... special attention.'

Choking, Angela nodded.

'And then when we were doing those posters and I saw how you could draw, I thought that was it. I thought you were into art and so drama really could help you out. I remember going home feeling really committed to finding a way to help you.'

A spasm of breath left Angela and his face darkened.

'That was all it was,' he said, his face suddenly bleak. 'And now you do this. You come here, putting me and my family at risk.'

A sliver of fear sliced through her; she wasn't sure what he meant.

He went to the kitchen and began to open cupboards and slam them closed. She wondered what he was going to do to her. He opened a biscuit tin and slammed it onto the kitchen surface. Change inside rattled like a snare drum. He stood there, hunched, flushed, counting coins and then dropping them into his pocket. There was no sound from the children in the living room.

Nick walked back towards her and pointed at her with a mean, cruel twist to his face, his eyes no longer brown but black.

'Stay here.'

He ran upstairs and Angela waited as he had ordered, staring at her feet and then touching the plaster. Her wrist stung.

His feet sounded on the stairs. He was holding something in his hands, a bowl or a cup. He set it down near the phone and it was only then that she realised it was a piggy bank. He opened it and began to pull notes from inside and then force them into his wallet. Angela wondered if the piggy bank belonged to one of the children. If it did, she felt sad for them. She hadn't thought he would be this way. His hands seemed to shake, raking inside the pig with his fingers.

Not looking at her, he picked up the phone in the hall, listened for a moment and then pressed one of the keys before hanging up. A cold feeling clutched her heart as she wondered if he had just called 999.

Eyes still black and forbidding he held out his hand; it was full of cash. 'Take this.' He filled one of her hands with coins and folded the fingers of her other hand over a pile of notes that were crumpled from being inside the pig. 'I called you a taxi. You'll need to give the address of your dad, mum or who-ever. That should be enough.'

'Will it be so much?'

'I think so, yeah.'

'I could get the train again. I think I can ...'

'I've called the taxi. You shouldn't be anywhere near here. It's too far to Croydon and you could get lost. It'll be here any moment. You take the money and go straight home, and tell *no one* that you saw me or that you were here.'

She liked this. Another secret between them. She nodded slowly, but he was still frowning at her. She stuffed the money into her pockets and the action loosened the dressing on her wrist.

He turned his back on her and opened the door, then stood on the doorstep, looking up and down the street. Light fell through the coloured glass of the door and made patterns on the wall. She watched his back and smiled to herself, remembering. She let her thumb creep into her mouth.

The warmth of Mr Dean's hand on her shoulder blades. His face close enough that she could smell his clean, minty breath. *Well done, Angela, well done.*

Jasmine on one side of him and Angela on the other, so that their hands were around his waist while a classmate took a photo. The muscles under his shirt, hard. The weight of his arm on her shoulder. That flutter under her ribcage because she was touching him and he was touching her.

The patterns on the wall disappeared and the hall darkened, a cloud or the sun moving behind the trees. Angela took her thumb out of her mouth, slick with spit, and let her hand fall on her stomach. Another memory blossomed in her mind.

His hand over her face, pressing so hard that it flattened her nose. Feeling his fingers dig into her skin, the sharp pain of them, nails on the sweaty inside of her thigh. Hot breath whispering, *don't tell.*

He came back inside but didn't completely close the door. He seemed agitated.

'I meant what I said – just you turning up at my house – being on my doorstep talking to me, means I'm breaking the law. If anyone finds out about this, I'll go straight to jail for a long time.' He spoke very quietly, leaning towards her. In the close space of the hall, she could smell him. She wanted to see him smile again, all straight white teeth and the sparkle in his eyes, but his face was serious, eyes dark with anger. 'Do you understand?'

'I won't say anything. I won't say I saw you.'

'It's another really terrible position you've put me in. Didn't you realise that? You must have known that.'

'I just wanted to see you again.'

'Why? You tell everyone that I'm a—' he swallowed his words, as if he had meant to swear, 'monster, and then you want to come round and see me.'

'I'm sorry.' She was sorry. She didn't know what she had expected. The fight with her father swirled in her mind again. *Why do you want to kill it? Did you have sex with him?* The flare of his nostrils and the smell of his sweat. She had wanted away from him. She had wanted to see that face she had drawn in pastel and charcoal – the eyes that in the picture had been bigger than in real life. She had wanted to feel kindness.

She glanced up at him – his straight nose and long eyelashes, his perfect lips, the line of stubble across his cheek. She would have liked to sketch him from this angle, in profile, frowning at the car in the drive. She picked absently at the dressing on her wrist as she listened.

She put a hand over the dome of her abdomen.

'Do you think I should get an abortion?'

He raised his eyebrows and ran a hand through his hair. 'I don't think that's something I can advise you on.'

'I think I'll probably get one. I'm just scared it hurts.'

She glanced up at him and noticed that his face was still red, as if he was ashamed. She just wanted to die. She felt cracked, like an egg, her insides leaking out. She wanted him to touch her like before, to tell her she was great. She had believed it for just a moment, when he said it. But then she had ruined everything, that morning in the hall after she had taken the pills and Donna was at her.

'Do you want me to tell the police that I was lying? Do you want me to tell them that you *didn't* touch me that way?'

'The damage is done. If you really want to help me, don't say that you came to my house. Don't say anything any more.'

'I won't say.' She bit her lip and then turned to him. 'Do you believe me?'

'I don't have any choice.' He had that face again – the expression of Max from *Scuttlers*, tied to a chair and waiting for the first blow. He hadn't been acting properly, Angela realised, he had just been showing what he looked like when he was really afraid. It wasn't acting; it was telling the truth.

'I'm telling the truth,' she said, 'I promise I won't tell anyone, ever.'

'Good.'

'Do you think I'm lying?'

Mr Dean said nothing, staring out into the drive, anxious for the taxi to appear.

'Everybody lies, you know,' she said quietly, looking down at her wrist.

Suddenly there was a sound of tyres on the gravel, and Mr Dean thrust the door open. A grey car was reversing into the drive.

'It's here,' he said, turning and taking her elbow.

Angela took a step towards the door and stopped, then looked up again into his face. 'Would you do me a favour?'

He raised one eyebrow at her. 'That depends on the favour.'

'Will you give me a hug goodbye?'

He hesitated, his face sad and frightened at the same time. Angela put her arms around his waist. He smelled so clean that it brought tears to her eyes. She felt him tense under her touch and then gently push her away.

'I just wanted a hug.' She felt glad for the few seconds he had allowed it.

'You need to go now.'

Angela walked down the drive and got into the back seat of the taxi. She gave her mum's address to the driver, and then turned around to watch Nick, who was standing on the doorstep, but he went back inside before she had even pulled out of the drive.

She got out of the taxi on the Portland Road, walked up to her mum's door and tried the handle. It was locked and she didn't have her key. She didn't have anything, except her phone and a few quid change from the taxi ride. She rang the doorbell then waited, heart pounding, unsure how her mother would react. She clasped her elbows, still feeling a shiver from Mr Dean's hug.

The door swung open. Donna didn't say a word but her face opened with relief to see her and Angela felt glad. There was still a faint mark on her cheekbone where Angela had stabbed her.

'I had a fight with Dad.'

'Really? What a surprise. Come in and we'll call him.'

'I'm not going back there.'

'Ever?'

In the kitchen, a glass of wine had been poured.

'I don't know. I want to stay here tonight.'

Her mother leaned against the kitchen counter and scrolled through the contacts on her phone. 'He's not going to like it . . .'

'I don't care,' said Angela.

There was something in her mother's relaxed disapproval that calmed her. Angela felt something pushing up from inside her. She wasn't sure if it was the baby or if it was all the things she had never told fighting to get out. So much had happened to her, and she had swallowed it all.

Donna was leaning against the kitchen counter, phone pressed to her ear.

Years since she had done it, but Angela leaned into her mother and put a hand around her waist. After what seemed like minutes, Angela felt her mother's arm encircle her. They stood like that for a minute, with Angela's head on Donna's shoulder. When she felt her mother's hand smooth the back of her hair Angela bit her lip to stop herself crying.

'There,' Donna said, 'there, there.'

Her mother's grip loosened as her father answered the phone. Angela stood up and folded her arms.

27

Nick

As soon as Angela left, Nick rushed to make dinner. His sister and niece were coming round and he had agreed to make pasta. Rusty needed walking but there was no time now, so Nick let him out into the back yard, and sent Luca and Ava out with him. They ran around and climbed up and down the slide, faces pinking with the cold.

Nick chopped onions and fried them, stirring in pesto and chopped tomatoes, glancing over his shoulder at the shouts of laughter from the yard. He was trembling and Marina would be home soon. He thought about sneaking another joint but there was no way to get time on his own. Leaving the onions to soften in the sauce, he found a half-empty bottle of Orujo at the back of the liquor cabinet and poured two fingers into a mug, wincing as he gulped the spirit back. He returned to the stove, feeling a little better, braced by the alcohol, shocked into a dull, wary calm. He turned down the heat on the pasta as Luca appeared at the back door, eyebrow raised.

'Dad?'

'Yeah?' Nick felt his smile forced, overly enthusiastic.

'Who was that girl who was here?'

'It was just . . . she was just . . . ' he frowned at the bubbling sauce, scraping chopped garlic from the board and stirring it, 'a local school kid collecting money for a charity. Just had to find some money for her. I took some from your piggy bank but I'll pay it back tomorrow.'

Nick glanced at Luca. He was still, hand on the doorknob, regarding Nick, his face impassive. Nick's nerves returned and he drained the pasta although it was a little early, needing something to do to distract from his lie. When he turned again, Luca had gone back into the yard. He sighed audibly, exhausted suddenly, as he poured the pasta and the sauce into a dish, ready for the oven.

Marina got home just before Melissa and Rebecca arrived. Nick had calmed down, the table was set and everything was ready. She smiled weakly at him when she came in, dark circles under her eyes. He put his hands on her waist and tried to pull her into him, but she tugged away. She walked upstairs, and he watched her go, loosening her shirt from her waistband. He looked down at his hand that a moment earlier had rested on her waist. Nothing was the same any longer. He wondered what she was thinking upstairs. He knew some part of her doubted him.

He served up quickly, as soon as his niece and sister arrived. Melissa and Rebecca sat on one side of the table, with Ava and Luca kneeling opposite. Marina was in her usual seat at the top of the table, her hair up, coaching Ava to eat.

'Daddy,' said Ava, twisting and starting to get down, when he got up to slice more bread.

'*Siéntate y acaba de cenar!*' said Marina, pointing. Immediately, Ava turned back to her bowl. The reprimand had been for his daughter, but Nick also felt her scorn.

Nick poked his niece in the ribs and then his sister as he returned to the table. 'Good to see you both.' Marina avoided his eyes.

He helped himself to some more pasta from the pan and sat down beside Marina, tousling Ava's warm hair and reaching to rub Luca's back. 'Is it good?' he said, picking up his fork.

'Pretty good,' said Luca, with a lump of sausage skewered on his fork.

'It was amazing,' said Melissa.

'Have some more,' Marina said, turning to get up, but Melissa stopped her.

'No way, I'm done,' she said, holding her sides.

Nick took a mouthful of food. He had no appetite and was eating almost as slowly as the children. 'One helping of Daddy's pasta's more than enough . . . ' he said, breathing onto the back of Ava's neck so that she giggled and brushed her skin with the back of her hand.

Under the table, he ran a hand over Marina's thigh. She gently moved her leg away from his grasp.

He cast his eyes over the table.

'So anyway ... back to what we were saying; the concert's on the twenty-seventh ... and you're so excited, aren't you?' Melissa said, addressing her daughter.

Rebecca smiled into her empty bowl, revealing her braces. She had become shyer in the past year, even in front of her family, the awkwardness of adolescence.

'Who you going to see?' Nick said, swallowing, looking across the table at his niece.

'Katy Perry,' she said, eyes suddenly shining with excitement.

'*Gonna make you roar . . .* ' Nick leaned across the table with his hand in a tiger's claw.

'That's not even the words,' his niece laughed generously.

'Who you going with?'

'Olivia, my friend from basketball. Her mum's taking us. We're going to try and get right at the front.'

'I've got a race, or I could've . . . ' Melissa shrugged.

Luca and Ava left the table, but Luca came up to Nick and tugged on his elbow. Nick lowered his ear. Fingers cupped over his mouth, Luca whispered, 'Should I not tell Mum about the girl in the hall?'

Nick's chest constricted.

Luca's eager little mouth reached for Nick's ear again. He got up, hand on Luca's head to steer him out of the kitchen into the hall. Nick was relieved that his sister kept talking to Marina, about her race.

'I'll speak to your mum about it,' he said, his face serious.

'Probably best if you don't mention it to her or your sister. Thank you for looking after Ava.'

'She looked sad, the girl in the hall.'

Nick felt his face sag. 'I don't think she was sad, just tired.'

Luca's expression was solemn, making his little boy face seem older, but then he nodded his head and smiled thinly. 'Okay.'

Nick exhaled heavily, all the blood in his fingers and his toes, as Luca ran off to find his sister.

In the kitchen, Nick began to stack the dishwasher, scraping Luca and Rebecca's leftovers into the bin as everyone left the table. As he was bent over, Nick felt Marina's cool hand on the small of his back. He turned, smiling, thinking she had forgiven him.

'What's that? Did you hurt yourself?'

Nick stood up. Marina was pulling at the back of his T-shirt.

'You've got blood on you.'

He held his breath, realising that it must have transferred from Angela's wrist when they embraced.

'Is it blood? I ... uh, don't think I cut myself.' He avoided her eye, but felt his face begin to burn. He took refuge in the dishwasher, but he knew that Marina had seen, and that she wouldn't let it go.

Nick had expected Marina to return to the blood on his shirt the moment that Melissa left, but he was saved by the onslaught of family activities that took them to bedtime. As soon as his sister left, it was bath time and Rusty needed walking, and then there was the news and family calling from Spain. Just as Nick and Marina were getting ready for bed, Luca appeared at the bedroom door, pale-faced and pulling on his lip.

'Accident?' said Nick.

Luca nodded.

Nick ruffled the little boy's hair. 'Don't worry about it, little man. Let's sort it out.'

He changed Luca's sheets, then stayed and rubbed his back for a few moments until he settled again. Nick felt responsible for the bedwetting. Luca had always been bright and sensitive. He didn't miss much and Nick knew that his troubles were affecting his son.

He put the sheets in the wash and then went into the bedroom and began to undress. Marina was sitting on the edge of the bed wearing an old T-shirt, putting cream on her brown legs. He stripped down to his boxers and got into bed.

'Why were you strange earlier?' she said, turning to him suddenly. 'About that mark on your shirt . . . you blushed.'

There was no point in lying.

He inhaled and smoothed the fine hairs on his stomach with one hand before meeting her eye.

'Don't freak out.'

She turned and locked eyes with him, waiting.

'This afternoon Angela came to the house.'

Her brown eyes widened. 'Angela Furness . . . *the girl?*'

He nodded. 'She just turned up. I had to get her a taxi home.'

'*Oh Dios mio!*' she covered her eyes with one hand, springing up from the bed. 'That is against your bail!'

'Don't you think I know that?'

'Did anyone see?'

'Only Luca, Ava I suppose, and the taxi driver. I was terrified.'

'If the police find out ... If she says ... if someone saw ... Why would she come here?'

'She was ... weird. I don't know what's going on in her head. She started clawing her wrist when I told her she shouldn't be here. That's what the blood was. I put a plaster on it but I think it must have transferred onto me somehow.' He decided not to tell Marina that Angela had actually embraced him before she left. He sighed, looking into the palm of his hands.

'All she has to do,' said Marina, eyes glassy with fury and hurt, 'is tell *one person* and you will go to jail. Do you understand?' She held up a finger that quivered before him. 'Her mother, her father ... just one person.'

'I didn't do this. *She* came *here*. She put me in this position. Once again, I had no choice in the matter.'

'Keep your voice down. Luca is probably still awake.'

Nick leaned back against the headboard and closed his eyes. 'I don't believe she'll tell anyone. I don't think so.'

'You don't *think*—'

'She told me she was sorry ... I believe her.'

Marina put her head in her hands and Nick tried to tug her towards him. She sat down on the bed, but shrugged his hand from her shoulder.

'Try not to worry, okay?'

*

The next day was Friday and Marina was working from home. Nick picked up Ava from the childminder and then Luca from school. When they got home, Marina was sitting cross-legged on the floor beside her laptop, the living-room carpet strewn with reports on children in need. She began to tidy up as they entered, hiding the pictures of refugee children crying, and case studies on young girls who had been trafficked across Europe.

Luca charged into the room, reiterating all the stories he had just related to Nick in the car: he and his best friend Jack had caught a spider in the playground and taken it into class where it had escaped into another child's bag, never to be found again. Ava held up her painting – so close that the still-wet green paint of the grass marked Marina's sweater.

As Marina took her work things into the kitchen out of the way, Nick got down onto his knees and began to wrestle the children: tickling Ava until she screamed as Luca sat on his back with a choke-hold around his neck.

The children's laughter was loud, and so close to his ears that Nick didn't hear the phone ring. As Luca fell gently to the floor, Nick lifted his daughter's top and blew a raspberry on her belly.

'Nick!'

Marina stood at the living-room door with the phone pressed to her chest to muffle the sound. Nick frowned, sitting up on his heels, out of breath.

'Again!' Ava called from the floor.

Nick pressed a finger to his lips to hush them as he got up.

'It's the police,' Marina whispered, eyes imploring.

Nick pressed his teeth together as he took the phone from her and left the room.

'Hello?'

'Nick, it's Detective Sergeant Brookes. Can you talk right now?'

Dread flushed through his body. 'Yeah, I ... sure ...'

Marina was at his side. He felt her hand slip into the back pocket of his jeans as she leaned in close and he turned the receiver so they could both hear. His hand trembled.

'I wanted to call you personally, although I'm sure you'll want to talk to your lawyer, too. Your police bail was due to run until the end of the month but because of insufficient evidence we will no longer be pursuing the investigation into the accusation of sexual assault.'

Nick frowned and parted his lips. Marina had not heard or was as stunned as he was – she was still leaning in and looking up into his face.

'So ... what you're saying is ...'

'It's over.'

'But ...' Nick straightened and Marina's hand fell from his pocket. He heard a congratulatory tone in the detective's voice, as if she expected him to be relieved and grateful. 'I mean ... can I get some kind of explanation? Why was I accused of these things? Is there evidence that she was abused by someone else?'

'You know everything there is to know. We have insufficient

evidence to pursue the investigation into the allegations against you.'

'So . . . I'm no longer on bail? There are no restrictions? I can work in schools again . . . as if anyone would ever hire me.'

Detective Brookes had been trying to interrupt him and now her voice was clipped. 'You are no longer on police bail and are no longer restricted from being alone with children.'

Nick breathed through his teeth. There was a ball of rage at the pit of his stomach. 'And my record – it's clear?'

She cleared her throat. 'You have not been charged with any offence. You do not have a criminal record.'

'I know that, but what's happened to me these past months . . . this investigation . . . will it be known? Will it be on my record?'

Brookes cleared her throat. She spoke slowly and quietly. 'You have not been charged with any offence, but if you apply for disclosure, a check on your name will bring up your arrest with a note that there was insufficient evidence to pursue charges of sexual assault of an under-thirteen. Any future police checks on your name will flag that up . . . but if you were under more suspicion, a different report would be issued.'

'Insufficient evidence. It doesn't say I'm innocent.'

'That's right, but you can go back to life as normal. There are no more restrictions placed on you and the investigation is over.'

Nick swore under his breath, and swallowed. 'Yeah, right. Thank you,' he said, eyes burning. He hung up.

'Did she say what I thought she said?'

'Yeah ... it's over. It's all over,' he whispered, the phone heavy in his hand.

Marina's eyes filled with tears. '*Que alivio*,' she murmured, pressing her face into his chest.

He put an arm loosely around her shoulders, resting his chin on the top of her head, then gently removed himself from the embrace. He put the phone back on its stand and stood in the hall, hands on his hips. She reached for him again, but he moved away.

'What is it?'

'What is it?' he turned to her, wide-eyed. 'This is not okay. They put us through this. Our whole lives have been turned upside down. I've not been able to work, we had to ask my parents to look after the kids even though I'm right here, *right here* ... people writing articles and calling me a paedophile online, hurting our child, breaking windows, nutters we haven't even met threatening to ... rape you ...' He covered his face with his hands.

'Keep your voice down. I know how you feel, but let's not be bitter. Let's be happy that it is over.'

'Are you fucking kidding?' Rusty's ball was lying in the centre of his bed. In a single movement, Nick bent and picked up the ball and threw it with all his strength at the hall wall. The ball ricocheted and Marina put her elbows over her face to avoid being hit.

'This is not right,' he whispered. 'It's not fair. I didn't do a damn thing wrong. A girl makes something up and I get dragged over the coals. It's just not fair.'

'I know,' said Marina, hands facing down, pacifying. 'But we have to move on, or else . . . '

His throat hurting with a sour mixture of rage and relief, Nick pulled her into him. He had to forget and forgive the past months, but did not know how.

Part Three

'The rape joke is that time is different,
becomes more horrible and more habitable,
and accommodates your need to
go deeper into it.'

Patricia Lockwood, 'Rape Joke'

28

Angela

She was on her way to school. The day was dark and drizzly and Angela walked slightly hunched over, with her hands in her pockets and her backpack low on her shoulders. She hadn't got up in time and was still hungry, having had only half a bowl of cereal. There were crisps and chocolate in her bag but it was so wet she decided to wait until she got to school. The rain dampened her hair and it began to cling to her face. Angela nudged it aside with the heel of her hand.

Some of the kids had umbrellas but they were the losers. The cool kids just got wet. The weather didn't matter. Her clothes were damp but she didn't care. All she thought about was getting to school and having something to eat.

She watched her baseball boots fall on the pavement, feeling the splash of the puddles soak through the fabric to her socks and feet. Suddenly there was a pair of burgundy Doc Martens before her. Angela stopped and looked up. It was Jasmine, her brown hair exploding in bunches at the side of her head. At first Angela started, glancing behind, in case it was an ambush and she was going to be beaten up by a group of kids, but Jasmine was alone.

'What's up?' said Angela, trying to sound tough.

You couldn't see where Angela had ripped the patch of hair out. It had all grown in, or else the way Jasmine had combed the bunches, it didn't show.

'You're not really pregnant. That's a lie, too.'

Angela tried to push past her, but Jasmine grabbed her elbow and spun her on the pavement. Angela faced her old friend. She didn't want to argue. It was too wet and she was too hungry, but Jasmine was all jaunty angles: hip and folded arms, sloped shoulder and tilted chin.

'Leave me alone.' Angela pushed past her again and went on her way.

'*Leave me alone!*' Jasmine pulled on Angela's backpack and she felt it jerked off her shoulders. It landed heavily in a large puddle.

'Fuck off.'

'No, fuck you, you lying bitch.'

They started screaming at each other. Other kids just avoided them and gave them a wide berth, heads down against the rain. A truck passed and drenched them both in a dark wave of dirt and rainwater.

'In your *dreams* Mr Dean shagged you. You just make

everything up. How would you even know that you're pregnant? You always look pregnant.'

Angela punched her softly in the shoulder, where it didn't really matter, but Jasmine recoiled and then slapped Angela's face, really hard. It shocked her. The wet slap in the cold rain. Instead of striking her back, Angela put a hand to her cheek. Jasmine looked furious – all the whites of her eyes showing, her full lips twisted. The raindrops were resting in her hair, like small jewels.

Angela turned her back on Jasmine and started walking to school as fast as she could. She didn't have the energy for a fight this morning.

'He always liked me more than you. My mum saw the selfie he took with me and said it was clear he was leering at me.' Jasmine was walking just as fast, spitting insults in her ear.

'Whatever,' Angela threw back, putting her hands into the pockets of her hoodie.

'It's true. No one fancies you, not Mr Dean, not Adam. I talked to Adam . . . '

Angela turned for a moment then kept walking.

'He told me all that stuff you said about you two hanging out and making out in the park was bullshit. He said he never touched you.'

Angela hunched over even further. She hadn't been lying. Everyone hated her and so they didn't want to believe her. She was all alone. Walking as fast as she could, Angela ran up the steps that led up to the main building of Croydon Academy. There were twelve steps, and normally Angela took the long way round to save the effort, but today she just wanted to be inside fast. The teachers didn't like her either, but at least they would stop Jasmine hounding her. Her weight and her school bag meant that she couldn't climb as fast as she wanted. She was sweating and her thighs hurt as she tried to speed up. Jasmine was still behind her, like a dog snapping at her heels.

Liar. Bitch. Fatso. Dirty skank.

She was nearly at the top step, the toe of her Converse finding damp concrete. Just then Jasmine tugged at her bag again and Angela slipped backwards. Her hand reached for the railing but the metal was slick with rain. She toppled, crashing into Jasmine, who jumped to the side, then hit the steps with her back before her legs somersaulted over her head and she rolled to the bottom, the hard steps hitting deep in her side and then her forehead, the bone of her arm.

There was a puddle at the bottom of the steps and Angela rolled into it, curled into a ball on her side, not able to get up, her bag still hooked over one shoulder, pinning her arm back.

'Are you all right?' Jasmine said, walking halfway down the steps.

Angela had no words, or rather no air in her lungs to carry them out of her mouth. She propped herself up on one elbow. There was a sharp crushing pain in her stomach and she wondered if she had broken a rib. She put a hand to her lip and saw blood on her fingers. She had bitten her lip when she fell.

Suddenly Jasmine was at her side, taking her schoolbag and then tugging at her arm.

'I can get up by myself,' Angela said, moving onto her behind, then using the railing to get to her feet.

Her knees stung as she tried to get up. Her leggings were torn and black from the wet ground. It was hard to stand up straight and she wrapped her arms around her abdomen.

She couldn't be sure, because her body was so hot now, blood pumping through her so hard that her head throbbed, but she thought her period had started. There was a heavy, aching tug on the inside of her thighs. She looked down as dark wetness flowed from between her legs, soaking her grey leggings. She parted her lips and looked up at Jasmine. Her face had changed, from hate to horror.

'What is it? You shouldn't have worn those leggings, you idiot.'

Angela swallowed, a strange taste in her mouth, metallic, rusty, right at the back of her throat.

'Have you got other stuff to put on?'

Angela's hand was a claw fast around the railing. She was freezing cold all of a sudden, trembling from her scalp to her knees.

'You can put your hoodie round your waist. Come on, I'll take you to Mrs Hegel.'

Mrs Hegel was the teacher responsible for pastoral care. All the girls knew that if they needed to talk, she was the person to go to. Angela had barely spoken to the woman before. Gently, Jasmine took her elbow.

'What's happened to you now, Angela?' said Mrs Hegel, with that patronising voice that all teachers used.

'I fell down the stairs.'

Jasmine was quiet, her face suddenly long and cautious.

'I slipped. It's wet,' Angela sighed, not wanting to explain any more. She could feel she was still bleeding, hot and wet on her thighs.

Mrs Hegel's face became pinched with concern and Angela thought she was appalled by the blood on her leggings, but she asked Jasmine to leave and then picked up the phone and called the nurse.

'I'll get the nurse to come here. It's probably best.'

Angela sniffed and nodded. She sat beside Mrs Hegel's desk, two hands over her stomach. She swallowed tears that ran down the back of her throat, salt and slick.

'I know that you're pregnant, Angela – have you been to see a doctor?'

'No, my dad made an appointment. I'm supposed to go this week.'

Mrs Hegel winced, her lips pursing. Angela wondered if she didn't believe her either.

'I think when the nurse gets here, she'll want you to go to hospital straight away.'

Angela said nothing but raised her eyebrows. She was sick of going to hospital.

'If you're bleeding, it might mean there's something wrong . . . ' Mrs Hegel's eyes softened and she put a hand on Angela's. 'Shall I call your dad?'

'Call my mum,' Angela said, the word *mum* choking her.

29

Stephen

No charges had been lodged against Nicholas Dean because of insufficient evidence.

Stephen turned on the burglar alarm and locked up his flat. He had imagined this moment over and over, but now it was time to act.

What are you going to do? Donna had challenged him. He would have felt better doing it with his own bare hands, but even this way, he would get satisfaction from knowing that justice had been done.

It had been easier than he thought. The man that Stephen contacted on a cheap Nokia pay-as-you-go phone had been easy to find. He was called Simon Hunter and registered to the address he had lived in before prison, with his wife and three children.

'Five hundred pounds. A hundred up front.'

'I'll do it for a thousand, three hundred up front. I'll need to watch him – get him when he goes out. There's more risk in the daylight.'

'All right, a thousand.'

'Is it a woman? I don't do women.'

'It's a man.'

'Do you want him cut?'

Stephen had taken the cash from his bank account in five separate random amounts, just in case. Now he felt the slight weight of the notes in his inside jacket pocket, next to his heart. He was wearing sweat pants, a baseball cap and had the hood of his top pulled up over the hat. He walked away from downtown Croydon, past Norwood Junction station, frowning against the wave of marijuana smoke that dissipated as he walked by a crowd of people dominating the pavement by the bus stop. The road was narrow and busy and smells assaulted him, heavy and clinging: exhaust, kebab, dry cleaners and pizza places.

It was a relief when he saw the park and the narrow road opened up to its green expanse. He entered and walked with his hands in his pockets.

There was an ash tree with a hollow trunk near the railway line, in the far corner of Ashburton Park. Stephen had noticed it over the years, taking Angela to the swing park when she was little, or playing basketball with his colleagues. He had described it exactly to Hunter – how he could feel around the rim of the bark and then up inside the tree, the spider's webs and leaves giving way to the dried-out darkness.

The park was perfect. People came and went, but there was the cover of the trees and no CCTV.

Stephen walked slowly across the grass, not drawing attention to himself. It was the afternoon, and few people were around – even the children's playground was deserted. He walked past the old youth club defaced with graffiti, the tall trees swaying in the distance alongside the ripped wire fencing that ran along the rear side of the railway track. One side of the old convent library was covered in scaffolding. As he passed the building, Stephen looked up at a motto engraved in sandstone above one of the arched doors: *God be our help.*

The money was in a polythene bank bag and Stephen had handled it and the money inside only with gloves. He took it out from his inside pocket as soon as he entered the darkened corridor of high trees, then tucked it quickly up inside the hollow ash as he passed.

His heart thumped in his chest as he stood behind the hedgerow by the bowling club. Silently, he remonstrated with himself for the nerves. He wasn't afraid of being found out – he had taken no chances – but didn't like asking for help. He didn't relish divesting his power to another person. He wanted to hurt Dean himself.

Suddenly, through the tunnel of trees, Stephen observed a man – medium height, balding, a small comfortable gut, dark jacket, jeans and trainers. He was unremarkable, apart from the fact that he stopped briefly at the ash tree and reached inside.

Stephen walked home and had just turned the key in the lock when a text in the basic phone vibrated in his pocket.

Three hundred received. Will text when complete.

Stephen went inside, hurriedly turned off the burglar alarm, and then poured himself a finger of whisky. He had taken a risk for Angela. Not for the first time, he hoped that she had been telling the truth.

30

Donna

Donna plumped the pillows and folded the duvet onto the sofa, then tucked Angela in, setting a little table at her side with juice and chocolates and her iPad. Now that she'd had a bath, Angela was pale, and with her wet hair slicked back, her face seemed blank and bloated.

Donna had had to leave work yet again to go to the school, where she had found Angela filthy and bloodied after the fall.

'Do you want me to put a movie on for you?'

She shook her head, pillows at her back and her sketchpad on her knee.

'Just shout if you need anything.'

Angela nodded, lips pressed together.

'Are you in pain?' Donna put a hand on her forehead.

She shook her head.

'I'll get you a sweater to put on over your pyjamas.'

Upstairs, Donna took an old sweatshirt from one of the bottom drawers, then sat down on Angela's bed and put her head in her hands.

Grief flooded her.

Tears curled over Donna's chin and she nudged them away with the back of her hand. Looking down, she saw a white box poking out from under the bed. Stripped of its duvet, the mess underneath Angela's bed was clear to see. Donna leaned down and saw that it was her daughter's old jewellery box: the same jewellery box she had loved as a little girl, watching the ballerina twirl as the tune played. Donna reached down and stroked the box with her fingers, but had learned her lesson there. Angela was entitled to her privacy. After all she had been through, she was at least entitled to that.

Donna stood and looked at her reflection in Angela's wardrobe mirror. A tired, middle-aged woman looked back at her. How had her life turned into this? Everything she had been raised to want was now twisted and warped, mocking her. She turned away from the mirror. She was standing in the exact spot where Angela had been when she vomited after taking the pills.

Donna put a hand over her mouth. She was a terrible mother. She had been angry that morning, angry with her daughter for trying to kill herself. It had been an inconvenience. Now she knew why Angela had been so desperate.

The doctor in the emergency room had been clear.

'I can confirm that your daughter has had a miscarriage. It may have happened naturally, but considering the circumstances in which it occurred, it is more likely that the fall caused it.'

Angela had been monosyllabic about the accident, but she had said that Jasmine had tugged on her bag on the stairs, causing her to lose balance. She closed her eyes, teeth resting on her knuckles, remembering her words to the doctor.

'She was due to have an abortion at the clinic tomorrow. The police were aware of it ... She won't tell me *who*, and I need to know.'

The doctor had smiled sympathetically – a thin, weary smile that Donna imagined she had offered many times, to the dying and the distraught. It consoled without true comfort. 'The best person to tell you who the father is ... is Angela herself.'

Slowly, Donna descended the stairs, the sound of the television just audible through the closed living-room door. She watched Angela from the bottom of the stairs. She was sketching a face, head resting against the sofa. Angela had Stephen's hair and eyes and the shape of her face was the same as Stephen's mother, who had died shortly after their wedding. As puberty took hold in Angela, Stephen became more visible in her daughter's face – nose and chin. It was as if Stephen was not content with claiming their daughter's heart, he had to claim her body, too.

'Who you drawing?'

'No one. Just a face.'

Over her shoulder, Donna recognised the face as Nicholas Dean. It wasn't so much that the sketch resembled the man, but rather that the sketch resembled all of Angela's previous attempts at drawing him.

The charges had been dropped. The CPS were not going to prosecute him. Donna didn't want to aggravate her daughter when she was so vulnerable, but she needed to know, once and for all, what had happened. She was willing to risk another disagreement and Angela running back to her father's; she had to know.

She ran a hand over Angela's slick hair. 'C'mon, love, let me dry your hair.'

'It'll dry on its own.'

'I know that, but come and I'll dry it for you.'

Angela sat by the dressing table in her mother's room, looking at herself in the mirror, while Donna sat on the bed and gently brushed her daughter's hair, curling it under at the ends, as she had done when Angela was small.

'That feels nice.'

Donna smiled. 'You always liked getting your hair brushed and dried. I used to put you to sleep running my fingers through your hair. Do you remember that?'

Angela nodded and Donna moved the brush under the warm air of the dryer, careful not to tug as her daughter moved. She stroked from the root and curled the hair under, using the dryer to set it. Angela's face in the mirror was peaceful, relaxed.

'I remember when you were at nursery and when you first went to school. You always used to insist I brushed your hair and put it in a ponytail. You wouldn't let your dad do it.'

'He used to pull it. Accidentally. It hurt when he did it.'

Donna smiled, taking her time and brushing the wet strands, then working the dryer from the roots down to the ends.

'Are you feeling better, or still sore?'

'My legs and my back hurt, especially the first time I lie down. If I don't move it's OK.'

'I can put a duvet on top of your mattress tonight. Help to make it softer.'

Angela nodded, lips pressed together.

'Are you still bleeding?' Their eyes met in the mirror.

'It's stopped now, I think.'

'Best to still wear the pad during the night.' The hospital had sent them away with huge, thick, sanitary pads.

Angela tilted her chin up – a strange, aggressive nod.

Donna worked the brush through her hair again, lowering the heat of the dryer to make the whole process last longer. Angela closed her eyes in pleasure at the sensation.

'I was glad that you came home to me. I never wanted you to leave. Not really.'

Angela opened her eyes. 'You said you hated me.'

'I'm sorry. I didn't mean it.' Donna ran the brush along the nape of Angela's neck. 'Maybe we both said and did things that we're not too proud of.'

Angela nodded vigorously, so much so that Donna had to loosen her grip on the brush so as not to tug the hair. 'I'm sorry I hurt your face,' she said, fiddling with jewellery on the dressing table.

'That's all right.'

Her words brought a thin-lipped smile from Angela.

'I lost a baby, you know, before I had you.'

It was dangerous, and Donna didn't really want to talk about it, but she needed Angela to talk to her about what she knew.

'Not as bad as what happened to you. I had an abortion. I had planned on telling you, if you had gone through with ... ' Donna stopped, watching Angela's eyes in the mirror for a reaction.

'You mean, like a brother or sister?'

Donna lowered the hairdryer and ran the brush through her hair. 'No, it was before I met your dad. I try not to think about it, but it was with someone who hurt me ... a long time ago. I was older than you, a young woman.' Donna smiled at the mirror, and the image of their two faces blurred because of the tears that pricked her eyes. 'But I don't think it matters how old you are. It's something that's not supposed to happen and so it's hard to ... deal with.'

'Did you want the baby?' Angela was unemotional, blue eyes dark and fierce, but there was an eagerness in her voice.

'I didn't know,' Donna swallowed, being honest, 'I wasn't ready for it. I didn't want to be pregnant, that was all ... but the abortion was hard. I did it on my own. My mum wasn't there, as you know, and I didn't have girlfriends to go along as I hadn't told anyone about it.'

'Why didn't you tell?'

Donna turned the hairdryer back on, keeping the heat

strong but the jet on low, so that she could continue styling without the noise. 'I guess because it wasn't a boyfriend. It wasn't someone I was with. It was someone who ... hurt me and then suddenly things were happening to my body that I had no choice about. The doctor told me I was pregnant. It was in my body and I had to deal with whatever consequences there were ... but that had been forced on me by someone else.'

Donna watched her daughter's eyes carefully. There was still no glimmer of recognition.

'Who was it ... that hurt you?' Angela spoke carefully, her face still closed.

'It was someone I trusted. At the time I thought I had to obey him. He was as old as my father. I worked with him. He was in a position of power ...'

Angela's hair was dry. Donna drew the brush through it a few more times, and Angela closed her eyes to each stroke.

'That's horrible,' said Angela, opening her eyes and smiling at Donna in the mirror.

She smiled back.

'You were ... raped?'

Donna held her breath, and nodded.

Angela lowered her gaze and Donna couldn't resist any longer. She bent down and hugged her daughter, folding her arms in front of her chest. She opened her eyes and looked at their reflection, tears streaming down Donna's face. Angela was passive in her arms, neither welcoming nor spurning the embrace.

'I wish we had something else in common,' Donna half-laughed, knuckling tears from her cheeks.

'We don't have that in common,' Angela said plainly, her face suddenly frozen.

'What do you mean?' Donna took time to react to the tone, tasting tears in her throat. She let her hands rest on her daughter's arms.

'What about Mr Dean?'

'He didn't rape me.'

'But he sexually assaulted you?'

Angela shrugged, her face at once angry and full of pain.

'Who made you pregnant? You must know, darling.'

She nodded, but only once, so that it was less a confirmation than an acknowledgement. Their eyes locked in the mirror.

'Who, then? That boy from school? Adam?'

Angela shook her head. 'Jasmine said I was a skank, because I went with him, and because of the thing with Mr Dean. No one believes me. Jas didn't believe I was pregnant. Everyone just hates me.'

'Well, *I don't hate you*,' said Donna, sinking to her knees and taking Angela by the shoulders. 'I believe you. I love you, and I'm sorry if I wasn't there for you, but I want to make things better. You can't go on like this anymore.'

Angela reached out and touched her thumb to the scar on Donna's cheekbone where the pen had cut. 'I made a mark.'

'It'll go away in time – but this business will not go away. I need you to talk to me, Angela. I need you to tell me the truth.'

She sighed, chubby hands in her lap. 'I can't tell you.'

'Why not?'

'I promised I wouldn't say.'

'That promise doesn't count. You're just a little girl – you're not supposed to be pregnant.'

'I'm not a little girl,' Angela flashed, recoiling from her touch suddenly, half-turning back to the mirror and picking up the brush. There was a deep flush on her throat and cheek and Donna knew she was close to talking. If gentleness didn't work, then provoking her might.

'I know. I know that. It's not what I meant. I mean you're young and you should be enjoying life, enjoying school and your friends, not going through all this. You don't owe this person that hurt you anything at all. He has no right to ask you to keep it secret. Tell me who it is, and I promise I won't let him hurt you *ever* again.'

'You can't.'

Donna took her by the shoulders. 'Of course I can, darling. I'm your mother and I'll protect you. I won't let anyone hurt you.'

Angela smiled, a strange bitter smile that was soaked in sadness. 'No one else can tell what he's really like. He's a good actor. Everyone always believes him. They would never believe me.'

'*I* would believe you. Are you talking about Dean?'

Angela said nothing, looking down into her hands. 'Can I stay here then?'

'Of course. You mean, go back to the old arrangement?'

'Yes. I just want to stay with you.'

Donna was still on her knees before her daughter. Angela leaned forward and put her arms around her mother. Donna pressed her close. 'This isn't finished, darling. You need to tell me what happened. Whenever you are ready, I will listen, okay?'

Angela nodded and turned towards the mirror, teasing her styled hair over her forehead with its ugly green bruise.

31

Marina

She could have done without a big family dinner today.

Marina ran towards the barriers at Waterloo with only two minutes to catch the Farnham train. Her head was aching from smog, the rush-hour crowds and a day of work that had left her neck and shoulders tight with tension. She scanned her Oyster card and then stepped onto the train, just before the doors closed. Scanning the carriage for a seat she felt a wave of fatigue. She had had an argument with Theresa just before she left work and now felt ill.

'Don't take this personally,' Theresa had said, with her ubiquitous wincing smile.

'Of course it's personal; how else am I supposed to take it?'

'It was a purely pragmatic decision. Things are crucial right now, with the political arena the way it is. We can't expose ourselves to potential scandal ...'

*

Marina managed to get a seat wedged in the corner of the carriage. She put her briefcase on her lap. There was no time to go home and change; she would need to go straight to Betty and Tom's. The whole family would be there, and Nick had texted earlier to say that his sister, Melissa, would collect Marina from the train.

Marina sighed and closed her eyes as the train lurched into movement. The carriage was a febrile chamber of body odour and heady cologne, making her headache worse. She just wanted to be home and in her sweats, cooking and drinking wine while Nick bathed the children and put them to bed. She loved her family and she was almost as close to Nick's parents as she was to her own, but there was still that requirement to be polite, to help out, and to be *happy* despite everything that was wrong in their lives.

What had happened today wasn't Nick's fault, but after his arrest somehow they had both stood accused. Somehow the crime he had been accused of had also become her culpability.

She opened her eyes in case she fell asleep and missed her stop. The guard was passing and Marina flashed her travel pass. She was trying not to think about it, but nevertheless, the conversation with Theresa returned to her.

Marina had been dealing with some last-minute emails when the Chair of the Board of Trustees called her into the small meeting room. As usual, the cut of Theresa's clothes was expensive, her make-up exact and her jewellery heavy. She was at least twenty years older than Marina. Nothing about Theresa was ever out of place, not a hair or a smudge or a colour mismatched.

'Would you like a coffee?' Theresa asked and Marina sensed something in her tone, a placating eagerness that immediately unnerved her.

'I'm fine, thanks.'

Theresa clasped her long thin fingers on the table. 'I wanted to speak to you about this in person. I think official news of the appointment will go out some time tomorrow, but I wanted to make sure you heard it from me first.'

Marina had raised an eyebrow, unable to think what Theresa was hinting at.

'We've appointed Martin Chalmers to manage the day-to-day operations of Care, and I hope he'll join us next month. I think he's fairly well known in the sector; you might know him. He'll report to me directly and we're hoping for the time being that he'll take the helm here.'

Theresa smiled and Marina tried to respond but felt the strain on her face. 'Are you . . . am I being fired?'

'Good God, no, Marina.' Theresa reached out to her, bony hand flat on the table. 'You do a sterling job, but in the current climate I think that Martin will be a . . . steadier figurehead.'

'So you're bringing him in above me? He has less experience than me. I'm expected to report to him?'

'No, of course not, that would get too complicated. You can continue to report to me, but Martin will take on some of your strategic role and, as I said, will be our new figurehead.'

Marina felt her lungs losing air. 'Why?' her voice was almost inaudible.

Theresa's eyes narrowed. 'I thought you might have seen it coming with the DfID bid – we've not had government investment at this level before – it is a significant endorsement but we are at that tricky stage; trying to grow from a middle-sized to a bigger charity involves greater scrutiny, greater accountability . . .'

'*I know that.*' Marina felt anger and hurt swirling inside her. 'I worked for that funding. I won that—' She fought to keep her voice level and to purge the emotion from her tone.

'I know, but you also know what goes hand in hand with accepting the funding. The director will need to undergo *full security clearance*. This requires you to reveal all your personal finances, relationships and past relationships. It really is intrusive and makes many people uncomfortable.'

'I am fully aware of that, but I can withstand scrutiny.'

'Well,' Theresa cocked her head to one side, like a bird on a lawn sensing a predator, 'it has the potential to bring things out into the open in . . .' she licked her lips as she struggled to find the word, 'an uncomfortable way.'

Heat rose in Marina's cheeks. Suddenly she sensed the truth that Theresa had been circling around. 'Bring *what* out in the open?'

'If it had been *anything* else . . . if he had been accused of robbing a bank . . .' Theresa's eyes crinkled up – an attempt at humour, which fell flat.

'But . . . it's over,' Marina said, hearing her breath in her throat. 'The investigation is no longer to be pursued. They've dropped everything. He's innocent. No charges. It's finished.'

Now Theresa's face was placating, patronising – a thin-lipped smile below her sparkling granite eyes. 'I know, but the press and the uproar in the community, the parents' forum . . . not to mention the fact that someone obviously specifically connected Child International with this debacle of yours . . . '

'It's all over now.' Marina's cheeks were burning.

'It might actually have been better if he had been charged, but this way . . . insufficient evidence, the parents still having no answers . . . it leaves us open to attack, or even to having the funding withdrawn. I came up with this solution and I was sure that you would support it. Your role has only been altered very slightly – it's a sideways move in reality, and I want to take this chance again to say what an asset you are to us.'

The train shuddered and Marina had to take a deep breath to stop angry tears from spilling. She cleared her throat and flicked through her phone in a desperate attempt to distract herself from her thoughts. There were no new texts from Nick. She took another long, deep breath, mouthing the words, *not his fault*. But then whose fault was it? Her career had been hobbled, through no fault of her own. She blinked quickly, and then kept her eyes closed, remembering again the images she had seen on the computer. There was no evidence that he sexually assaulted or raped Angela Furness, but he may well have fantasised about it.

Marina opened her eyes.

A text arrived from Melissa saying she was already waiting at Farnham station.

Melissa hooted her horn as soon as Marina left the platform. She waved and began to walk towards her sister-in-law's red Audi.

'Hey sis,' said Melissa, leaning over and planting a kiss on her cheek as Marina put on her seatbelt. 'Good day?'

'Not bad,' Marina lied. 'How was yours? Thanks for coming to get me.'

'No bother. It made sense,' said Melissa, straining to the right before pulling out onto the Approach Road. 'I texted Nick to say I'd be passing. I had a client cancel on me.' After a lucrative career in finance, Melissa was now a personal trainer. 'It means Nick doesn't need to leave the kids with Mum and Dad again.'

Marina pressed her teeth together in annoyance. It was only a fifteen-minute drive to the station so Nick would only have left the children with them for half an hour. She knew Betty and Tom had felt obligated while Nick was still being investigated, and probably Melissa was protective and indignant on their behalf. 'I'm starved,' she said, choosing not to rise to the bait.

'Well, you're in luck. I heard there's enough to feed an army as usual.'

The children launched themselves at Marina as soon as she walked in the door, Luca with his arms around her waist and

Ava encircling her thigh. She let her briefcase fall to the floor and did her best to smile at Betty, who was standing at the kitchen door. The house smelled of roast lamb. Nick had been helping his mother in the kitchen and came out with a glass of wine in his hand, all smiles and blond hair.

He helped her off with her jacket, plucked Ava from her leg and kissed her cheek. Again, Marina restrained herself. Anger swelled in her, but she stopped herself for snapping at Nick for beginning to drink before they had even discussed who would drive home.

'Give your mum a chance to get in the door,' Nick said. The children tore back along the hall and into the living room with their cousins.

Nick took her face in his hands. She lowered her eyes, knowing that if she looked at him, all her hurt and anger would be visible.

'Guess what?' he said.

She looked up. His eyes were sparkling with excitement.

'What?'

'Guess . . .'

'Darling, I'm not in the mood,' Marina said, taking his hands from her face but holding them. 'What?'

'Not only did I get a new contact for media training that's likely to bring in eight grand, but . . . wait for it . . . I have an audition on Friday for . . .' he held her arms, 'the *lead role* in a new West End version of *The Great Gatsby*.'

'Oh, sweetheart,' said Marina, hugging him despite the conflicting emotions pitching inside her, 'that's wonderful.' In his arms, she thought how she was genuinely happy for him, and needed his comfort, yet loathed the parts of him that had now been laid bare. Loathed. It was how she felt.

He hugged her back, running a hand over her shoulder blades.

'You all right?'

'Yeah,' she said, releasing him, 'just a bad day.'

He raised his eyebrows. She still loved his face and the way he looked at her, moving his brown eyes over her features, as if trying to read her.

'I'll tell you later.'

'No,' he put his arms around her waist, 'tell me now.'

She groaned and rested her head on his chest for second and then looked up into his face. 'Theresa's putting someone in above me.'

'What? How can she do that? You're at the top.'

'Not anymore. That big government grant – apparently I won't withstand the scrutiny.'

His face immediately darkened. 'Because of me.'

'No, no,' she tugged his hands from her hips, hung up her jacket and put her briefcase and keys by the coat rack. She kicked off her shoes. 'It was my own fault. I probably said too much, too soon.'

'But you had to, right? You were only being honest – declaring a potential conflict of interest and *Theresa was the one* that said it was insignificant.'

'Yeah, well, she's changed her mind. Honesty, it seems, is not always the best policy.' She offered a wry smile.

Nick picked up his glass of wine, which he had placed on the hallstand. 'Here.'

'No, I'll need to drive us home.'

'I'll do it. I've only had a sip. You win the wine prize tonight.' He kissed her and for a second she almost felt better.

She took a sip from his glass. The wine was warm, but she didn't care.

Dinner was roast lamb, cauliflower cheese, new potatoes and baby peas. As soon as the food hit the table, the whole family began to talk and load their plates. Betty had given Ava, Luca, Jennifer and Jack dinner slightly earlier, and they were now in the den with Jack in charge. Rebecca was at the dinner table, however, her long red hair loose and hanging over one shoulder as she ate slowly, giggling at the ritual teasing from her Uncle Mark.

Betty was seated next to Marina and smelled of cigarette smoke and hairspray. She ate little, but coaxed everyone else to fill their plates. Tom was drinking red wine, his cheeks and nose turning red as beets. Nick was happy and almost miraculously returned to his old self, Marina mused, as she put a forkful of cauliflower into her mouth. He was young again, boyish, mischievous, the family clown, the little boy they all loved.

What would his family think if they knew what she knew about him?

Marina smiled and drank wine and replied when she was spoken to, but she felt as if she were underwater. She was still so heavy from her day, and found the interaction an effort. Her throat ached, as if she could lose control at any moment, and so she had little appetite. It reminded her of the very early days when she had come to England as a student: sitting at dinner tables and at bars feeling tired from the effort of translating everything that was said to her.

She no longer felt that fatigue; she dreamed in English now, but the sense of alienation was familiar.

This was her family – her English family – the grandparents, uncles and aunts of her children, yet she felt alone tonight.

Reading her, Nick put his hand at the small of her back, but kept on talking to Rebecca, who was telling a breathless story about her performance in her school production of *Beauty and the Beast*.

' . . . and I totally forgot my words . . . and I felt, like, my face getting really, really red, and the light from the stage was so bright I couldn't see anyone.'

'That's the thing,' Nick interrupted, 'it's so bright, it makes you feel as if you're alone up there, when in fact in the darkness there are hundreds of people watching you.'

' . . . but then, all of a sudden I remembered my words. And it, like, felt, like, it had been *the* longest time, but when I spoke to my friends afterwards they said it was just, like . . . a dramatic pause or something and I'm like, yay, I got away with it.'

'Sounds like you got talent, baby,' Nick said, eyes smiling, pointing his fork at her.

Marina looked at her food. *Don't call her baby*, she thought, then admonished herself for being so critical of his every word.

'Finish that, love,' said Betty, holding the dish of cauliflower out to Nick, who obediently emptied the last of the vegetable onto his plate.

'So, how was Katy Perry?' Nick asked, but Rebecca's face fell.

'It's next week, but I might not be able to go. Olivia's mum can't take us now.' Rebecca looked nervously at her mother.

Nick looked at his sister for explanation. Melissa talked to the table, forking a piece of lamb and taking another potato. 'It's not a problem. I'll find someone else to take you both.'

'Why, what's wrong with Olivia's mum?' Nick asked.

'She sprained her ankle really badly and she's not supposed to put weight on it, so, I guess, standing for all that time ... and also she's kind of on a crutch, so it would be pretty difficult for her to be, like, in a crowd ... ' Rebecca visibly sighed, then began to eat her peas, one at a time.

'We'll work something out if we can,' said Melissa, stiffly. 'If not, I'm sure Katy Perry'll be back again soon.'

'Or we could go by ourselves?' said Rebecca so quietly that Marina thought she was the only one who heard it.

'You're not old enough,' said Melissa, quickly, curtly.

'We *look it*.' Rebecca raised a rebellious eyebrow at her mother, but coloured immediately as Melissa's stern gaze fixed on her.

'You've got the race, right?' Nick said, wiping his mouth with a napkin as he met his sister's eyes.

Melissa nodded.

'I'll take you, Becks. We shall *roar* at Katy Perry.'

Rebecca dropped her cutlery with a clatter. 'No way? Really? Oh my God, I've got to tell Olivia. That would be so great. Seriously ... that would be *so great*.'

'We're on, then. I'd love it.'

Everyone was smiling apart from Melissa.

Mark began to organise a collection of the plates, leftovers and cutlery.

Nick began to jive in his seat. '*I am the tiger and I'm gonna hear* . . .'

Rebecca rolled her eyes. 'Still wrong.'

'Will you two calm down?' Betty joked as Mark handed her the plates.

'Was that the *Rocky* theme tune?' Tom offered.

'Oh Dad, please, that was a *very* dated reference,' Graham joked. 'I shall begin your re-education next week.'

'It's quite all right,' Melissa said suddenly, over the clamour and chatter, her face visibly colouring with what seemed to Marina like anger, 'my race isn't that important. *I'll* take her.'

'But Mum?' Rebecca whispered before she was silenced by another caustic glance.

'It's fine. I don't want you to miss out on your concert.' Melissa was sitting erect in her chair.

Nick grinned, palms up on the table. 'But . . . I can take her. You don't need to miss your race. I'd love to do it, honest. We'll have fun, eh, Becks?'

Rebecca raised her shoulders in silent delight.

Melissa shook her head, but it was more of a shudder that shook her whole body. 'No, it's fine. I shouldn't have mentioned it. We have it covered, but thank you anyway for volunteering.'

Marina watched Nick's Adam's apple bob on his throat. His palms were still turned upwards on the table.

'What?' Nick looked at his sister.

Silence fell on the table and the hairs raised on Marina's arms. She wondered if her morose mood was skewing her perception, but then Melissa said, in a voice that was almost clinical in its coldness, 'Rebecca, can you leave us to talk? Go and see what your brother and sister are doing.'

Without another word, face red to the roots of her hair, Rebecca did as she was told and left the table.

'What is it?' Nick said, quietly, and Marina watched the confusion on his face.

Unaware of the seconds of communication that had passed, Betty proudly placed an enormous trifle in the middle of the table and Mark stacked bowls and spoons beside it.

'I was just offering to help,' said Nick. 'What's wrong? Why can't I just take her? You go to your race, Olivia's mum stays home with her feet up – everybody's happy – including, it would seem, Rebecca.'

'It's just not necessary,' Melissa said coldly.

'Oh for God's sake,' said Tom, picking up a serving spoon. 'Let's have some pudding.' He smiled and nudged Graham, who was in a confusion of wanting to maintain the beneficent equilibrium, his normal role, and support his wife. 'They're trifling over nothing, eh?'

No one laughed, but Graham humoured him, putting on a posh voice and echoing, 'A mere trifle, sir,' as he spooned a portion of the dessert into his bowl.

Melissa was undeterred. 'All right, I'll say it, if you want me to.'

'Say what?'

All the energy in the room was pitched between Nick and his sister. Marina was aware of the tug, an almost tangible force between the two.

'I don't think it's appropriate for *you* of all people to be taking two thirteen-year-old girls to a concert.'

'Me of all people? What does that mean? I'm her uncle.' His voice was now a whisper, as if it might crack.

'Yeah, well, I just don't think it's right.'

'You don't think *what's* right? Me?' Nick said, visibly shrinking in his chair. Silence mottled the room. His eyes fell to the table, hands in his lap.

Marina swallowed and then got to her feet, putting a hand on Betty's shoulder in apology for what she was about to say.

'Listen, we're gonna go. I've had a tough day at work and the kids are tired . . . ' Marina turned to Melissa. 'But you should say what you mean, you know, sis?' She arched an eyebrow. 'Not appropriate? Of course it's appropriate, but what you mean is that you do not trust your brother, your own blood.' Marina pushed her chair into the table. 'It's good to know, finally, whose side you are on. This man is your brother; you have loved him all your life. He is my husband, and this year has been a test for us, a struggle, but I tell you something . . . ' Her heart was pounding so hard she could hardly hear her words. 'I love him better than you do. I know him better than you do. You almost do not know him at all.'

Nick was open-mouthed beside her. Everyone was still for a moment, as if after an explosion. The words settled in each of their hearts, like dust.

'Let's go.'

Nick nodded, followed her into the living room, where she picked up Ava. He took Luca by the hand. In the hall, his parents were both standing, faces blanched with sadness. Nick hugged them both, but Marina could not bring herself to – not that she blamed Betty and Tom, but she could not be a part of this. She could not condone this spectacle any longer. It was like the *matanza* – and now she saw that Nick, and herself, their whole family, was the pig roped to a board screaming its lungs out.

Marina strapped the kids into the car, and then got into the front seat and put on her seatbelt.

They sat in the drive for a few moments, watching the house with the light in the doorway, Nick with the key in the ignition. Marina flipped down the vanity mirror and ran her thumb underneath her lids, sweeping away eyeliner that had smudged when her eyes teared. In the mirror, she caught Luca's eyes, watchful, concerned, all-seeing.

'Thank you,' Nick said to the windscreen, turning the ignition and switching on the headlights. 'How could she even think that about me? I just didn't know what to say, and then you said it for me. Thank you, *bonita* . . . '

She turned to him. 'Don't call me that. Take us home right now.' The anger that had waited inside her for so long was now rising. Her heart thudded as she waited for the car to start.

'What's the matter? Why are you angry? You were amazing in there.'

'*You're* what's the matter. Take us home.'

'But—'

'Take us home.'

Not saying another word, Nick reversed out of the drive and then drove in silence to Firgrove Hill. She kept her face angled away, glancing at him only when she turned into the back to check on the children. The muscle in his cheek twitched and she knew he was clenching his teeth.

In the back, Ava and Luca were serious and silent, sensing a row.

As Nick turned onto Long Bridge, they were nearly home. Marina unbuckled her seatbelt before he had even turned into their drive. She was shaking now, at the end of her tether – knowing that there was no other option than to let the children see it.

The bloodied pig, screaming for life and freedom, flashed in her mind.

He pulled on the handbrake and reached for her hands.

'Hey,' he said, pacifying, but she slid her hands from his and left the car, taking Ava out of her seat and setting her down and then ushering Luca out.

It had rained heavily while they were having dinner and now the gravel drive and the pavements smelled of the thrashing: wet earth and flint, dampened stone. The humid air felt too thick in her lungs.

'I don't understand,' he started, hands at his sides, palms

turned towards her, at once asking for a fight and attempting to defuse the tension. 'You back me up, and I'm grateful and now you're like this. I know you've had a bad day but—'

'Is nothing to do with bad day. Is you.' Her grammar always left her in extreme emotional states.

She pulled Ava and Luca towards her, one on each side. Palms of her hands on their warm heads. Luca resisted her slightly but she was only just aware of it, anger and grief and a sickening despair making her body rigid with tension.

'Yes, I took your side. I am your wife. I love you.' Her voice broke now, tears burning then chilling on her cheeks. 'But I cannot love what you did. I hate it and it's making me . . . hate you.'

His face blurred and she blinked the tears away. His whole body seemed to sag. 'Marina, you can't believe that I did that.'

'What am I to think?' She almost had no breath. It came to her in spasms. 'What you look at disgusts me. You disgust me.' She was aware of the crown of Ava's head in her palm and her young son by her side. She gulped, struggling to contain herself. 'I found another video on my laptop. You can't control yourself, can you?'

His lips pinched in what she imagined must be shame.

'It doesn't mean anything,' he shouted, loud enough that she flinched. 'It's just p—' He stopped, heel of his hand to his forehead, turning away from them in frustration.

Porn. Just pornography. It was what he meant but wouldn't say in front of the children.

'If it doesn't mean anything, why do you need it? Why, after all we have been through, you still want to watch those things? And why that, only that? Just that video. I saw you watched it twelve times. I couldn't watch it once.'

His shoulders sagged, the anger gone and his face sad now, tired out.

'Yeah, well, you're perfect, aren't you?'

'I'm not perfect, but you're my husband and their father so why must you look at it . . . does it excite you?'

Arms heavy at his side. 'Yes, it excites me, all right. That's all. But it has nothing to do with us. I want you to understand that—'

'I don't understand it and I don't want to. I don't want you in the house with us. I don't want you here.'

'What?' He took a step towards her, but she backed away, taking Ava with her. Luca stood alone between them.

The words had been said and now Marina was calm, waves of pain travelling through her muscles as her lungs heaved. She sniffed and wiped her face with one hand, not taking her arm from her daughter.

'You can't be serious.'

'Go back to your parents, your brother's, I don't care. I don't want you in the house with us tonight.'

She turned to go inside, but Luca was still rooted to the spot in the centre of the driveway.

'*Ven aquí. Ahora,*' she called to him and finally he turned and followed them in.

Inside, at the window, Marina watched as Nick stood rocking with his head in his hands and then got into the car and drove away.

32

Nick

'Melissa didn't mean that,' Betty said.

Nick sat at the kitchen table, head in his hands over a mug of lukewarm, milky tea. He didn't want to talk about it. He hadn't been home to Firgrove Hill for two days and was staying with his parents, but Marina had said he could go over later and pick up some clothes and see the children.

He heard the snap of his mother's cigarette case and then felt a light breeze as the back door opened.

'I dunno,' he said, looking up, 'I think she probably did.'

'No, she didn't. Your sister supports you. She just gets a bee in her bonnet sometimes. I don't want you getting down. You'll probably sort it all out this afternoon. Marina said she loved you ... twice ... once in front of us and again when she was annoyed with you.' Reluctant smoke drifted into the room on a stray wind. 'That's not what you say when you want to end a marriage.'

Nick rubbed his eyes with forefinger and thumb. *End* and *marriage* echoed in his chest, and caused a stark fear to grip him. And Marina hadn't been *annoyed*; she had used the words *hate* and *disgust*. He had told his mum something of what had passed between him and Marina. He'd had to – he was in their house with nowhere else to go – but there was no way to explain to his mother what Marina had really meant –why she found him disgusting.

The children were at nursery and school and Marina was at work. He had arranged to pick up the children and walk Rusty and then pick up some clothes while he was there. *As soon as I get home, you have to leave*, she had said, *no dinner, no talking. I need time to think. I don't want you there.*

Just the thought of losing Marina ruptured something inside him. It was like bursting a blood vessel, haemorrhaging. He wouldn't survive the loss of her – he was certain of that.

He sat up and gulped back the tea, which was now cold and tasted awful. His mother smiled at him from the doorway.

'That's it. Be positive. I bet she's had second thoughts already, two nights without you.'

'Jesus Christ, Mum,' he shouted, standing up and thrusting his mug into the sink. 'Will you just leave it? It's none of your bloody business.'

The strained, saddened expression on her face blanched him.

'Look . . . I'm sorry.'

She stubbed out her cigarette. 'It's fine, don't worry about it.'

He could tell he had shaken her. He went to her and took

the bones of her into his arms, simultaneously seeking forgiveness and resenting his need for it. He was sick of being sorry. He rubbed her back, her top sliding under the palm of his hand so that he could feel each of her vertebrae.

At Firgrove Hill, Nick nudged open the front door. His home was at once relief and reproach. Rusty woke from a sleep and scampered towards him, nails tic-tacking on the wooden floor of the hall.

'Hello, boy. We'll go out soon, okay?' Nick said, bending to tickle behind the little dog's ears.

He kicked off his shoes and walked around the living room and then the kitchen, opening the fridge and inspecting its contents, as if to find his absence in evidence somewhere. He opened the dishwasher. Marina had forgotten to turn it on when she left for work and stacked it with her usual haphazard lack of interest. The dishwasher had always been his job. With distracted pleasure, he took time to reorganise it and then switch it on.

He went upstairs. He had to do a video audition – a second call-back – over Skype for a small part in an American TV show, and decided that he would do that in the office before he took Rusty out, and picked up the children.

In their bedroom, he stood looking at the double bed, then walked to the chair by the window over which Marina had hung a worn T-shirt and a pair of tights. He touched the foot of her stockings and drew it to his face.

Feeling shorn, he took a holdall from the top of the

wardrobe and placed it on the bed. Marina had asked him to pack a few things, but he couldn't muster the will. He loved her. This was his home. He walked out of the room with the bag still empty on top of the bed.

In the office, Rusty settled at his side as normal. Nick drank a cup of coffee looking out of the kitchen window, remembering the first visit by Brookes and Weston all those months ago. He was no longer the same man that had opened the door to them, relaxed and happy and thinking of making love to his wife. He was wary now, wounded. Trust was no longer implicit.

Nick sipped the bitter black coffee. He narrowed his eyes as he watched the branches of the tree swaying in the yard. He was the victim. He was the one justice had let down.

He put his palms over his face, feeling fatigued. He had barely slept, missing his wife and his children.

Glancing at his watch, he saw it was two hours until it was time to collect Ava from nursery. He refreshed the browser on his brand new laptop. The police had kept his phone and laptop, and Nick had been so relieved not to be charged, that he had not even queried it and bought new ones.

He opened up a Word document that was the script for *The Great Gatsby* with his own part highlighted. The audition was next week. He typed some notes on emotion but then became distracted again. He opened his browser and checked the news and then the weather for the next few days. It was an hour until his Skype interview but he didn't want to prepare too much – often that put him off, caused the performance to be forced.

An itch of desire crept over him in the boredom but he

wanted to keep this new computer clean. He hesitated, as the itch grew stronger. He thought about doing something else: vacuuming the stairs, putting weed killer on the path. Instead, he let his hands rest on the keyboard and typed: *pornhub*. With his left hand he unbuttoned his jeans as his right hand navigated to sites that he knew from experience had the best free videos. Penitent, even on the threshold of longing, he chose something lightweight, soft-core, normal.

The woman that appeared before him was young, skin as tight as an apple. Her mouth was open and her eyes were closed.

He wasn't aroused as quickly as he normally was. Nick slowed down and opened another video, this one more violent. The woman was struck and made more noise. Mouth dry, Nick found his mind invaded by Marina, the dark pools of her eyes so like his daughter's, judging him.

He closed his browser and deleted his history.

He was suddenly trembling, swollen with shame.

He opened up his own photos and chose an old one, Marina in a bikini on the beach in Valencia, her birthplace, sand clinging to her bottom and her waist narrowing as she reached up to a bright blue sky, her stomach tight and brown. Once it had been enough for him – just this photo. He had been tantalised by the bows at each side of her hip, and how one was just coming undone. That had been the first time he went home with her: met her family. They had gone to Valencia at the end of the trip, for some time alone together. Sangria. Violent warm waves and hot sand. Seafood at night.

Again, it wasn't working. When he looked at Marina he saw her eyes, and everything that he knew lay behind them: her worries, her hopes, her fears, her disgust in him. He loved her more than he loved himself but he could no longer abstract her body from who she was. Once, she had been the object of his desire: in the bar where he worked, her round backside in her pale blue jeans, her wide white smile, her accent, the taste of her – spice and oranges. Now he knew her body so well he would be able to pick out one of her fingers, one of her toes, almost one hair from her head. Intimacy. He was intimate with that woman and he could no longer objectify her, no matter how hard he tried.

He buttoned up his trousers and closed the laptop. When he saw her in real life he wanted her, and loved every inch of her, but the *idea* of her, the *idea* was tarnished by the familiarity – her frown when he disappointed her, the loose skin below her ribcage after carrying the children, the dimples on her hips, the corns on her baby toes.

Nick put on his jacket and Rusty stretched in expectation of a walk, front paws out and rear in the air. He shook himself and then waited by the door for the lead to be attached. Nick checked his watch. There was time to take Rusty around the block. He just wanted to clear his head, and then do the Skype audition before picking up the children.

Outside the air was warm and hopeful: spring starting to smell like summer. Nick just wanted to take Rusty to the avenue of trees near the reservoir but the little dog had in mind their usual route, and tugged him towards the park on

Morley. Rusty stopped and sniffed at lampposts and bushes, while Nick checked his phone. He wanted to be back in time to warm up for the interview.

As Rusty urinated, Nick imagined standing on a lonely stage, the warm spotlight finding him. He tried to remember what it was like to lose himself in a character, to open himself up to something outside himself. It was hard, because he was still so preoccupied by himself. He wondered if he would ever be able to act again, if Marina did not forgive him.

He thought about Angela. They were more similar than he had considered. Both of them had been hurt. Neither had justice; both of them were victims.

Marina's face in the drive flashed before his eyes, telling him he disgusted her. He had not laid a finger on Angela Furness but had he been completely innocent? He had put his baby daughter to bed and then sought out images of girls being raped.

Rape.

He remembered looking up the word in the dictionary as a child, not understanding, yet feeling the titillation of it.

Such a gentle word, with that tender *p.*

As a young teenager he had found, and been transfixed by, an image of a statue, Bernini's *Rape of Proserpina.* Just a picture of white marble and yet Nick had been fascinated. His eyes had lingered on the hands of the muscular man, Pluto, fingers digging deep into the woman's upper thigh, as she tried to escape his lust. The anguish on her face contrasted with the steel force of the man's musculature, calves, abdomen. The deep impression of Pluto's fingers in her flesh foretold the rape to come.

As they approached the park, Nick was aware of a black car driving past him on the quiet school road, windows darkened. He had rarely walked Rusty at this time, and the park was unusually empty. After school or on weekends, there were games of rounders or five-a-side football, parents cheering from the sidelines. In the mornings there were joggers, and other dog walkers, but this afternoon no one else was around.

Rusty strode confidently at his side, his short legs and tiny paws reaching out with assertion. Nick smiled down as the little dog stopped at an interesting smell and then tugged back on the lead, doubling back and sniffing some more, before a careful, strategic pee, leaving his mark, establishing dominance. Dogs didn't question their own nature – they had no cause.

Just then, there was the sound of car tyres skidding on tarmac as the black car braked near the entrance to the park. Nick turned at the screech.

It happened so fast. He experienced it in frames, like a strip of film.

Two men got out of the car and walked towards him. One had a fistful of gold rings and the other slid a long baton from inside his jacket. Both men were taller than he was and although not heavy, seemed hard with muscle.

Nick swallowed as the men focussed on him, looking over his shoulder in case their target was behind him. They didn't speak and Nick had never seen them before in his life, but suddenly he knew that they were here to hurt him.

They were only a few feet away when he turned to run. He let go of Rusty's lead and ran further into the park, faster than he ever thought he could, energy hot in his muscles. The pathways were overshadowed by tall green trees that absorbed all the sound of the day: traffic, conversations. There was only his breath and the rhythm of his feet on the path.

Suddenly, Nick felt a hard crack at the back of his neck, between his shoulder blades. The force took him down and he fell on his hands and knees. Before he could get to his feet, the two men began kicking him so hard that he was slowly beaten into the undergrowth at the very edge of the park. His breath left him and he couldn't get to his feet. The pain in his ribs brought tears to his eyes. His stomach began to convulse as the muscles in his abdomen tried to withstand the blows.

The man with the rings leaned down and took Nick by the sweater, lifting him so close that Nick could smell the man's bitter breath and see the spit stretch between his lips, the tiny blood vessels in his small eyes.

'You're not going to touch another kid again, you disgusting prick.'

'I . . . I didn't . . .'

'I took money for this, but for filth like you I'd do it for free.'

The man's fist smashed into Nick's face. Again and again, so that he was blinded. His nose cracked and then there was another blow to his jaw that must have knocked him out for a few seconds or minutes, but when he came round again it was still happening. Blood in his mouth. The panting of the men as they beat him.

Then nothing . . . and Nick rolled to his side, blinded, ringing in his ears, the smell of damp moss, earth. Pain all over his body but mainly in his jaw and neck.

He tried to swallow but his tongue was thick in his mouth, metallic with the taste of blood. He couldn't open his eyes. They had swollen shut, but he knew he had to crawl and try to get help.

Because he couldn't see, his hearing was sharp. He thought he heard Rusty barking. His phone was in his back pocket and he reached out, trying to feel for it.

A blow landed on his forearm first and then his upper arm. Nick heard the crack and had never felt such pain – searing through him. He cradled his hand, gritting his teeth.

'Get his ankle,' Nick heard, then tried to move, to protect himself, but couldn't.

He screamed then. It seemed to come from deep within him, below his lungs, somewhere in his bowels.

He choked, not knowing if hands were around his throat or if his own blood was choking him.

The pain radiated through him. He saw Marina's face just before he blacked out. She wasn't smiling. She was in the driveway with Ava and Luca cradled under each arm, protecting her children from him. He remembered the smell of her tights and the unpacked bag on the bedspread.

How would she know where he was?

Would she even look for him?

33

Angela

Everything had gone back to normal. She was living with her mum and her dad was coming to pick her up this afternoon. She wasn't pregnant anymore. Alone in her bedroom, Angela took the diamond ring on the chain from her jewellery box and put it around her neck, as she had done that night when she took the pills.

From downstairs, Angela heard her mother calling.

The weight of the necklace felt good on her neck.

Treasured.

Precious.

Special.

Just for a moment, Angela felt as valued as she had when he had given her the ring. The ring meant she was beloved. She leaned back on her bed, pressing the ring into her chest.

Donna called again from below.

'Coming.'

Angela tucked the necklace inside her shirt, closed her jewellery box and pushed it back under the bed.

Downstairs, Donna was excited, holding a package that had arrived in the mail and she had already burst open. 'I ordered this for your birthday, and it's only just arrived. I can't believe it took this long, but maybe that was meant to be. Here you are, back home with me now.'

'What is it?' Angela smiled in anticipation.

'Do you want me to wrap it first?'

'No, it's fine.'

'Go through, sit down.'

Smiling, Angela went into the living room and sat expectantly on the couch.

'I didn't want to just give you money. I wanted to get you something you could keep.'

'What?'

'Close your eyes and hold out your hands.'

Angela did as she was asked, waiting, one hand tucked under the other until a small weight landed in her palm.

It was a little black box. She shook it and it rattled.

Carefully, she opened it.

There was a little gold coin on a chain inside.

'It's a St Christopher. Solid gold. It's meant to protect you. Keep you safe.'

'It's lovely,' said Angela, about to close the box, but Donna leaned over and took the necklace from its case, holding it up so that it turned in the light.

'Try it on. I got the slightly longer chain, so that it might last you until you're older. You're supposed to keep it on all the time.'

'I'll put it on later.'

'It's hard to do the catch. Let me help you.'

Donna was already standing up and holding the necklace open. Reluctantly, Angela held up her hair so that her mother could fix it in place. It was better now, with her mum, but there was still a feeling of strain between them, as if they were both trying not to have a fight.

'You're wearing a necklace already. Take that off first in case they get tangled.'

'No,' said Angela, and suddenly pulled away with force. The necklace that Donna had been holding open around her neck broke and the St Christopher fell to the floor.

'*Angela!*' That voice her mother had always used when disappointed. 'Look what you've done.'

'You were forcing it around my neck.'

One hand over her chest, pressing on the ring, Angela watched her mother as she picked up the St Christopher and then inspected the chain.

'It'll mend, I suppose.'

Donna was trying very hard not to cause an argument. Angela turned away from her mother, and leaned against the wall.

'What is that necklace, anyway? You never wear jewellery.'

'Leave me alone.' Angela had her back to her mother, but she felt her eyes on her, burning through her clothes and into her skin.

'Come here.'

Angela put her hands on her head, elbows in front of her face, warding her off.

Donna took hold of her shoulders and spun her round, jarring her shoulder blades off the wall.

'Leave me alone.'

'What are you hiding?'

Angela tried to twist away and pushed her elbows further together, but Donna reached inside the neckline of her shirt and pulled out the ring.

'Leave it. It's mine,' Angela shouted, twisting away again so that the chain broke. The ring was heavy and fell inside her shirt and Angela patted herself down, expecting to find it, but Donna was already on her knees.

'What the hell is that? It's . . .'

Too late.

Angela watched her mother's face, studying the ring. Recognition took hold, flooding her features, eyes, eyebrows and lips.

Donna held the diamond ring in her left hand. Now, in comparison, Angela saw how much larger her own diamond ring was beside her mother's engagement ring. Why did she still wear that little ring her father had given her, anyway?

'He's been at you, hasn't he? It's him, isn't it? All this time . . .' Donna's eyes were wild.

Angela's hair was over her face; she looked at her mother through strands.

Donna brushed the hair from Angela's eyes and held her face.

It was too much for Angela, so close to her mother's eyes, inhaling the breath that left her mouth. The truth stuck in her throat and stung her eyes. Close like this, Donna would see the truth inside her.

'I'm right, aren't I? It's him?' Donna shook Angela, fingers digging into her arm.

'No,' she screamed back, tears exploding out of her. It was different from the aspirin; different from the fire, different from the time she stabbed Donna in the cheek. Now the tears seemed to be coming from deep inside her. 'No. No. No.'

'Look at you. Look at the state of you. You're shaking. Look what you've been through. You can't keep this to yourself any longer. I'm your mother and I have to protect you – that's what I'm supposed to do. But I can't do that unless you tell me the truth.'

'No!' Angela cried, folding into Donna, against her will it seemed, but she no longer knew what her will was. It was a relief to find Donna's soft shoulder, the softness of her flesh, the smell of her, all of her childhood built around that smell.

'No.'

'I'm right. Just tell me that I'm right?'

Her mother's soft hands on her cheeks, smoothing away the tears and wet hair.

'Yes,' Angela whispered, her tears stopping suddenly. 'Yes.' The breath was lost inside her. She opened her eyes. Her mother was holding the diamond ring in front of her.

'This is your grandmother's engagement ring. He kept it to himself. He had it valued and insured and I only saw it once throughout our whole marriage, but I remember it. I remember how it holds the light. When did he give it to you?'

'A year or so ago.'

Donna nodded, her face grey but resigned. 'You were in your last year at primary? It was before all this, before fights and head teachers, it was way back then . . .'

Breath paused in Angela's throat but she nodded.

'And that was when it started, when he started . . .'

'I don't remember when it started.' Her voice was faint, her eyes staring into the distance. 'I remember when he used to look after me it was always different, but when he moved out it got worse. He said I was special.'

'Before you even knew Mr Dean, he gave this ring to you.'

She nodded again. 'He said he loved me and the ring proved it.'

'And the baby. It was his?'

Her mother's face had changed. It was at once placid and murderous. Angela had never seen her hold so much anger and calm at once. It frightened her.

Angela blinked: that was the only acknowledgement she gave.

'I remember now. I let you down. That morning after you took the pills. You tried to tell me, but I jumped in about calling your dad. You tried to tell me and all I did was say I'd call the one who hurt you.'

Donna looked down at the St Christopher still clenched in her palm.

'Give me your hand.'

Angela held out her hand; Donna pressed the medallion into it, and curled the fingers over.

'And that thing with Mr Dean? Did he *ever* touch you?'

Angela shook her head, tears salt in her throat. She wasn't sure she would be able to speak. 'I wanted to tell you but I was scared, and I couldn't take it back. I had to say it was someone, because I couldn't say his name. And me and Jasmine liked Mr Dean . . . he was better than all the boys in school.' Angela nudged the heel of her hand to her cheek, catching a tear.

'I said I was going to protect you, and I meant it.'

Angela met her mother's eyes. She felt a hot, quick fear, like a flame on paper, hungry, unstoppable.

34

Stephen

It was just after two.

Stephen had called a few times to see if they were ready and received no reply. He wasn't worried. Donna always let her phone lose charge, although Angela had also not replied to his messages. He hummed as he walked up to the door. His old neighbour, Dennis, was in the garden.

'All right, Stephen?'

'Just picking up Angel.'

'It's good to see you again.'

Stephen smiled and rang the doorbell, squinting through the frosted glass for the shapes of Angela and Donna inside. He felt good today, although he was one thousand pounds poorer. The loss of funds was a fair trade for justice. He had been told that Dean had been successfully hit. It had been clean. No one had been caught – in fact, Hunter had said that Dean had been left in the undergrowth and may not be found for a while, perhaps days. It could only have been more satisfying if Stephen had done it himself.

'Alright?' he called over to Dennis. 'Back to work you are. No rest for the wicked.'

'I'm just doing a little today. Some weeding. Clear space and then I know what I have to do; the canvas is clear.'

'You're doing a fine job.'

Stephen faced the door, impatient now, not wanting to continue conversation with Dennis any longer.

He was just about to press the doorbell a second time, when the door opened.

Donna looked worse than usual: wild greasy hair, ruddy face and large wide eyes that seemed crazed.

Stephen put his hands in his pockets and rocked back lightly on his heels. 'Is Angel ready?'

'Come inside.'

Something about her eyes – leery, maniacal – made him wary.

'It's all right. It's a nice day. I'll just wait for her out here. Is she getting her things?'

He strained his neck a little, over Donna's head, looking for a sign of his daughter or the sound of her fairy elephant feet on the stairs.

Suddenly Donna took a step towards him and poked her forefinger into his chest so hard that it felt like the impact of a rubber bullet. Dennis glanced up over the hedgerow.

'You filthy, disgusting pig.'

She was whispering. It wasn't her normal anger: hurt and indignation. This was rage – calcine, incinerating. The blaze of it drove him back from the doorstep.

Still a whisper. 'You're never going to touch her again. Never going to lay a finger on her, never going to talk to her, or see her, you are never, never . . .'

Stephen didn't counter her, only hoped that she would keep her voice down. Dennis was stooped over the hedge, eyes on the primroses, ears on the conversation. Stephen had always known how to take Donna down in an argument – she was so vulnerable, so easy to criticise, to hurt – but not today. He heard her words, and his hands began to tremble, but he managed a smile, tried to shrug it off. She couldn't mean what he thought – it was just Donna, hung over, ranting.

'Wipe that smile off your face, you sick, sick man. You're a policeman, for God's sake. I'll kill you for doing this to her. She's only a little girl.'

His instinct was to get back into the car and drive away, but Angela had to be inside the house and ready for him. She had to be waiting.

'Angel?' he called, almost embarrassed to raise his voice like that in the street. She came. She appeared at the door, but she didn't have her coat on. She didn't have her rucksack in her hand. She just stood at the door in her bare feet, her stomach sticking out.

'Understand?' Donna said.

She was like a wild thing.

Stephen put his hands on his hips. 'Angela, get in the car, sweetheart.'

'Your mother's ring? That big old rock that you wouldn't let me have when we got engaged. Your secret's out now.'

Again Stephen attempted a slack, nonchalant smile. His bowels knew what she meant, but his brain was still hopeful. She was jealous. 'Well, she's my only daughter. My mother would've—'

'Your mother's turning in her grave, that she brought filth like you into the world.'

Stephen sighed, hands in the air. 'Look, have you been drinking?'

She was now so close that he could smell her, but it wasn't wine or cigarettes that made him turn his face away. There was a blinding glow of illumination in her eyes, as if she could see right inside him.

Suddenly, Donna turned from him and pointed at Angela. 'Get back inside. Get back inside, right now.'

Stephen tried to smile, slipping his hand into his pocket as if to suggest he was calm. He told himself it was just the same old Donna, using Angela as the pawn in their relationship.

Remarkably, Angela didn't push past her mother and into his car, but instead slipped back inside as she had been told. As she vanished from the doorway Stephen suddenly felt eclipsed.

'Look,' he began, 'I don't want to have an argument.'

She laughed then, a strange bitter laugh. 'I'm not going to argue with you, Stephen. You raped our daughter.' Tears flooded her eyes suddenly, making them seem crazed. 'You filth.' Spit left her mouth with the word.

Throat dry, Stephen glanced towards the car. He felt an urge to curl up, hide. He couldn't look at Donna. She had been so easy to break but now he felt powerless before her. Fear flushed through him. He didn't want to be here, couldn't bear to hear her voice or see the stark accusation in her eyes. He turned left and then right, as if calculating his escape. Dennis was busying himself in the flowerbeds, but Stephen sensed he was listening.

Donna's face was fierce, her eyes black as stones and her mouth turned down.

'I thought it was me,' she said. 'I thought *I* was the bad mother. And you know what? I *did* let her down ... but not anymore.' She leaned close again and he could smell the wrath of her breath.

'Donna, please.' His mouth was so dry he could almost hear his lips parting.

'Don't *Donna* me. You can't talk your way out of this. I'm going to make sure that you never, ever hurt her again.'

Chilled to his fingertips, he turned his back on her and walked to the car. As he reached the door, he felt her fist between his shoulder blades. He gasped, winded and off balance, more from her words than the blow, a hand on the roof of the car to steady himself.

'That baby was yours,' she said.

'I didn't think it was possible,' he said, facing her again, tongue sticking to the roof of his mouth. 'I thought she was too young.'

'She *was* too young,' Donna whispered.

She wrapped her cardigan around her, a gesture that had always made her seem insecure, but was now terrifying, as if she were gathering resolve. He felt himself trapped within the vortex of her anger, helpless, stuck, like an insect in amber, unable to move or even look away from the glare of her eyes.

She raised her chin and looked at him down her nose. 'You know better than me what they do to people like you in prison.'

Stephen almost fell into the driver's seat. His tyres skidded on the road as he drove away.

35

Marina

'But what do you mean, I cannot see him now?'

Ava was in her arms, screaming loudly in her ear so that Marina couldn't hear. Luca was silent and pale at her side, but squeezing her hand too tightly, making her fingers numb. Ava was heavy and Marina had to wrench her hand from Luca to move Ava to the other side of her hip.

'His condition is critical and there are no visitors allowed at this time.'

'I'm his wife!' She was crying now. She had tried so hard not to, in front of the children. 'Please … I need to see him.'

'We will let you know as soon as that is possible.'

She sat down, sobs breaking her body as she tried to comfort her daughter.

'Is Daddy going to die?' said Luca, his face pale but dry-eyed.

'No, no.' Marina pulled Luca into her and wiped a hand over her face.

*

Rusty had been found and reported lost before Nick.

He had not picked up the children from school and Betty had been called, but when Marina got home and found the holdall on the bed and Rusty missing, her first thought was that he had taken the dog and gone off on his own.

Nick had been in the undergrowth of Morley Park, unconscious, but Rusty had been found whining near the reservoir with his lead hanging, and taken straight to the RSPCA. Finally, another dog walker had seen Nick's boot, kicked free of his broken ankle, and peered underneath the lower canopy of the trees before calling an ambulance.

He had been taken straight to surgery and Marina had been called.

On the plastic chairs, she hugged both of her children. Her phone rang constantly and Luca took over answering it: granddad, Melissa, Mark. Betty and Tom texted to say they would come and take the kids. When finally it was her parents, Luca passed the call over.

'I can't talk right now,' she cried, Luca stroking her plaited hair. She wanted to tell him to stop, that he was a child and shouldn't be the comforter. 'I still haven't seen him. I still don't know what's happening.'

'*Gracias, cielo*,' she said, kissing his forehead when she hung up. Luca returned a thin-lipped smile.

'Mrs Dean?' the doctor called.

It wasn't her name, but she didn't care. They all sprang to their feet.

*

The nurses looked after the children while she went to him. He had a broken jaw and eye socket, although his eye had been saved. His nose was broken, as was his radius and tibia. His beautiful face was swollen beyond all recognition.

'*Mi amor*,' she said, tears chilling her cheeks.

His lips were dry and he struggled to speak but a tear left his eye and she caught it with her forefinger before it reached his bruised cheekbone.

'Don't say anything. I love you. The police said they will try to talk to you but the doctors say it may be a while before you are ready.'

His hand reached for her and Marina took it. His fingers were grazed and bloody, as if he were a bare-knuckle fighter, and yet they were protective wounds. She kissed each bruised knuckle, then smoothed the hair from his head.

'You're going to be okay,' she said. 'Whatever has gone on between us does not eclipse us. You have to get better. You are my children's father. You are the man I love.'

'I love you. I'll get better. I'll *be* better.' His words were slurred and she could sense the pain he felt when he spoke.

'The children want to see you. Can I bring them in?'

'Do I look okay?' She watched his bloodied iris slither under the lid.

'You look horrible, but they need to see you. Just like I did – they need to see you're alive.'

Marina spoke to the children, squatting in the corridor, each of them curled into her arms.

'He's all right, but he has to heal. Just like when you fall over and skin your knee. You can't get up on the bed and touch him, but you can talk to him. You can tell him that you love him. It will make him feel better.'

Marina walked into the hospital bay with both of their small hands in hers. There was no way to explain why this had happened. He was there and he was broken, but he was going to be okay. There was nothing else she could tell them, or tell herself.

Epilogue

Two Years Later

Donna apologised and asked if she could squeeze in. Couples nodded obligingly and stood so that she could work her way to the single free seat. There were whole rows free at the back, but she wanted to be near the front.

She had only just sat down and taken off her coat, run a hand through her newly lightened hair, when the curtain was drawn back.

In the first scene, Alice was asleep. The spotlight found her, pale blue dress and golden wig. In the darkness, a white rabbit appeared and Alice chased it and then followed it down the rabbit hole.

The lights went up on the stage. Donna covered her mouth with one hand. The set was wild and colourful, the crazy mind of Wonderland. There were black and white stairs going every which way, like an Escher print; lush colourful forests of leaves and flowers, a huge looking-glass in the middle, with the gold frame shining and detailed. It had meant months of work for Angela, gold leaf in her hair, paint under her fingernails.

Donna sat forward in her seat, straining to see. She only had a small part, one of the Cheshire cats, but she had worked on all the scenery and designed a lot of it herself.

Music burst into the room, and then other characters appeared – the caterpillar, the pigeon, the mad hatter.

All through the legal proceedings, this play had been a lifeline. Her art teacher had asked Angela if she would design the set. Working away with her brush and pencils behind the scenes had been just what she had needed at this time. She had had to testify on video camera with a social worker beside her. She was getting counselling now. Stephen pleaded guilty and so it was easier than it might have been. She had not been put through a trial or cross examination and Stephen had been kept on remand until the sentencing hearing. He had been sentenced to fifteen years' imprisonment. Angela would likely be in her late twenties by the time he was released.

'Miaow.'

It was her! Angela! Wearing an elaborate purple mask that she had finished painting just the night before. The hall carpet was still stained with purple and blue paint.

'Look at the state of that,' Donna had joked, treating the stubborn stain.

'You know when I grow up?' Angela had said, slumped against the stairs, paint on her forehead, 'I think I want to go to art school.'

When I grow up. She had almost lost her twice.

What could growing up mean, after all she had lived through? Donna hoped it meant being happy, being loved. In the darkness, Donna smoothed the skin above the knuckle on her ring finger, where her wedding ring had been. The same man had hurt them both so much, but Donna still felt responsible.

After her father had been sentenced, Angela had come to Donna with one closed fist held out towards her.

Close your eyes and hold out your hand.

Donna had done as she asked and soon felt the weight of the antique engagement ring in her palm. 'What should we do with it?' Donna had asked, the hurt and revulsion still fresh at the back of her throat. Her fingers remained open, unable to clasp and hold that thing.

'Don't care,' Angela had shrugged.

'We could sell it. Go on holiday,' Donna had smiled painfully, willing every ounce of succour within her, wanting to give strength to Angela. Now she understood how her little girl had treasured that ring, as she had held dear the chance of her father's love. What she feared most for Angela was that love itself would always be tarnished for her now because of the hard, bitter promise in that ring and the violence that Stephen had offered in the guise of love.

Angela shook her head. 'Let's throw it out. I don't want it. Even the money,' she stopped and bit her lip. 'But . . . if you want it, you can. I don't mind.'

Together they had gone outside and found a drain on the

Portland Road. When Angela let the diamond ring fall from her fingers she crouched quickly to hear the plop of its fall into the dark sewer water beneath.

'That's done then,' Angela had said as Donna took her hand. Her fingers were freezing.

From the back of the stage, Angela spoke her only line: 'Every adventure requires a first step. Trite but true, even here.'

Donna put one hand over her chest, feeling herself swell with pride at her daughter.

Could it be that Angela was going to be all right? Could it be?

*

'Just stay in the car. I'll be back before you know it,' said Nick, as Ava whined that she wanted out of her car seat to come with him.

This afternoon, the family were going to drive to Bristol to see Mark and Juliette. Nick parked on a double yellow line as he ran into the chemist to pick up his pain medication. He was lucky; there was almost no queue and he was back in the car in minutes, yet there was a ticket on the windscreen.

When he turned the engine back on Ava's CD began again and he quickly cut it off.

'Daddy!' Ava complained.

'Not now, we're nearly home,' he said, anger flaring in him.

In Firgrove Hill, he reversed into the driveway and was

about to get out when he saw Marina, changed into her jeans, locking up the house. He watched her in the rear-view mirror: her round backside, white striped top, sunglasses pushed into her hair. He loved her, only it was harder to make her believe him now.

'Ready? Sorry I'm late.' He put a hand on her thigh when she got into the car.

'Dad got a parking ticket,' said Luca, smiling nervously.

Marina turned to face Nick, eyes wide, memories they seldom mentioned almost visible in her large brown irises.

'Good start to the weekend, huh?' He tried a smile.

She turned from him and put on her seatbelt, brought her sunglasses down over her eyes.

'Let's get going,' Nick said into the rear-view mirror, waiting for his children's smiles.

Before he pulled out of the drive, he leaned towards her, lips just parted for a kiss.

'*Llegamos tarde,*' she said, the muscles in her neck tensing. '*Es un camino largo.*'

Relenting, he kissed her cheek. She was right. It was a long road ahead, and he hoped they would make it.

READING GROUP QUESTIONS

* What are the main themes explored in the book?

* At the start of the book, did you think Nick was innocent or guilty? Why did you think this?

* How well does the author draw the characters in their domestic settings?

* Do you think Nick was treated fairly by the legal system or by society?

* Discuss Nick's family's reaction to his situation.

* Do you think Nick is a good father?

* Discuss Angela's relationship with her mother.

* What was the biggest shock in the story?

* Who do you think the 'little liar' is?

* What do you think is the moral of the story?

AUTHOR Q&A

What was your initial inspiration for *Little Liar*?

In writing this novel, I wanted to explore sex, power and trust and how these themes interact in wider society but are also reflected in personal family relationships and dynamics.

Were you influenced by any current debates or news stories when writing?

Yes, but current debates have often centred around famous names in the worlds of media, politics, sport, arts and entertainment, while ultimately this is a discussion about *every* woman and *every* man. I wanted to explore gendered power dynamics in more 'everyday' environments and in private spheres such as the home and the family.

Did writing this book entail a lot of research?

I was grateful for the help of a Solicitor Advocate, who had advised me before, when I was writing *The Guilty One*. He guided me on procedural issues in this novel, but any errors of fact or emphasis here are, of course, my own.

Despite our system of justice in the UK being innocent until proven guilty, society treats Nick as a guilty man as soon as he is accused of the assault in the novel, with the allegation alone having devastating consequences on his life. What did you want to convey by writing from the viewpoint of the accused, as well as the accuser?

I am drawn to controversial, emotional subjects for my novels and like to explore all hues of the theme through my characters, often because I can see both sides to the story.

As in my first novel, I am again exploring ideas of guilt and innocence, but also what it means to be a victim. I was keen to challenge stereotypes here – Angela as the accuser is not an archetypal victim and Nick at the beginning of the novel is seen as the perfect family man, made a victim by the accusation.

Why did you choose for Angela and Nick to come from different socio-economic backgrounds? What were you trying to explore about class?

Each of my novels deal with class on some level. In this instance, I think the fact that Angela and Nick are from different socio-economic backgrounds serves to underline the power dynamics between them.

Why did you title the novel 'Little Liar'?

In *The Guilty One* everyone was guilty in some respect, and similarly here, there is more than one liar in *Little Liar*. I like the title because it is accusatory but the tone is somewhat teasing. Sexual allegations often resort to one person's word against another and as a society, I think we are in the midst of a revolution which is altering the way we respond to that.

Both Angela and Nick are innocent and guilty of things in the novel. Do you think there is a clear line between innocence and guilt, being a good person or a bad person?

In my stories, again and again, I challenge notions of good and evil. I think these are labels which some people find comforting, but the reality is that good people can do terrible things and vice versa. In *Little Liar*, I think this goes one step further – particularly if we consider the character of Nick. Only towards the end of the novel does Nick really begin to consider how his thoughts and actions make him guilty, even as he vouches for his innocence. In fiction, characters that are only good, or only bad, tend to be very dull, so I always seek to create flawed characters that are nevertheless easy to relate to.

This is the third book that you've written, following on from your acclaimed novels *The Guilty One* and *Redemption Road*. In all your books you examine childhood and the lasting impact of experiences in childhood, particularly trauma. Why is this a topic that interests you?

I remember a *New York Times* review of *Redemption Road*: 'childhood is a perilous country in Lisa Ballantyne's novels ...' In some respects that is true. As a reader and a writer I am very interested in how our childhoods impact on our adult selves. Experiences in childhood are often very intensely felt and ultimately shape who we become and how we view the world. I remain fascinated by the nature–nurture debate and how these two forces combine to make us who we are as people.

Can you tell us anything about the new novel that you're writing?

My new novel is a portrait of an extraordinary woman's life as she struggles to turn the trauma from her past into a positive force.

Have you read Lisa Ballantyne's gripping and emotional bestseller, *Redemption Road?*

The crash is the unravelling of Margaret Holloway ...

Trapped inside a car about to explode, she is rescued by a scarred stranger who then disappears. Margaret remembers little, but she's spent her life remembering little – her childhood is full of holes and forgotten memories. Now she has a burning desire to discover who she is and why her life has been shrouded in secrets. What really happened to her when she was a child? Could it have anything to do with the mysterious man who saved her life?

Read on for the opening of *Redemption Road ...*

1

Margaret Holloway
Thursday 5 December, 2013

Margaret Holloway wrapped her scarf around her face before she walked out into the school car park. It was not long after four o'clock, but a winter pall had shifted over London. It was dusk already, wary streetlamps casting premature light on to the icy pavements. Snowflakes had begun to swirl and Margaret blinked as one landed on her eyelashes. The first snow of the year always brought a silence, dampening down all sound. She felt gratefully alone, walking out into the new darkness, hers the only footprints on the path. She had been too hot inside and the cold air was welcome.

Her car was on the far side of the car park and she wasn't wearing proper shoes for the weather, although she had on her long, brown eiderdown coat. She had heard on the radio that it was to be the worst winter for fifty years.

It was only a few weeks until her thirty-sixth birthday, which always fell during the school holidays, but she had so much to do before the end of term. She was carrying a large handbag, heavy with documents to read for a meeting tomorrow. She was one of two deputy head teachers at Byron Academy, and the only woman on the senior management team, although one of the four assistant heads below Margaret was female. The day had left her tense and electrified. Her mind was fresh popcorn in hot oil, noisy with all the things she still had to do.

She walked faster than she might have done in such wintry conditions, because she was angry.

'*Don't do this,*' she had just pleaded with the head teacher, Malcolm Harris.

'It's a serious breach,' Malcolm had said, leaning right back in his chair and putting two hands beside his head, as if surrendering, and showing a clear circle of sweat at each armpit. 'I know how you feel about him. I know he's one of your "projects" but—'

'It's not that ... it's just that permanent exclusion could ruin him. Stephen's come so far.'

'I think you'll find he's known as Trap.'

'And I don't think of him as a project,' Margaret had continued, ignoring Malcolm's remark. She was well aware of Stephen Hardy's gang affiliations – knew him better than most of the teachers. She had joined the school fresh out of college, as an English teacher, but had soon moved into the Learning Support Unit. The unit often worked with children with behavioural problems, who had to be removed from mainstream classes, and she had been shocked by the number of children who couldn't even read or write. She had taught Stephen since his first year, when she discovered that, at the age of thirteen, he still couldn't write his own address. She had tutored him for two years until he was back in normal classes and had been so proud of him when he got his GCSEs.

'He was carrying a knife in school. It's a simple case as far as I can see. He's nearly seventeen years old and—'

369

'It feels like you're condemning him. This is coming at the worst time – he's started his A Levels and he's making such good progress. This'll shatter his confidence.'

'We can't have knives in school.'

'He wasn't *brandishing* the knife. It was discovered by accident at the gym. You know he carries it for protection, nothing more.'

'No, I don't know that. And that's beside the point. This isn't as dramatic as you're making out. Kids drop out of sixth form all the time . . .'

'But he's not dropping out. You're forcing him out, after all he's overcome. Seven GCSEs with good grades and his teachers say his A Level work has been great. This is just a blip.'

Malcolm laughed lightly. '*A blip, hardly what I would call it.*'

Margaret swallowed her anger took a deep breath and answered very quietly. 'This decision will have a huge, huge impact on his life. Right now he has a chance and you are about to take it away. There are other options. I want you to take a step back and think very carefully.'

'One of us does need to step back . . .'

'I've said my piece. All I'm asking is that you sleep on it.'

Malcolm's hands fell into his lap. He clasped them and then raised his thumbs at the same time as he raised his eyebrows. Margaret took it as assent.

'Thank you,' she managed, before she slipped on her coat.

'Drive carefully. There's a freeze on.'

Margaret smiled at him, lips tight shut. Malcolm was young for a head teacher: early forties, a keen mountain climber. He was only seven years older than Margaret and they were friends of sorts. They didn't often have differences and he had backed her rise to the school leadership.

'You too,' she had said.

The conversation tossed and turned in Margaret's mind as she walked to the car. She thought about Stephen with his violent older brother and collection of primary school swimming trophies. She thought about Malcolm and his insinuation that her viewpoint was personal, emotional.

The snow had become a blizzard and flakes swarmed. She was thirsty and tired and could feel her hair getting wet. She saw the car, took the key from her pocket and pressed the button to open the doors.

As the headlights flashed on the new snow, she slipped. She was carrying too many things and was unable to stop herself. She fell, hard.

Picking herself up, Margaret realised that she had skinned her knees. Her handbag was disembowelled and the papers for tomorrow's meeting were dampening in the snow.

'Jesus Christ,' she whispered, as her knuckles grazed the tarmac chasing her iPhone.

In the car, she glanced at her face in the rear-view mirror and ran her fingernails through her dark cropped hair. She had worn her hair short since her early twenties. It accentuated her big eyes and the teardrop shape of her face. The snow had wet her lashes, and ruined the eyeliner that ran along her upper lid in a perfect cat's eye. She ran her thumb beneath each lid. The lights from the school illuminated her face in the mirror, making her seem paler, childishly young and lost.

She turned the key in the ignition, but the engine merely whined at her.

'You have got to be kidding,' she said, under her breath. 'Come on. You can do it.'

She waited ten seconds before turning the key again, blowing on to her stinging knuckles and wondering if she might actually self-combust if she couldn't even get out of the *bloody car park*.

Often, she took the Tube to work but there was disruption today and she hadn't wanted to risk being late.

She turned the key again. The engine whined, coughed but then started.

'Thank you,' Margaret whispered, pumping the accelerator, turning on the lights and the radio.

She put on her seatbelt, turned on the heaters, exhaled, then glanced at Ben's text on her iPhone before she turned on to the road. *We need milk, but only if u get a chance xx*

The wipers were on full, the snow gathering at the corners of the windscreen.

She turned right on to Willis Street and then after the Green Man Interchange she took the first exit, signposted *Cambridge and Stansted Airport*. It was just over a half-hour drive from the school to Loughton in good conditions, but because of the snow and the heavy traffic today, Margaret expected it would take her forty minutes or more to get home.

Under her opaque tights, her skinned knees were stinging. The sensation reminded her of being a child. She banged the back of her head gently off the headrest, as if to shake the worries from her mind.

Ben would be making dinner, but as soon as she had eaten it, it would be time to take Paula to her acting class in the local community centre, where Margaret would sit drinking weak machine coffee, preparing for her meeting tomorrow. If they made it home early she would be in time to stop the fight that Ben and Eliot, her seven-year-old, always seemed to have around bedtime, when her son was reluctant to relinquish his iPad.

She was a young parent, or young by today's standards: twenty-five when she married Ben, and twenty-six when Paula was born, with Eliot coming only two years later. Ben was a freelance writer and worked from home and Margaret sometimes felt jealous that he saw more of the children than she did. Often it was Ben who welcomed them home from school, and most days during the week Ben cooked dinner and helped them with their homework.

Heading home, she always felt anxious to see them all again.

At home, on the mantelpiece, there was a black and white photograph of Margaret reading to her children when they were both small. It was her favourite family photograph. Ben had taken it, snapping them unawares. Eliot was tucked under one arm and Paula under the other, and their three rapt faces were pressed close together, the book blurry in the foreground. Not tonight because she had to go out, but most nights Margaret still tried to read to them.

She indicated and then pulled out on to the M11, just in front of a lorry. Both lanes were busy and she kept to the inside. There was a jeep in front of her and a lot of the splashback landed on Margaret's windscreen. The traffic was travelling at sixty miles an hour, and the road was damp with dirty slush.

Margaret slowed down further as visibility was so poor. Caught in her headlights, the blizzard swirled in concentric circles. When she looked to the left of the windscreen, the flakes darted towards her; when she looked to the right they reformed to focus in on her again. The snow building up on the corners of the windscreen was blinkering her. She could see the red of tail lights in front, but not much else except the illuminated, swirling flakes.

Margaret was not aware of what hit her, but she felt a hard jolt from behind and the airbag exploded. She put her foot on the brake, but her car collided with the jeep in front. The noise of metal crushing took her breath away. The bonnet of her car rose up before her and everything went dark. She braced herself for great pain, holding her breath and clenching her fists.

No pain came. When she opened her eyes, there was the sound of car alarms and muffled screams and, underneath it all, the trickle and rush of water. She ran her hands over her face and body and could find no wound, although there was a dull ache in her chest from the airbag. She tried the driver's door, but it wouldn't open, even when she shouldered it. She reached for her handbag but it had spilled onto the floor. Her car was contorted and dark and she couldn't see where her phone had fallen. She leaned over and tried to open the passenger door but the impact had damaged that too.

There was a glow from behind the bonnet as if something in the engine had caught fire.

The snow continued to fall, filling the space between the bonnet and the windscreen, so that it felt as if she was being buried. The lights that remained grew fainter. Margaret rubbed on the side window to clear it of condensation and pressed her face against the glass. She could see shapes moving in the darkness, oscillating in the oily puddles reflected by car lights. The shapes were people, she decided. There was also a wavering yellow, which almost looked like flames.

'It's all right,' she said to herself, out loud. Help would come. All she had to do was wait. She slid over in the seat and searched with open palm on the floor for her phone. She found almost everything else: her lip gloss, a packet of tampons, ticket stubs for an Arcade Fire concert, and two hairbrushes.

While she was bent over, head to the floor, she became aware of the smell of petrol: a noxious whiff. It reminded her of hanging out of the car window at petrol stations as a child. She strained to peer out of the small clear corner of her side window.

The grass embankment that ran along the crash barrier had been replaced by a strip of fire.

Margaret's breath suddenly became shallow. It rasped, drying, in her throat.

If she was right, and her fuel tank had been ruptured by the collision and the engine was on fire, then there was a chance that the car would explode.

She wanted to speak to Ben but was now glad that she couldn't find her phone. She wouldn't be able to conceal her fear.

Ben. Just the thought of him brought tears to her eyes. She remembered the smell between his shoulder blades in the middle of the night and the quizzical look in his eyes when she said something he disagreed with; the hunched way he sat over the keyboard in the study when he was working on an article. Then she thought of Paula, impatient to go to drama class, her dinner finished and thinking that Mum was late *again*. She thought of Eliot, lost in a game on his iPad, unaware of the danger she was in, or that his mother might be taken from him.

She looked around for objects that might smash the glass and found a weighted plastic ice scraper down the inside of the driver's door. She used all her strength and succeeded in making a crack in the window.

All she could smell was petrol and her own sweat – her own fear. The car alarms had ceased but had been replaced by the flatline of car horns. She realised that many more cars must have crashed. The flatlining horns would be drivers slumped against their steering wheels. Through the small triangle of cleared window she could see the shape of the fire moving.

'No,' she screamed, pounding her fists and her head and her shoulders at the window. 'NO.' She knew the insulating snow meant that no one would hear her. She twisted round and stamped at the glass, pounding with the soles of her flimsy shoes. It hurt but the window held fast.

She didn't want it to end here. So much was unfinished. There was so much she still needed to know, understand, *do*.

Suddenly there was a man by her door.

If you enjoyed this extract, you can buy *Redemption Road* now in paperback and ebook.